THE ENDS

JAMES SMYTHE is an award-winning writer of eight novels for adults, and three for young adults. He also writes for television and film. He lives in London with his wife and son.

JAMES SMYTHE

THE ENDS

Book Four of The Anomaly Quartet

HARPER
Voyager

Harper*Voyager*
An imprint of HarperCollins*Publishers* Ltd
1 London Bridge Street
London SE1 9GF

www.harpercollins.co.uk

HarperCollins*Publishers*
1st Floor, Watermarque Building, Ringsend Road
Dublin 4, Ireland

First published by HarperCollins*Publishers* 2022
This PBO edition 2022
1

A catalogue record for this book is available from the British Library

ISBN: 978-0-00-754189-8

Set in Sabon LT Std by Palimpsest Book Production Ltd, Falkirk, Stirlingshire

Printed and bound in the UK using 100% renewable electricity by
CPI Group (UK) Ltd

MIX
Paper | Supporting
responsible forestry
FSC
www.fsc.org
FSC™ C007454

This book is produced from independently certified FSC™ paper to ensure
responsible forest management.

For more information visit: www.harpercollins.co.uk/green

PART ONE

1

What if we don't have time? If there's no way of controlling forward momentum, the sense that something happened in the past, so its tense changes, its relationship with us alters. Something happened, it affected us, and we learned from it, and we grew, perhaps. If we don't have time, something happened, but maybe also it will happen again. Maybe we can't learn from it, because it's not that simple any more. So: what if we simply no longer have time?

My days begin the same. Every day, every day the same. I wake up, and I breathe, the first breath to make sure that I still can, the second preceding a gulp to check for blood in my mouth; and I reach over, right hand to left, to feel my pulse; and I wonder if I have slept at all. I need to know if I was asleep or dead; if I am still the age I was when I went to bed.

I look at the sun, rising in the distance, and I can still look at it. I don't have to turn away, for fear of being blinded. There are floaters afterwards, yes, and I can't hold the gaze longer than a few seconds; but there's still something between me and it that allows me to look.

Don't stare directly at the sun, we were told as kids, you'll go blind.

There aren't nearly as many reliably solid truths as there once were.

Using the bathroom takes longer than once it did. I am slower, and I clean up after myself, wipe every surface down. Clean the glass after I have showered. It feels inconsequential, to be clean, to be tidy, when I'm the only person to see it, appreciate it, but it's a structure. It provides a structure, knowing that to begin with a wash will help, that to shave your face, to bring you back to humanity in that small way, will make a difference. To sit on the toilet and understand that the body is doing what the body should be doing, or needs to be doing. The sounds from next door are the same every morning. A loop you can set your clock by, as they used to say: because it starts so definitely, a voice that cries out to signify its beginning. A silence to signify its ending.

Their story is the worst part of living here. It breaks me, or it did. There was a time when it was ruinous, when it affected me. And then that feeling faded, I suppose, and now it's part of the house, part of the landscape. Like it used to be living beneath a flight path. You notice them at first, and then . . . don't.

My neighbour is a man on his own. His name is Austin. He had, or has, I am not sure, a wife, Susan. Austin had been in hospital; they let her bring him home the day that the enveloping happened. The world went lawless, really. I had been in hospital as well, for tests. I was back at home, feeling sorry for myself. Waiting for results that wouldn't come, not in the normal timeline, not until well after the chaos hit. But we had both been in hospital, both for the same sickness, even if I didn't know it yet. He was so much further along than I was, of course. He was careening towards his end.

So Susan brought him home, to die in his house. We watched them wheel him in, through the front door, depositing him as if he was just some delivery, then going; and we heard her talking to him, her voice low and soft, carrying through the walls. Birdie said to me that we should bake something, and I told her that we had done more than enough. That we should let them be, he was clearly palliative, they needed their peace. Rubbing my hand, where they'd taken the blood samples. We thought it was anaemia. We hoped it was anaemia. There had been a drop of blood, a cut that wouldn't heal. I had looked online, and there were alternatives that didn't bear thinking about. The reality never entered my mind, not at that point.

'She won't have time to cook. She'll be looking after him,' Birdie said.

'She might not be hungry.'

'She'll need to eat. Keep up her strength.'

'But the Anomaly,' I said. That day, the day we knew it was meant to envelope us, the news was off. There was that cycling Do Not Panic message on the screens and the phone lines were all blocked. All we had was our own sol2r batteries, though we knew we could run weeks off those. Potentially indefinitely, if the sun held after we were enveloped. That was a worry at the time. And Birdie tutted, rolled her eyes.

'We don't know what will happen,' she said. 'What if it's nothing? Then you've just sat around when you could have been doing something—'

'No, no, you're right,' I said. 'Of course, you're right.'

So Birdie baked a pie. Shortcrust, so thick. That layer between it and the meat, where it's less baked, where it's somehow intangible: the looseness of it, the fabric of the pie. And the smell of it, of the crust ever-so-slightly sweet, the stew so savoury. Birdie always added soy sauce to the stock, wanting that intensity to it. The two smells mingling. I hold on to those smells. She delivered the pie and made me stand with her on their doorstep. I had my hands in my pockets, because I was ashamed about it. There is nothing that you can say. Has never been. What words, to soothe that sort of pain? Even with my mother, and the distance between us, when she went, there wasn't anything.

Austin was quiet. We could see the door at the far end was closed, we imagined him behind that. Susan answered, and she stared at us as if she had never seen us before.

'What?' she asked.

'We brought you this,' Birdie said. 'We thought—'

'We heard about Austin,' I said. 'I mean, of course, we're so terribly sorry.'

'There's no need,' she replied.

'We're fine,' she said. 'Look: I would really prefer you just left us alone.'

'Well, if you *do* need anything,' Birdie started, but she cut her off.

'I won't,' she said, then she shut the door.

I remember that conversation perfectly. How burned in her eyes were, deep set, absolutely determined. Building her up to something. Funny, how some things remain with such clarity. How loose memory can be.

Ask me if I remember being a child, and I do.

Ask me if I remember Birdie leaving me, and I do not.

Not the exact moment. She was there one minute, and then she was gone.

We lay in bed and Birdie soothed me, her hand on my chest, running through grey hairs. That I remembered – the act of looking down, of surveying my body like cresting hills and rolling moors of pale flesh, the rivers of lilac, the soil of browning moles; my work, landscapes, dragged into my own body image – the grey hairs that I remembered being a thick blackness. And yet here, grey, or silver, even, if we're being generous. Those hairs pulled out in the movements of her fingers, through and through, back and forth. Even with everything happening, I am still getting older. Some people do not; I do nothing but age.

I am not who I was back then, but then I am also the same. I have been alone so long; I have been myself for so very, very long.

We lay there, and Birdie stroked me, as if I was some sort of comfort animal, and we listened, because in the quiet we could hear him moaning, groaning. He was dying, and we could hear it. The sounds of him just waiting to die.

Birdie and I had a daughter who had died a year or so previous. Rebecca, her name was. She didn't make any of those sounds come her own ending.

We were enveloped sometime that night. Lying there in that darkness, listening to Austin fading out. There wasn't a sound from the Anomaly or anything, nothing to mark it, so we didn't know, we didn't quite realize. We lay there all night, listening. You could only hear the sound if you strained, really. It was a hum, in the background.

I remember thinking of Rebecca, and the white-noise machine we'd had for her when she was a baby.

Then the sun started to come up, and we heard him shout

out, 'Do it, do it, do it!' Six words, clarity in his voice; and then he was silent. Birdie sat bolt upright, and she said for me to shush, even though I wasn't saying anything, and she listened.

'I think he's dead,' she finally said, a few minutes of silence later.

We didn't mention his request; his invocation. We didn't talk about it. We got up, and got dressed, and we looked at the sky and it was different. The sky was different, that subtle, inky shimmer.

'It's here,' Birdie said. 'It's really here, then.'

We walked, or we must have. The world was broken, irrevocably, in that moment. We wandered around, and we helped people who needed help, and everything tore itself apart. So many people were dead in the run up to the enveloping, we didn't quite know the scale, but so many. Our part of the city, of Los Angeles, was a ghost town.

When we got back to the house, Susan was in the street. She was shaking, shivering almost, in the heat. She looked like somebody who had seen a ghost. There was no other way to describe her.

'Are you okay?' Birdie asked. Susan shook her head.

'He's alive,' she said. 'He's alive.'

I looked through the windows behind her, and there he was, groaning, moaning. His death throes. He was alive, definitely, twitching on his gurney.

'Did they say how long they thought it would take?' Birdie asked, but Susan shook her head, over and over.

'You don't understand. He was dead. And now he's alive. I killed him, I fucking did it. I did just what he asked.' His request of the hours previous. 'I did it, I did it for him and he died, he was fucking *dead*, but now here he is. He's alive.

And he wants me to do it all over again. I can't do it again, do you understand? I can't do it.'

We heard them, through the walls. She shouted at him, begged him to die. He said, again, 'Do it, do it!' But she didn't, whatever it was that she had done the first time. Instead, she waited, and we waited; and then he went quiet.

There was silence again, but by then the rumours were swirling about the new rules of our world; the new rules of dying. We understood them, even if she didn't.

The groaning began again. Six hours until he begged for death. A loop that began the same way, every time. We got to know that first groan, the first one after the Anomaly enveloped us, playing out the same every single time. We got to know the intonation of his pleas. 'Do it!'

Susan shot herself a few days later. But she didn't think it through, of course; because then she was right there with him again, her own loop beginning anew. There to hear it with virgin ears, there to go through that very first dreadful realization of what the Anomaly meant to her, and to him. To them.

To listen to it all play out as we were still grieving Rebecca; as I was starting to understand what was wrong with me. My first bleeding coming so soon after that, and we thought that was it, that my own death would be accelerated. I imagined myself with a month, say, of life, looping that month eternally. Birdie looking after me, growing older, always having to tell me how long I had left, because she would know to the hour, the minute, the *moment*.

That wasn't what happened, though.

Susan ended his loop, his cycle, a few times for herself before she gave up; before she took to ending her own life, the futility of it. She learned, eventually, from talking to us;

from leaving herself notes. Working out what must have happened. And then she left him to die alone, going off somewhere by herself. She looped back a year later, presumably some sort of accidental death that sent her to the start of her loop; and then once again, thirteen years after that. She came back, and she learned what had happened. I told her, I had to. Birdie was gone by then, she had left, and I told Susan that it was endless, that Austin couldn't be saved. I had tried, in fact, while she was gone: I had tried to help him, in every way. It was impossible.

Thirteen years is a long time to loop.

I would always hear him through the walls; that muffled moan, and then his invocation. 'Do it, do it, do it!' We both would, but then Birdie started sleeping with earplugs, so that she didn't even really hear it any more; and I just got used to it. It's strange: there was something almost comforting to it, after a while. Because it was so constant, and when I was alone, when Birdie had left, it was something else there, someone else, in the darkness, or the light, but there, absolutely infallible, absolutely unchangeable. His final moments, inevitable.

Austin was on one loop; Susan was on another. Both of them were out of time with each other, and yet, when they both were dead, they came back at the start of their shared loop. That same moment. Time lost, time found; time dragging itself into sync with other versions of itself.

Everything repeats, and it never, ever ends.

Our daughter, Rebecca, was born when the Anomaly was at the edge of our atmosphere, slowly creeping. Skulking, somebody once said. We knew that it was coming, that it would reach us, but nobody knew what would happen when it did.

Or, maybe, nobody *told* us what would happen. And we spoke about having a kid, about whether it was the right thing to do or not. We were barely twenty, young compared to some, but we knew that we wanted one. An accident that also we never even considered anything less than perfect timing.

Then she was born, this cradled bundle of muslin and puckered skin that felt so unbearably soft, so utterly undamaged by the world, and we knew we were right. She got older; we watched her. She was a little kid, and we spoke about trying for a second.

Then she died, and we stopped speaking about it. Our world, our personal world, stopped turning.

Then, months later, nearly a year later, the planet was swallowed.

You wonder, in those moments, what logic there is. What logic, what reason, what possible cause. Some people think it's alive, or sentient. Some people think we made it in some lab somewhere. Some people think it's a god, and they worship it.

I have to believe it's nothing: it's chaos, chance. It's something that happened, that isn't punishing us, and that we had no part in. We fucked the planet with the way we behaved; we ruined each other with our words and deeds.

I have to believe that the Anomaly is just that, an Anomaly; because otherwise, how do we come back from it? Is there any way at all to come back from it?

2

The telephone rings. It never rings.

'You're still alive, then.' My sister's voice. Half-sister. Crackly, satellites that haven't been maintained in too long carrying the call. A miracle they still work; it makes you wonder if somebody's up there maintaining them, on their own loop. Fixing satellites for eternity.

'Martine,' I say. 'I am alive, yes. And so are you.'

'I'm not the one who's dying.'

'We're all dying.'

'Excellent. Good work on turning this to shit before I've even begun—' she starts, but I stop, back-pedal. She's quick to scare. We aren't close, not really.

'I'm sorry, I'm sorry. Please. It's nice to hear from you.'

'I'll bet.'

'I mean it. Are you okay?'

'I'm fine,' she says. 'I'm fine. London's under the yoke of a cult leader, we're all baking, the house needs some repair that I simply cannot be bothered to do, but otherwise it's fine. How's the City of Angels?'

12

'Still haven't found any,' I say. I hear the smile on the other end, her skin against the handset. A joke we've made for the longest time. I think we both probably find comfort in the repetition.

'Listen to me, anyway,' Martine says. 'I saw her.'

'Her?' My voice in my ears. Like blood pumping, suddenly, and hard. I know who she means. I still have to ask.

'Birdie. Birdie, your erstwhile wife, I saw her. She's here.' Martine's voice drops to this quiet hush, this calm that I can't even begin to process; because, how could she be calm? How could she be quiet? Birdie left, she left, and no word, and now—

'Where?'

'Back here.'

'Here.'

'You're repeating yourself in your old age.'

'We're the same age,' I say, on autopilot, brain whirring, 'and we're not exactly decrepit—'

'Dying makes you age faster,' she says. There's no answer to that. 'Do you want me to say anything to her? I could go and find her again—'

'It's definitely her?'

'I know her. She's dressed in the drabs, though. I think she's fallen in with the Knot crew.'

'She didn't like that stuff.'

'People change.'

'Birdie didn't,' I say. Martine snorts.

'Everybody changes. Or they have the capacity to. Look, she's here, she's *beige*, she's in with the Knot. Pettersen gets them all, you know.'

'He didn't get you.'

'Well, no. But I've always been a woman of refined taste.' I could hear the smile.

'I'll come there.'

'You'll come here!' She laughs, a spit of laughter. She sounds more forced-posh than before. Her Ts sharper, her Ss more sibilant. 'You won't come here, you can't. What are you going to do, commandeer a plane?'

'Maybe a boat,' I say.

'A boat! You idiot. What if you have a, what do you call them? Episode? What if you have an episode?'

'Then I have an episode.'

'You can't be near other people.'

'I won't tell them. I'll keep my distance. And it's only if I bleed, I haven't had one of those in months. Months and months. I can't even remember the last one.' That's a lie: it's been two months. Maybe a few days more.

'How are you feeling?'

'I'm fine,' I say. 'Fine, I suppose.'

'You suppose.'

'I'm tired. I'm worried about dying. I'm worried about living. The neighbourhood's dead, I think, abandoned. A few people, but I don't really leave the house.'

I am quiet, and then: 'Do it, do it, do it!' Austin's begging voice.

'Is that him next door?'

'Yes,' I say. 'The windows are open.'

'I don't know how it doesn't drive you mad,' she says. Even as callous as she is, that's how it gets thought about now. Death doesn't quite sting the way it once did, not when it's normalized, or when it's missing the chaotic nature it once held. Now, death is more like chewing: an action we repeat without thinking, more complicated than breathing, but still there, constant, over and over. 'I would have sound-proofed the room,' she says. 'I would have put egg cartons—'

'Where are you even getting that many egg cartons from?' I ask, suddenly bitter.

'The shop. Or anything else, anything else at all. Not egg cartons, cardboard, or newspapers, or foam—'

'Foam.'

'I would have soundproofed the room, or better yet, his room, do his room.'

'I don't want his last moments to be spent wondering why it's changed,' I say.

'You're soft,' she tells me. 'Do you speak to him?'

'Sometimes,' I say. Sometimes I sit with him, and I try and make him feel better about what's going to happen to him. I don't know if it helps him.

'He's dead already, let him be.'

'Maybe he doesn't want to be alone.'

'Well, he is. And so are you.'

'At least I had somebody. At least we both did. Not toxic like you, driving everybody away. At least if we die alone we once knew what it was like to not be.' I feel triumphant in that; but, of course, the game has gone too far. She is quiet. If it wasn't for the crackle of the satellite line, I would think she had hung up. I feel bad; I try to drag it back. 'Where did you see Birdie exactly?'

'High Street Ken. If I see her again, do you want me to say something to her? She didn't see me, I was careful, I'm always careful these days. You never know.'

'You're risk-averse.'

'Of course I am.'

'Don't say anything to her. I'm coming.'

'Ha! I'll believe it when I see it.' She hangs up, the dial tone noisy, blaring. I hold the handset. My hands weak, my knuckles weakened to pale white. My skin is tracing paper, my veins thick tar blood, lines all over my body. A circulatory system that's failing, but looks like it's still doing its job.

Birdie is in England. She's in England, and I don't know how, or why.

I am in California, now. I have been here for a while. I was, when I was a kid, in Sweden, and then Florida, and then London; and then, when I was able to leave home, I became somewhat nomadic for a few years; before, finally, I settled in California. I first met Birdie in London, and then we travelled, and then we settled. We found these little houses with a balcony and a neighbour on either side, and the beach only twenty minutes away, if we walked fast and pretended that cars didn't exist. Rented houses with thin walls, a kitchen that came off a living room, a space at the back that wasn't quite a garden, a terrace for drinks, I suppose; for socializing. The landlord died, because he was prepared for the Anomaly; because he bought into the idea of killing himself when it landed. One of the quickest loops I've encountered: poised for it to come, like a New Year's countdown.

He is not alive long enough to collect the rent.

The bedroom has a low bed, for what was once solely aesthetic purposes, but which now works perfectly for my back, my legs. My general sense of weakness. I lie down. A brief pause, while I think. Because plans need to be made. I need a sense of moving forward. That wasn't always the case. I am – perhaps was – an artist. Back before, I would be meticulous. I needed to capture the moment I was seeing absolutely. There was nothing abstract about my work; rather, it was meant to elicit the response of seeing the thing at that exact moment, at that exact time. I'm sure, for Birdie, it was annoying: I would suddenly announce that I had to get something, to sketch what we were seeing. Inspiration hitting. If I'd been a photographer, it would have been so easy, but instead I got my pencil, my notebook. I saw something new, and I tried to grasp it, to make it everlasting on the paper. I moved, I constantly moved, and I saw new things, and I captured them.

I don't really paint any more. There's nothing new. Everything is static.

But Birdie being somewhere, being in England, presents an opportunity: to move again. To travel across America, to find my way back to somewhere that I once called home. There's a route, of course. A way that these things are done. A ship, that's easiest. A seven-day crossing, cargo ships and passenger ships, doesn't matter which. I'll need money, I know, but there is some, different currencies. Some people still use it, many don't; but I have no option. I have nothing to barter. I have a lockbox, with cash inside it. Rarely of value. Birdie's old jewellery is better of course; but again, limited. And the pristine items, of little value to anybody but yourself.

Here's a Star Wars figurine in its packaging, for the full experience: of opening it, of smelling that waft of crass plastic. Darth Revan, his arms hiding a lightsaber, a sliding lever to push it out. You make the noise with your mouth, approximating its warm vmm; and you move his arm, up and down. A perfect trigger. My mother got it for me from Disneyworld, when I was a kid.

Then a hag stone that I found on the beach. I remember the day; I remember feeling the hole in the stone, my fingertips finding it. Worrying it, wondering how it got there.

Rebecca's hospital bracelets; from when she was born, and when she died.

Memories have to either be popular, or absolutely personal. They have to be. The collective unconscious means that the popular is worth more to more people. There are millions of Star Wars figures in bargain buckets, their paint worn, their lightsabers missing; there are trillions of stones on beaches, un-rare, un-lovely. Worth nothing to anybody, really. Only to me.

I take everything from the lockbox. The money, the figure, the stone, the bracelets. One that we fixed together; one that she fixed together herself. Not a good memory, but a memory: of how she clipped it on, clicked it. The sound of it, and then she pulled at the cuff.

'It won't undo,' she said. We knew that it wouldn't leave her wrist, not unless we cut it off; and we knew that we would only cut the translucent bracelet off in one of only two scenarios.

Either way, it's taken off only when you leave.

I have a backpack. It is all I can manage, all I can carry. My back's not great. When the fits come, which they do, infrequently but invariably, they make me shake. My whole body feels as if it's tearing itself apart. A few changes of clothes – they all hang off my frame; there's no point in wondering what looks best, but rather about practicality, how small they will roll, how hard they will wear – some clothes and my notebook, my pencils. Specific pencils, my pencils; and a Field Notes notebook, with the paper to weather any conditions. I think about the sketches I'll make, that I'll never turn into paintings. Black and white and greyscale, never to have colour injected into them. There's nobody who wants art, not here. Nobody wants moments preserved, now. Just look out of the window, everything is preserved for you.

We used to be fragile and human, and then we changed. Now, look at us: we are eternal. Pettersen, the man who runs

London, the man who started the Knot – a church, a twisted version of faith – once said that we had evolved; that we are gods now, able to overcome death. That the Anomaly was our key to realizing our true power.

My father was a fan of his. In those latter days. He went to his talks, his churches, his preacheries, his lectures, and he dragged me along. I was a kid, and I had only recently lost my mother, and he took me with him. He would say that if she was meant to come back, she would come back. Tying knots in ropes, to wear: eternal, a loop. This was when there were only rumours about what happened inside the Anomaly. Before statements, when there were leaks: person *x* on mission *y*, coming back terrified. The internet buzzing about what exactly happened up there in space, or latterly, the atmosphere. My father clinging to the edges of the computer screen as he read the stories, back when it wasn't yet imminent, but close enough.

I hated Pettersen. I hated my father for taking me to watch him; for giving himself over to the Knot, when I needed him so much.

There is a copy of one of Pettersen's books in the house. Birdie found it, not long after the Anomaly came. We were out, and there was a little wooden box of books outside somebody's house, *Library Of The Sun* printed on a little sign above it, and she took the book.

'We should know what he believes,' she said. 'Better to know your enemy, right?'

She was grieving. I was grieving. Everything was broken. She read the book cover to cover, and I said, 'Am I losing you to him as well?' I was half-joking. A quarter-joking.

'Of course not,' she said. She finished it. A month later, she read the book again.

She read it a few times. She said, 'I just want to understand him, I suppose. What he thinks. Not that I believe it, but it's interesting, to see things from this side. The way that they think, you know?'

Then, one day, she was gone.

There are conspiracy theories about what was known about the Anomaly and what was not. Because we were not told; or, rather, the *public* was not told. Back in the old days, when the threat was nuclear war, say, there were stories of bunkers, of tunnels, enormous panic rooms running the length of cities, veins from a dilated iris. They remained, of course, super-structures under our feet; but the purpose shifted. When it started to become clearer what would happen when the Anomaly did reach us, when the governments were forced to admit that the rumours might be true, the use of those tunnels changed. *Safety tunnels* was the phrase that the theorists used. Nothing to cause death, no source of accidental anything. Down there, there are no weapons. There are no loose cords to trip over and fall. There's medicine, instead, and food processors, that any lumps in food might be denied the chance to present a choking hazard. Safe tunnels as a conspiracy theory; even our conspiracy theories are nice and comfortable, some return to plush ease and no fears. We conceptualize ideals, and now our ideals are quite simple: don't die, and don't let those we love die, and stay away from death in all of its forms. The important, the wealthy, the rumours go that they're living down in those tunnels, eating processed slop, not moving really, being careful not to hit their heads in case they die and loop. They're wrapped in bubble wrap, waiting for the Anomaly to leave.

The Anomaly: a mass in space, undefined, unending, so

gargantuan that it was impossible to know where it ended, and where the rest of space began. And so old: first discovered back when my grandmother was young, as it slowly eked its way across our solar system. It swallowed everything that went into it: spaceships, sent to explore it; subsequent missions, echoing the first, meant to find proof of life after the fact; then as it came close to us, edging its way to our planet, either a target or simply detritus in its path, our space station, the last bastion of defence. We tried to expel it, with weapons and bombs and devices that used techniques nobody was allowed to know about, as our enemies would be listening, as if they didn't have something better to be doing. The most interesting arrogance of our planet came when it was months then weeks away from us: the West felt like that would be when Korea, for example, would make its move. Or Russia: were they finally rebuilt? Was this their chance?

But here was the reality: it came from outside, and moved towards the sun. Swallowed the celestial objects that came near it, like plankton into the mouth of a shark. The planets coming and going, in and out of the Anomaly, in and out; and the scientists watched, from Earth. Most of us didn't know. There were no stars, sometimes. That was the tell. For years and years and years, sometimes, some parts of the sky had no stars.

Then we were nearly there, Earth's orbit so close it was as if we could reach our hands up from the planet's surface and touch it.

It enveloped us. One day, the whole solar system was swallowed. More, maybe. Who knows. The sky blotted a little. This ever-so-soft haze, which at first it was easy to mistake for LA being LA, but revealed itself over time: inky-blue chemtrails of smog dancing when the light catches them at the right angle. Light that we're not even sure about.

And from inside it, we can't see stars, not any more. Not a single one.

That doesn't matter. That doesn't matter at all. I get bogged down in details. Capture the moment, put it on the paper: that's all about details. I think about things as representations; as abstractions, or replications. Facts are, somehow, intangible.

I say goodbye to every surface. As if the kitchen has a power of its own – this is food, sustenance, this knife the way I sliced my apples. I say goodbye to the bathrooms, countless hours of pain in there. In the early days, when Birdie was still here, and I was trying to hide what was happening to me, the bathroom was my refuge. She knew, I'm sure. She would have heard my being sick, masked with coughs, with the flushing of the lavatory. The taps running full pelt, showers at all times of day. Clothes washed before she even saw an inch of them. She asked me how I was, and I told her lies, and she accepted them. That is what I needed. She understood.

She asked if I was scared. I asked if she was. Both of us lying, I think, in our responses.

I run my hands along walls I have leant on. Turn handles I have barely ever turned, as we didn't close doors for years of living here. I remember the faucets that were tighter than others; I remember, with my palm, the draughts through windows. Sealant that we spoke of replacing, that we allowed to gently blacken. Push with a finger, nail bitten to the quick, to let it compress, to exhale. To watch the imprint my own fingertip leaves in the putty. My bag is already heavy on my shoulders.

There are photographs here, but I don't recognize them any more. They are so long ago, for me. They are not memories, but rather impressions of memories. I have kept them up, but I have never really looked at them.

I look at one, of me and Birdie and Rebecca. The three of us, holding each other, laughing. Something was coming, we were in denial. It was, then, so easy to smile, and to pretend.

I go outside, to the street. I walk next door, where Austin is nearly dead again. The sounds he's making quieter now. I tell him that I'm leaving, but I don't think he hears me. I say, 'I wish that I could have done more for you,' but I don't really know if I'm talking to him or to the past, in general. Everybody. Me, Birdie, Rebecca.

I turn back to the wall that runs alongside my house, which the windows in the master bedroom look out onto. I don't know when I noticed it, but it can't have been long after Birdie left: somebody had painted words, massive words, in this shade of doom black, onto the wall outside the front of the house.

Time means nothing.

You are free.

Don't look back.

A message left by somebody to the people of the city, post-Anomaly. I don't know who would want to write this; and I have wondered, in the past, if it wasn't left for somebody on this stretch. All of us, something to abandon.

I hear Austin shout:

'Do it, do it, do it!' I stare at the words: they have always bemused me, but they were here, waiting for me; waiting for me to have a reason to listen to them.

I am free, and I don't look back.

3

I imagine, sometimes, describing life to an alien visitor – an exercise I remember from being a kid in school – and those aliens wondering why we have built such large walkways between houses. Such a curious use of what little space we have. No cars here now, or not legal ones, at least. It didn't take long for cars to be outlawed entirely, removed from the streets. As illegal as guns became in that moment: how do we preserve our lives? Some fought, of course, fought both sides: because they loved to drive their fast cars, and they loved to shoot their big guns. They argued, private property, licences for those who wanted them, even if they required strict checks; but really, there was little support. As soon as everything could become a weapon for a death more terrifying than it had previously been – such a strange concept, because surely death should have been enough? but no – the locks went on. Cars were impounded; guns smelted. Who could have predicted that it would take something as simple as the loss of personal linear time to finally take action and protect people from guns? The streets were emptied, and the sun has baked the tarmac, and now it's a stew of new darkness, actual darkness, flowing with the yellow and white of old street markings, bent around, manipulated by the rise and fall of the ground. Like a swirl of Play-Doh, multiple colours blended together, inseparable after that moment.

I do not often walk, these days. I do not often leave the house, as I can't make it too far. My legs ache, my bones ache. Birdie once said, 'You keep acting like it's a symbiotic relationship or something. It's not you and the disease, it's you, and then the disease has latched onto you. It's a fucking assault, is what it is. It's a terrorist, holding you hostage while it tortures you to death.'

'Please,' I said, 'let's not talk about this. Not now.' It was my third ever bleed, blood coming from every pore, this slow seep of pale pink. We thought, then, it was so slow that maybe I had a short while to live. We prepared for me to come back, to loop. We didn't know how much I would stretch it out.

'Well, if we can't talk about it now, when can we? If not now, when?' Birdie was good at not crying in front of me, because – we laughed, about this, and other things – because, she said, 'If I start crying, then you might. And you'll cry blood, which is worse than tears. You win that one easily.'

I have stages and steps. I am going to die, I know that. I should already be dead. Everybody else, every single one who caught this thing, as best as I can tell, went within a year, two at most. The majority died within days.

I have lasted decades. That cannot keep, it simply cannot. Everything ends, even if it starts again. And before I die, I know this: I have to find Birdie.

I want to know why.

*   *   *

There is a man near the boardwalk, with a sign in his hand. On one side, the visible side as I approach him, it says *Golf Golf Golf Sale*, with a picture of a pitted ball flying, and scrappy lines to indicate movement tracing its path. He sees me coming – there's nobody else here, not a soul, so my footfall makes miniature echoes – and he turns. He's sweating in the sun, his coat too large for this weather. No shoes, his trousers ripped at the knees, intentionally, to turn them into shorts. Unfinished. He spins the sign so I can read the hand-scrawled message he's put onto its rear.

We can all be saved, it reads.

'From what?' I nod at the board.

'My friend, you ask the question, and I have the answer.' His mouth is rancid, rotten to the hilt. Dripping black tar teeth, or what's left of them. Dentistry has been abandoned in the end times; teeth won't be what kills us. 'We can be saved from . . . life.'

'A radical thought,' I say. A curmudgeon, at my age. Not elderly, but infirm, maybe. The curmudgeonly infirm.

'It is, though, it is. Have you ever contemplated: what if we are all dead already? What if this is the afterlife, eh? Or purgatory!'

'Oh, don't,' I say, 'the oldest twist in the book,' but he persists.

'What if we *died*? The thing arrived and we died, and this is purgatory. I can quote you the Bible, but I won't bore you with it—'

'I've read it,' I say. 'There's nothing in it about an Anomaly.'

'Jesus was a prophet, not a soothsayer. He spoke in ambiguity, of revelation, of the unveiling; and that, my friend, that is the Anomaly.' He misses the final A from the word. *Anomly*. 'We are the Anomaly. All of us.'

'We didn't die,' I say.

'How can you be sure?'

'Because I am dying now, and dying while dead would be unbearably cruel.'

'God *is* cruel,' he tells me. 'This is how peace comes: from the acceptance of that as a fact.' He jabs at the air with his thumb over a closed fist. A politician's move. 'We can explain God as easily as we can explain the Anomaly. Here's the delusion we have,' he says. 'That we were ever in control of anything. We made clocks, right? Clocks to tell us that time was moving forward, but that's not why we do anything. That's not actually at the core of humanity. Humans like control. We say, oh heck, we're just doing a thing because we can, fucking *exploring*, or *discovering*, whatever; but that's bullshit. Bullshit. We made clocks, right, because we wanted a sense of control over this thing we didn't understand. The planets, the tides, the fucking moon, we didn't have control over them, so we made something to force it to abide by us. It was brutal and preternatural and insane, insane, and we went, here's your fucking shackles, here's your numbers. We invented numbers, we invented time, we invented the shackle of the clock. We invented birthdays! Birth-fucking-days!'

'Birthdays mark a full rotation of the Earth relative to yourself,' I say.

'Bullshit. We don't know where we are. Maybe, maybe, the sun is moving around us. We have imposed these rules—'

'I should go—'

'Yeah, yeah. Everybody leaves.' He stares at me. He flicks his tongue between the maw in his mouth; pushes his tongue to the barrier of spittle, the bubble, where his teeth used to be. 'You know, I got secrets. I heard a story that there was a spaceship crashed, you know? One of the first to go up

27

there. The crew were still alive, they came back to Earth, but they were like fucking ghosts, or demons. Demons. You read about them in the Bible, I bet you did.' I don't say anything. There are always stories like this: somebody leaves, they don't come back, then they do. They come back changed, by what they've seen, by what happened to them.

I have lost too many people to pay attention to them now.

The man steps closer to me. I flinch backwards. 'You got anything I can have?'

'No,' I say.

'You're lying. You're lying. That watch.' He looks at my wrist. An old Timex, that my father had, that my mother gave to him as a present when they first met. The only thing he kept of hers. I think he lost his mind, but still, he kept that watch. When he left, he didn't take it, so I did. Sometimes I feel it, the weight of it, slipping down, the crown pushing into the meat of my thumb. 'You could give me that watch, if you like.'

'It doesn't work.'

'So give it to me.'

'What's the point? You don't need it, it doesn't work.'

'Give it to me,' he says again. Not raising his voice, and not forcefully. More: like a child, asking for another lolly.

'That's not a threat,' I say. 'If you like, I don't like.'

'I'm hungry, and you look—' He stops himself. 'I don't wanna die again. Simple as that, shit, I have kept on dying. I don't want to die again.' Shakes his head. 'You died, right?'

'No,' I say. The wrong thing to say, I knew it the moment the word left my mouth.

'Shit, okay, okay. Well, then: there's a lot to lose.'

'How do you mean?'

'If you died now. You've walked a long road.'

28

'Is that a threat?' I ask.

'I'm hungry,' he replies. 'Where were you? Point of entry?'

'At my house, just down there.'

'Give me the watch,' he says.

'No,' I say.

'Think of it as an investment. Give me the watch, and if you die – I'll be here. I'll have it. I can tell you what happened. If I've got the watch, that way, you'll know it's me. You'll know I'm telling the truth. I can show it to you.'

Things don't change. People move; the things on them move. The things they leave behind, they remain, like an echo. Stories abound of people using that, duplicating things, copying them. Like cloning. Take a watch, kill me, if I was wearing the watch when I started the loop, another will be on my body. Take the watch, you've got two watches.

There are rules. The rules are as intangible as the Anomaly itself.

The man is jittery. He's too jittery, his skin waxy, his teeth gone. I wonder how many times he's died. I wonder how long he has in each loop.

I peel the watch from my wrist – it catches my skin, and it bleeds, just a trickle of water-thin blood, and I freeze, I hesitate, in case it's not the skin catching, in case; but it is, it's a hairline cut – I peel the watch off and I hand it to him. He slips it on, the clinking of the strap.

'This is nice,' he says. 'I'll make sure to tell you. To find you, to tell you, if you come back, okay?'

'The watch doesn't work,' I say, again.

'I don't care,' he says. 'You're lucky you found me, you know.'

Aren't I just. A hustle, just as there was always hustle, as there will always be hustle. I was never able to pull anything like that off. I was a terrible liar, really. Too many tells. I assume this man was born hustling, he'll die hustling, he'll come back hustling.

If he's wearing my watch when he dies, when he loops, it will disappear. The Anomaly doesn't leave corpses; doesn't leave detritus. I wonder where it will go. Somewhere that's nowhere; until I die, and then it will come back to me. Watch heaven, maybe. No: watch purgatory. It feels strange, seeing it – my father's watch – on his wrist. Because my mother got it for him, and so that's something of her: her taste, more than my father's. He stopped wearing it when they divorced; started again when she died. Or, after she died. I remember a woman, on our doorstep, confronting him. Telling him, You failed her. You fucking failed her. I remember her swearing. I was a teenager, I forget my age exactly. Young. It feels a long time ago. And she was there, my mother's co-worker, who actually made it home. Standing there, furious, her own stuff going on, you could always tell. Her own chaos, the Anomaly coming, so much to do; but she took the time to come to our house, and tell my father off.

'You fucking destroyed her,' the woman said. 'I knew her when she died, I knew her. *You* destroyed her.'

'Where's next for you?' the hustler asks. He pulls something from his pocket, holds it out for me. An offering: half-chewed jerky, some sort of meat that I absolutely cannot trust the pedigree of. Teeth marks in the ends of it, though he has no teeth. Somebody else bit the jerky before he did. I wonder how he hustled that from them. 'You want some?'

'I'm fine,' I say.

'You look hungry.'

'I'm dying,' I tell him again.

'Oh, sure, sure.' He puts the jerky to his mouth and starts to suck it; then puts his fingers to the watch, turns it around on his wrist. Pokes the crown, changing the time of it, setting it to a time that won't change now. It doesn't even matter, I think; and I start to walk, away from him, down the promenade.

A T-shirt on the boardwalk, stretched over an awning: *We are not open*, it reads.

My shoes are not cut out for the task of travelling across the country, I don't think. I probably need some new shoes, which means foraging or looting or stealing or bartering, and I don't know which will be easier. Probably when I get out of the city, that's the best: they'll last me as far as the hills, out to the countryside. I don't have a map; I should get a map.

The library is a hub: of life, of art, of commerce. Seven floors changed and turned into something other than what it once was. The books – all of them, everything, more added when they're found or foraged or donated – across two floors, piled deep but not high, to avoid the risk of tower collapse, injury, death; food traded on one floor, clothes on another; education on another, advice another, lessons another.

The books are one in, one out, simple rules. Anything defaced is devalued and worthless. Even cracked spines and torn covers mean that the thing is repurposed: to toilet paper, to papier mâché, to decorative wallpaper. The curators of the library are revered: they know what you want, and they catalogue everything themselves, everything in their heads. An inventory of genres. Clothes are traded: here's where the new comes from, seamsters working there to transform any old fabric into something new, working from patterns in the books. I helped them, once, fetching those large foot-pump sewing machines, after we lost the electricity. Even when there are bursts of power, they never go back: just press the accelerator, over and over, this steady rhythm. Education, advice, lessons, they're traded for: either the teacher needs their own education, or they need other help. Teach me to fix a sol2r panel to a roof? Or, will you take the risk to fit a sol2r panel to a roof? Very few people work with electrics any more, the dangers are too great; those skills are valued highest of all.

I'm by the front doors when I see Janine and Peter. They live here. We've met a few times: I come by maybe once a year, maybe twice. Not wanting to push my luck. Good people, trying hard to do right by this place. Standing outside, cleaning down the tiles out here. Too much dust puts people off; and they need to do it early, so that the water dries before anybody risks slipping on them. The sun here, it only takes minutes to dry.

'Hello,' I say.

'Hey, hey, sunshine.' That term of endearment doesn't quite carry the joy it once did. 'You doing okay?' Janine puts her hand to her head, a sunshade for her eyes; but she still squints. Peter's on the floor cleaning. He looks up, smiles.

'I'm fine. Thank you. I need a map,' I say.

'A map. Okay, sure. We've got—' Janine nudges Peter. 'Go and help Theo, there's a pile in c-seven, c-eight, unless it's world maps?'

'I don't really know: the United States, certainly. And, I don't know. Where do ships go to? From New York, I mean.'

'You're taking a trip?'

'Yes,' I say. 'I'm going to where I grew up. England.'

'No shit! You gonna be coming back?'

'That's the plan,' I reply.

I don't know if it is. There is no plan.

Janine nods. 'Okay. Well, we'll get you some maps, and if you don't look like you're going to make it home, you just keep them, okay? A gift, from us to you.'

'Thank you,' I say. Of course, if I'm not making it home, it's because I'll be sick or dead, that's what Janine's implying; and the maps won't exactly be much use after that. I won't have a clue where I've come from.

Peter takes me inside, past the desks as they used to be. Security gates, red blinkers that no longer blink. A sign on the wall, kept up because it's funny, it's actually almost funny: *No handguns allowed.* A chuckle from Peter as he walks past, because there's always a chuckle. He likes to think about how things used to be, and how adaptable he therefore is. He moved on; and we move on, past books, piles of best-sellers. Past the apocalyptic section, still one of the most visited, even now; as if readers might want to see how it could have been worse. I once took out a copy of a novel called *The Road*, which was miserable and beautiful, and somebody else had scrawled in it, at the end: *At least we do not have to endure this.* Past the historical, the romantic: thumb-flecked pages in those. To the nonfiction, and the books of photographs, a monument to how the world used to be. Here's all the animals that are now extinct. Panda bears staring out from the covers of glossy coffee-table volumes, hanging from bamboo, eating that same bamboo. And then to the maps: those rotating stands, piled full of them. Ten or so, all spinning as Peter runs his hands past them and they twirl, tubular ballerinas made of concertinaed paper. Plucks a few from the one closest to him.

'This is a roadmap, continental America. This is with some of the cities. Are you stopping off?'

'Not if I can help it,' I say.

'You might have to. I don't know how hot the desert gets these days, but, jeez. Must be pretty hot. How are you doing the South?'

'I haven't thought that far.'

'Okay. I can make some calls. There's a bus, I know that? One of the border-runners. I can call him, if you like?'

'That might be good, actually.'

He nods at me. Hands me the maps. 'Here's some for the cities. You're taking a ship?'

'I think so.'

'Then New York, that's where they're all leaving from. Florida for some, but don't go down there. Too much chaos. And I'm assuming that you want to avoid the camps.'

'I do, if I can help it.'

'Okay, then, so: New York. Have you been?' He runs his fingers through his beard, splaying them, as if they're a comb.

'Not since I was a child.'

'It's fine there, fine. Cooler than here, so people are packed in like little tinned fish.' He shrugs. 'Boat from there'll be Spain, maybe? Or Ireland, you could get to Ireland first, on some of the boats.' He pulls those maps out from other rotatables. 'Where else?'

'I don't know. I'm going to London—'

'Whee. Long distance, long distance. I don't have a street map for there. Here's mainland Europe. Not detailed, but if you need main roads, they'll give you some idea of where you're headed. You can trek up through France, I reckon, if it's south. Go north, get to the Channel. Then England, that's London. One long road.'

'Thank you,' I say. I put the maps into my backpack, into the sleeve at the rear that was meant to be for a laptop. Next to my notebooks, my pencils. Optimistic with those.

'Sounds like one hell of a trip.' We walk out of the library. In the young adult section, three teenagers sit. They're reading, lounging on the floor. Reading, nothing more, as if there's all the time in the world. The books so old, and I wonder if the worlds in them are recognizable to them now.

Outside, Janine stares at us. Her hand again to her forehead, even though the sun is behind her, there's no glare, no need for the shade.

'You find what you're after?'

'Peter was very helpful,' I say.

'He gives that impression, but really,' she says, 'he's just faking it.'

'Oh, I don't know.'

'I've been with him since we were ten. I know,' she says. She hits his arm. He laughs, feigns death from the combat. Falls to the floor, rolling, howling.

'Ow, ow, this is it,' he says. 'The end cometh!' Strange to joke about death. Maybe we're there now, socially. Maybe we're past the awe of it; or the fear. Maybe it's just Janine and Peter.

'Hello?' A voice that belongs to none of us three. From the side, from the road. A woman, in her thirties. Maybe older. Walking to us, and she's unafraid in the moment – we're wary, usually, with strangers, all of us, trained to be – but she's not, she's fast. I step back instinctively, because I don't know what's wrong with her. There is always something wrong, always something. 'Please help,' she says. She's clutching her left arm with her right hand. Pulling it tight into her body, trying to fold herself smaller.

Janine steps forward. 'What's the matter? Hands out, you got something we can't see?' Worried about a weapon, something that could harm us. End our loops. Janine and Peter, together since they were ten.

When they die, it'll be together.

'You should stay where you're standing,' Peter says, and I step back again.

'I don't understand,' the woman says. 'I don't understand what's happening, where am I? Where am I? This is Los Angeles, isn't it?'

'Oh, God,' Janine says, understanding. 'Okay. Hello, darlin'.' A sudden country twang to her voice, soothing and comforting. Like some old song, minor key, inviting you in. Her voice altered, maybe to how it once was, a twinge of her youth come back to soothe people who need something pure, something soft. 'Come and sit here, sit with me, and I'll talk to you about it, okay?'

She's just come back. Peter and Janine are the unofficial guiding lights for those who have just started their loops again, around here. It's a real skill, telling them what's happened. Breaking that news. Peter runs inside to make coffee or tea, something warm: chocolate, the girl asks for, and Peter nods. 'I think we've got some, you stay put, let Janine take care of you.'

I stand there at the side, neutered and useless. The poor thing.

Janine sits with her, on a bench to one side, and takes her hand. 'What's your name?'

'Shannon.'

'Shannon, okay. So you remember—'

'What's happened to me?'

'Fuck. Fuck.' Janine stretches the words out, and rubs her

eyes with her forefinger and thumb. Digging deep, so deep I think it must actually hurt. 'This doesn't get easier. You remember, okay. You remember the Anomaly?'

'I remember, yes.' Shannon looks around. 'It's here? Was it last night? That's why everything's different?'

'It's here, yeah, for sure, it's here. We've got a pamphlet, we'll give you that. There's a pack, we've got a whole pack.' Janine looks to me. 'Can you fetch me one?'

'Of course,' I say, and I run inside, or walk as fast as I can, my approximation of a run: feeling every bit of me rise and slump as I do, my skin as if it's lost muscle, as if it's no longer clinging to the bone as I would like it to. I helped fill the packs one day, when it was decided that they would be useful. Here's what's happened; here's what we know. Here's what you need to know, to carry on, to move forward.

We are in a post-apocalypse. Or more: a post-post-apocalypse. You don't understand what that means, so please, let this pamphlet explain it to you. It is, certainly, not what you expected, not what any of us expected.

The pack is in a bag, a paper bag. Printed, marked, with contact details and names: Janine and Peter, a few others from the community who put themselves forward as the North Star, should guidance be needed. Some telephone numbers, and a guide for how to use them. A guide to the locations of old Blue Box telephones, in case you're not set up for the satellites. And inside the bag, other things: potato chips, because you might be hungry, a bottle of water. A whistle, a flare. People will come if they see the orange smoke. Orange means, *Please help*. That's the rule, that's what's been agreed upon. And a note inside: *Please do not panic*, it reads, *You are going to be okay, and you are among friends*.

I take one of the bags back outside. Shannon is sobbing,

and Janine has her arm around her. I approach slowly. Foot by foot. Pass the bag to Janine, who smiles at me.

'Shannon was saying that she's got a daughter,' Janine says.

'Oh,' I say.

'She's only seven. She'll be so afraid.'

'Right.'

'Perhaps you could find her? She lives— Where does she live, Shannon?'

'Peymont. Seventeen Peymont. Or that's where—'

'Okay,' I say. Cutting her off. It's the kindest thing to do, rather than letting her unpack it any more. 'I'll go there, see what I can find.' I smile, but Shannon doesn't, not even in that comforting way that lets somebody else know that they trust them, even if only a little.

Seventeen Peymont Street is a nice house, the sort that affluent families owned back when affluence was an aspiration: a way to display your hard work, your success, however moderate. A fence around it, painted and faded black. Inside, concrete slabs and gravel micro-gardens. This was once a bonsai paradise, by the look of it; a swimming pool, thin, long, the sort you do lengths in rather than frolic. Huge darkened windows across the front, glass and black steel. The door hangs wide open, and I step through. It's hot, a steam-house. Plants everywhere, but tended to, tended for. Ferns, which they say are cleansing. I had ferns in the hospital: I stared at them, at the bugs on them. The flies, those minuscule flies. I wondered, then, if flies were new, or somehow they were all simply looping. How long did they live for? How many generations could be born in one of those life cycles? How were we not simply overrun by them?

There's more in here that reminds me of the hospital: a bed with a switch, to raise or lower it. To bend it at the middle. This one is wired to something running out of the windows: I don't need to look to see the temporary power setup. There are bottles of medicine, and some sort of home-made chemistry works in the kitchen – it's a thing of beauty, granite and marble and concrete. Somehow, the cold lines of archaic brutalism turned into functional work-surface and cupboard areas – along with tins of food, long-life, preserved. An incongruity here, that you see everywhere: we're prepared for anything, and yet living in the space we once lived in with no preparations, with no cares. I run my hand along the countertop and find rubber corners: those sticky things you place down for toddlers, to proof it. This counter is too high for a toddler; we are too concerned, or this person was.

A photograph of a family hangs on one wall. Posed by a river, the sort of river you wouldn't go near now: raging, rocky, one gust of wind and that's it, a life spilled. The woman, Shannon, a little younger here, with a husband and a young daughter.

'What do you want?' A high voice, from behind me. Afraid, but it's only momentarily; until I turn, and she sees me, and she sees, I'm sure, that I am not a threat. Even if I were, you can smell how brittle my being is; how easily I would snap, and how satisfyingly. A woman in her mid-thirties. She looks scared. There's a towel on her head, post a shower or a swim, and she's holding a knife. Small, sharp. I raise my hands. Nothing in them.

'Shannon,' I say, as if the name will be a password.

'What about her?' She looks past me, craning her neck to see into the room with the bed, the one-bed hospice constructed here.

'She found us, or we found her. By the library. She asked me to come here.'

'She's my mother. She can't walk.' She looks at the door, where a wheelchair – an old, stable thing, the sort that doesn't run itself, that relies on others to make anything happen, really; and I imagine Shannon, frail, twisted, folded into that seat, her arms crossed, her legs under a blanket, even in the heat. There is hair on the floor, around the bed, around the chair. Decay: we can smell our own. I watch as the daughter realizes what has happened, as it crosses her face. I think of that gag, playing with Rebecca: a swipe of my hand across a smile, turning it into a frown, then back again, then tongue out, then sobbing, then mania, then any expression that I can think of, all in an attempt to make her smile.

Stealing her nose; the awe on her face.

Shannon's daughter's own face collapses, from one expression to another. No magic there, no illusion. 'I wasn't watching her, I didn't hear anything. She's gone? Is she okay?' she asks.

'She's confused,' I say.

'Yeah. She—' She stops talking. No words.

'What was wrong with her? I mean: what killed her?'

'Cancer.'

'Oh. Did she want—'

'To die? No. She was looking forward to her time again. I've got a daughter as well, now.' Shannon's daughter pulls her wallet from her pocket, opens it, brings out a picture. Three generations of women, and they're all similar: the through line of Shannon in them. 'This is us.'

'I'm Theo,' I say.

'Astrid. Good to meet you.' She shakes my hand, and then wipes a tear, and I reach for tissues, for a box of them from the counter. 'I don't know if I should be happy or sad, you know? We've been through a lot.'

'You have. How long was she sick for?'

'Ten years. I mean, not quite, but nearly. Ten.'

'It's a long time.'

'It's forever.'

'She won't know who you are,' I say. 'That will be hard for her, because she thinks you're still little, I think.'

'I was seven when it came. You know how old my little girl is?'

I smile. 'I can guess.'

'This is so going to fuck her up.'

'It'll be okay. She knew the Anomaly was coming. She might not have known what it was going to do, but that moment—'

'Yeah. Do you have kids?' she asks.

'I did,' I say. There's a weight to the past tense, and she reads it. 'Before.'

'I'm sorry,' she says. 'And here's my mom come back, I shouldn't be complaining.'

I smile. 'It's life,' I say.

Out of nowhere, she reaches for me. It's a surprise, and I flinch, her arms suddenly wrapped around me.

I can't remember when I was last hugged. No, I can, that's a lie: Birdie. She would have been the last. When I last felt a hand on me, a hand on my chest. The warmth of somebody else, and I didn't freak out, didn't push back. Don't come near me, because if I bleed, then there's a chance.

I'm not meant to be contagious. It's not the contagious kind. It's the kind that kills you fast, so I am defying every expectation. I don't want to be somebody else's death blow.

She sobs, into the shirt I'm wearing, I can feel her tears soaking through to my chest; the part of me where I feel like the skin is at its most thin, closest to bone, closest to blood.

'We should go and find your mother,' I say, but Astrid doesn't move, and I'm not going to be the one to make her.

As we're walking, she asks what's wrong with me, and I tell her. Her eyes widen. She shifts away from me a little.

'You can't catch it,' I say. 'It's the wrong strain. The right strain.'

'Oh,' she replies. 'You've come back? With it?'

'No,' I say, 'I'm still here. Still the original.'

'But you should be dead,' she says.

'So the doctors told me.'

'You're not.'

'I've been pushing my luck. If that's what you'd call it.'

'You should have died. Come back without it. I know somebody who did that.'

'I had it before. Before the Anomaly, so there's— I mean, the virus is how it ends. For me.' I can hear the clarity in my voice. There was a time it would have cracked, delivering that news. Saying that.

'How does that feel?'

'Desperate,' I say, I think.

'Did you know? Before, I mean.' She doesn't know how to talk about this; I do not know how to talk about this.

'I did,' I say. 'My daughter, we had a daughter. And then she needed our blood, but mine wasn't any use. They told me then. That was six months before.'

'Fuck,' she says. 'So you were first wave. Before they even told anybody?'

'Yes,' I reply. 'Second wave, but yes. And I didn't die, which made me an Anomaly myself. Everybody was sort of scared of me, I think.'

'We live in such a bubble,' she says. 'This place, you know? We're in such a bubble. Like, Mom didn't even necessarily think she would actually have to deal with this. She thought we might be clear, that it might have gone before—'

'I wondered that myself.'

'And now?'

'I don't know.' I look up at the sky, and it's still there: this sheen, this veil. The blue, slightly false now. That illusion, of light, of colour. 'We're still in the same path, the same orbit. Nothing's changed.'

'No.'

'So I don't know how long it will take. I'll die when I die.'

'You aren't going to kill yourself? Get it done?' She seems genuinely surprised. 'What's from here, only downhill, right?'

'I suppose,' I say. 'But—'

'I thought about it, with Mom.' She doesn't seem sad. Just logical. I think of the chemistry set in the kitchen. A witches' brew, designed for the cessation of misery.

'I don't want to come back,' I say. 'Not like this. Not like anything, really.'

'Not as if you've got a choice,' she replies.

'I was waiting,' I tell her. We are close now, the library looming over the houses. Once, these were all full; once, there was a bar on this corner, and a shop. And there, a man selling churros and Mexican drinks from large whirling glass drums, tumblers full to the brim with crushed ice.

'Waiting for what?'

'For death,' I say. 'There was – there is – a chance that the Anomaly will pass before I die. I mean, there has to be that chance, doesn't there?' She's quiet; she lets me speak. 'I've wondered if that's why the diagnosis was wrong in the first place. Maybe that's why I didn't die yet, maybe that's why I'm still here. You know when,' I correct myself, 'you remember when you were busy, or there was something important. And your body would fight off a cold because you had work, or a holiday—'

'That's a virus, though. Not something caused by a biological weapon.'

'Yes. I mean, fundamentally, I'm sure it's not correct. But maybe that's what I'm holding on for.'

'We don't know it'll ever leave. This might be it. That's what Pettersen says.'

'I don't pay attention to him.'

'He might be right.'

'He's not. There's science, that's more important. He's guessing, and manipulating the situation to his own ends. He's making it up, and there's nothing there to actually hold on to.'

She shrugs. 'My mother believed it.'

'She wanted to come back,' I say. 'She wanted to.'

'And she did. She gets a do-over, like he said she would.'

We see Shannon, then, standing outside the library. She's got a mug of some hot drink in her hand, nursing it even though it's ninety degrees out. She looks over to see her daughter, this woman who looks so like her, who looks so much like a copy or a clone or a duplicate; and yet, they're so distinct.

She cries as Astrid approaches. She knows, of course she knows. Even if she doesn't actually understand yet; even if the logic of it, as alien as it is to us, will have to be explained to her, over and over and over.

4

The map of the state is marked up with handwritten scrawl and icons, a legend for those icons attached to the map's top corner. It's built for walking, really: nobody uses cars, not unless they're sure there's no chance of a crash or anything else going wrong. There's a man trapped in a loop near San Diego who's in the car, suffocating, and he's only awake for seconds, not long enough to save him. We don't risk cars. Mechanics are few and far between, so they're flaky. Better to walk. Safer, somehow.

The markings show where there's food; and here's trusted people; here's the de-marked zones, don't go near these, there's either dangerous people in them or mass death loops that are inherently dangerous, or there's just something else generally wrong with the area. Marks where transport will leave from, at these approximate times, scratched through, changed, altered. Here's the names of people to use for said transports; if they have different names, do not trust them. Some of the churches will try to get you here, here, here, here, stay away from these spots, these roads, these corners. A fold-out table of descriptions of people: *tall, skin too pale, beard to top button; she's wiry, like pipe-cleaners, hair to match, eyes pale and wild; this one man is unpleasant to look at, like you know his intent from the way he walks, stay clear, his hands are large.* All the writing is too small, crammed into the space available. Another piece of paper, taped to the bottom of the main addendum: *My son is missing, if you see him, please tell him to come home, he looks like this*; and then a drawing, a remarkably rendered pencil sketch of a young man, dark eyes, black hair in this swoop across his forehead, his mouth slightly open as if sucking in air through his teeth. A glimpse of large front teeth, like slabs.

I trace my finger along a route: away from the sea, which seems to be the thing. Point myself in this direction, and walk. Stick to these streets. Those who came before me have marked street signs and corners: black scratches on the walls mean to stay away, to leave well enough alone. Walking with stones in their hands, to scratch as you go.

I haven't left this part of the city in twenty-five years. I haven't left the state in longer. I haven't done any of this before.

I fold the map up, and I begin. I start to walk. It's past midday, and I am hungry already. I should stop, to eat; but I do not, not yet.

5

I'm nearly at the bus station, which in reality is an old TGI Friday's, or the parking lot of one, and there are still houses here, and shopping areas, whole streets ripped free from the tethers of the grid, turned into small mall areas, like islands, drifting. Walking past them is strange, because there's nobody here, and there should be. There are no tumbleweeds, just vacancies. I wonder how many of them are dead; I wonder how many of them have stayed dead. If they regret what happened, what they chose, what they did.

I wonder, in the moments before they died, if they hated Pettersen. If they're looping, stuck in that hate.

I have hated him enough, over the course of my life. For what he did to my father – the avenue that he led him down, that led him away from me – but also what he did to the rest of the world. The lies, the misinformation. Taking advantage of people who were scared, who felt desperate. Everything was crashing, and he told them to take off their seatbelts, to trust in him. Those who survived the virus outbreak, they trusted him that they should die in the loop. Find eternal life through eternal death. And now they're in the perpetual loop. Some got their timing wrong, and they died; some were injured, and they survived, maimed.

Pettersen walked away, though, of course he did. He said he tried to kill himself, but that he was saved, he didn't know how. He said that he was a prophet, now, there to *live*. He told his people – those who believed in him, but not enough to actually do what he said when it meant killing themselves – to congregate on London: find their way to making a new city, with him as some sort of self-appointed mayor. No, more: a tsar.

He rules them, and I don't know what that means, but he's their ruler. Maybe they hate him, but he's a necessary evil for them. Something to believe in, people are always desperate for something to believe in.

There are eyes on me. They follow me as I walk down the middle of the street, as I scuff my shoes on the ground, my strength fading a little. I have eaten a pear, from a tree, miraculously; I have eaten stale potato chips and an orange that I took from a tree in somebody's front garden, and I have drunk water, home-mix Gatorade, more water. I don't stop, I didn't stop. I risked indigestion, because I honestly wouldn't know it if it happened to me. Every part of me hurts, every part is a low background hum of discomfort. The feeling of constant internal collapse. My brain is so used to back-benching the pain, what's a little more? So I keep walking, even as I feel their eyes on me. I hear footsteps; I hear the clambering of hands on walls, slap, slap, as they follow me. Sticking to the rooftops: here, low bungalows and single-storey apartment buildings, and I can't see them in my periphery, and I don't want to turn, because I don't want them to know that I know. I don't want them more confident. I want them to see that I'm weak. Slim pickings, no chance of anything good. Not even a good fight. I feign more of a limp; or, I allow myself the limp I try hard to bury the rest of the time. A slope to my gait. Let my foot drag a little, and the relief; and the scrape of it, worn rubber on concrete.

The street opens up into an intersection, tree-lined, where the trees have taken back the verges. Top of the list of things we let slip was trimming and maintaining the order we tried to keep to make things feel as though we were in control. We had lost control, so rewilding occurred. It was almost funny: that people couldn't make it happen, endlessly fighting and fighting, when all it took was the apocalypse to let nature get a hold back on the city. The trees grew, the grass grew. It was only weeks into our new reality that somebody realized that grass worked, looped, just as we do, and weeds likewise. So we stopped killing them. Why fight a fight that can't be won? Let them grow. Let them do what we cannot, or do not have a choice to do.

Some people say that this is the point: that we destroyed the planet, and then along came the Anomaly to help save it. To stop us breaking it over and over with our ceaseless stupid choices. Deus ex machina.

I cross the street. The tarmac here rippled and cracked, the effect of the melting-then-hardening that's happened. A lot of it, so it's pronounced. Peaks and valleys of grey stone; as if you would set a fantasy novel here, give it a volcanic name, a quest to lose yourself within it. And I rush, but I see their shadows: as the sun sets behind me, slipping into the ocean-horizon, it casts them across me. Three of them, something in one of their hands: a paddle, maybe? From a canoe, something like that.

'Hey,' one of them says. Quietly, as if he's testing me. His voice that unfortunately too-familiar ragged meth-smoke croak. 'Hey, hey, walking dude. Stop it, come here. Walking dude, stop walking.' I feel my bones creak, locking, almost.

Not here, not now. Please, not like this.

I don't want to die now. I didn't even make it out of the city.

'Yes?' I say. I stop. I turn. Three of them, two male, one female. Details that I wouldn't notice, but they're forcing me: standing, staring at me. Two shaven heads, one matted crow's nest; too much leather for this weather, too much ratty old denim; eyes that flit, over my body, my face, but rarely my own eyes; and yes, that oar, for some reason. Half an oar, as if that's the most intimidating weapon that they had to hand. It's brandished. Dragged behind a little, as if it's weightier than it is. Everybody feigning here.

'You lost?'

'I'm not lost,' I say. 'I'm walking.'

'Where?'

'Just walking.'

'Okay. Okay, you know what this is? What we are?' His voice is so broken it's a wonder it still works. As if he's speaking through some sort of digital manipulation. He doesn't wait for me to answer. 'We're not going to kill you,' he says; although, for them, that's the threat. That's the punishment. Actually, death here, it's not the end. Yes, you've made it this far, but still: death carries nothing with it. It's a loss of experience, not a loss of breath, of everything. 'We're not going to kill you, you understand?'

'I understand,' I say.

'We're going to keep you, okay? We've got places,' he says.

'You should be scared,' the woman of the three says.

'I am,' I say. Maybe I shouldn't admit that, but those are the words, that's what I hear from my lips. From somewhere deeper, somewhere guttural.

'But that doesn't have to happen. You dig?' I wonder what he would have been, or what he was meant to be. He's in his mid-twenties, which means he's very likely not here for the first time. Not unless he was born in this, and even then. There's a tattoo on his cheek, like those old tears that the gangs used to have, that started off as apocryphal murder tallies and ended as latch-on hipster bullshit. But this is a moon, waxing, full, beginning to wane. I have drawn moons, painted moons; they are as much a marker of time as anything. Reliable. The moon, our moon, still doing what it always did. Everything around it, near it. Even as the sky's not right, at least it's still up there.

And I realize: his moon is a tally. He's been around a few times, more than a few, and he's not aging. I wonder if this gang take it in turns: burning out, destroying themselves. Imagine what you can do to your body if you embrace the expendable nature of the self. I did cocaine, when I was younger, when we were travelling. I did some other drugs, before they went entirely chemical. Think of the destruction. He continues: 'You can give us your pills—'

'And don't say you don't got them, because you're old,' the other man says.

'I wouldn't insult you,' I say.

'Fuck no, you wouldn't.' He spits, and whacks the spittle gob with the oar as it falls. Reflexes that I maybe didn't expect, so exact I wonder if it was actually an accident.

'Your pills, whatever they are. We'll use them, and you don't need them.'

'They're painkillers,' I say. They'll take them either way:

better I reason, or try. 'I'm dying, and I need painkillers, or it will become too much.'

'Shit,' the female says, backing away. 'You sick? Can we catch it?'

'No,' I say. 'No, I'm sick, but you can't catch it.' Another mistake, talking not my forte. I could have scared them off. *Run, run, I bear a plague.* 'My ex-wife, or she's still my wife. She's alive, and I've been trying to find her. I want to tell her I'm sorry, because I think I pushed her away.'

'The fuck do I care about your fucking, I mean. Your wife? Your ex-wife, Oh, boo hoo, I need to find her, I'm dying—'

'Shawn,' the female one says. 'Like, give him a break.'

'Fuck off, Tanya. Give us your painkillers. What are they, codeine?'

'Morphine,' I say. 'Some naproxen as well. For when it's not so bad.'

'Legit?'

'Factory-made,' I say. 'Out of date. Obviously.'

'Give them to us.' I kneel and rifle in my bag. I'm prepared for this. This is a rule: always have expendables. I take a bottle of my pills, which says morphine on the script stuck to the side, but in reality is aspirin, a glut of aspirin. Hand them to Tanya, because she seems the most reasonable, and the one who wants to not be doing this the most. She rattles the bottle. 'Good choice,' the one called Shawn says. 'Good choice, you get it. Because we would have kept you alive, you get that?'

'I get it,' I say. 'I don't need the specifics.'

'Fuck you.' He kicks me: his boot, the heel, denting into my forehead. A surprise to me, because I thought they would pass without incident, they got what they wanted; and a surprise to him, it's clear, from his face. 'Oh shit,' he says.

'Let's go,' says the one whose name I don't know.

'C'mon.' Tanya grabs Shawn's arm and pulls him away from me. I'm on all fours, in the middle of the road. The tarmac coarse under my fingers, and I'm in agony, in actual agony: a different sort of pain than I'm used to, where it usually feels like backache or toothache or something deeper, somehow. This is stinging fire, this is wet agony. My vision blinking red, and I swipe at my head, the feel of an insect on my forehead, on the cusp of my scalp; but it's not an insect, not a creature, but a flap of something. I feel it: thick, curling in on itself, a flap of my skin. How thin is it that his boot would dig a trench, rip a line of it away from me? I pull it, because instinct makes me pull it, and that's a whole other agony, an immediate pain. I think I scream, but I can't be sure. There's a lot of blood on the floor, my hand in it as I start to crawl: away from the road, away from the plants. My hand on weeds, jutting from concrete that's erupted, miniature volcanos. And a rumble: something else, something louder, something that feels like it's getting closer. Is this it? Is this the ending, is this the way I die, I wonder? Is this what it feels like? Hands wet with blood, my vision red, and this rumbling, as the ground seems to vibrate under my touch—

The rumbling stops. An engine. The clunk of a door opening, then feet – booted feet, clomping weight, somebody walking harder than they naturally would – coming closer to me. The whole world shakes.

'You okay?' Her voice is calm, measured. She squats next to me. 'You're not going to attack me, right? This isn't some ruse, you're not going to rear up, knock me down.'

'No,' I say. I force the words out.

'There's a lot of blood.'

'Don't—'

'You don't want me to help you up?'

'Don't touch it. My blood, don't touch it.' I force the words out. I think of a movie, *The Elephant Man*. Poor soul, his words like drinking thick soup.

'Okay.' I feel her stand up. The light, the air. 'You got the bleeds?'

'Yes,' I say.

'Okay. I've got gloves, I'll put them on before, then I'll help you out.' She sounds calm, still. I try to say something else, about the gloves, but she pre-empts it. 'They've been checked, I check the integrity before I even pack them, I'm not an idiot.' She pauses. 'And I know,' she says, 'you're not calling me an idiot. I get that. But don't worry.' The sound of her pulling on the gloves. The snap of rubber. Her hands then on my arms. 'Woah, woah,' she says, as I try to push myself to my feet, using her as ballast. 'You're not strong enough, okay. Let me take the weight, that's fine, that's fine.' She shuffles me to the back of her vehicle. Helps me to sit down on it. A gate, folded down, and I have to push backwards, almost fall up onto it.

'Thank you,' I say.

'No problem. Somebody attacked you?'

'For my medicines.'

'Yeah, yeah. I know who it'll be. Three of them?'

'Shawn' – the word lisped, fat-tongued and bloody – 'and Tanya and another one.'

'Yeah. They live here, they're feral as fuck. Taking advantage.'

'You can't blame them,' I say. She laughs.

'I mean, you totally can. I've got to clean this wound, okay? You'll get an infection fast otherwise. Skin's too thin, so I'm going to—' She looks for something, the sounds of her moving things around. 'I've got disinfectant here, but it's going to hurt like shit. This is a big wound, you know.'

'He kicked me.'

'Shawn? He's a primo grade-A dick. You know how many times he's been killed? People hate that guy. They love to kill him, that's the truth of it. Hey, stay still, this is gonna hurt.'

'I'm Theo,' I say.

'Pleased to meet you, Theo. I'm Rhonda.'

'Like the song.'

'Sure, help me Rhonda, just like the song. Here we go.' She puts the disinfectant on. The pain is searing: a blistering agony, and I buck, I feel myself buck, but she pushes me down against the stuff in the back of her truck, one arm holding me steady, almost across my chest, almost an attack; the other hand with this cloth soaked in something that reeks of hospitals, of the cleaning fluid they use in hospitals, that you smell when you're there overnight, sleeping in a small chair, hoping for news, woken by that smell.

Rhonda stops. 'I need to pick out something,' she says. 'There's gravel in there.' She pulls a little knife from her pouch, and she holds the tip to my face. 'Don't move,' she says.

My memory shifts: away from Rebecca, to my mother, working on my knee when I was a child. How she dug around in this wound I made from falling onto gravel, from skidding, tearing the skin, getting the minute stones stuck into the flesh; and how she used a needle, and she said, I'm sorry, over and over, to keep it clean, to wash it out; and afterwards, she apologized again, I know this hurts, honey, I know, I know, before the iodine, orange staining my skin, dripping into the white of the sink, washing away, and there wasn't even any blood in it, by the end.

These people I love who died; and I am still here.

Rhonda wipes my eyes. A wet cloth across them. 'This is just water,' she says. 'I sterilize it myself, so it's clean, I can promise you that. That better?'

'Yes,' I say, but the pain is still absolutely tearing through me. 'Thank you.' She's older than I imagined from her voice. Forty, maybe. Dressed in casual fatigues, the sort they sold in surplus stores. She holds a bandage up.

'We should wrap this, okay? I would glue it, but your skin's pretty fucked up.'

'It's fine,' I say. She starts to wind the bandage around.

'After this, we'll get you a crash helmet.' I laugh, and it hurts. 'Don't do that,' she says. 'Not part of the deal. I'm fixing you, you don't get to make my job harder than it already is. Stay still, okay.'

I look down at the truck bed I'm sitting on. Dark green. Tarpaulin, some tools. Canisters of biogas, a sol2r panel hard-wired into something that's running to the side, that's been carved through the metal of the truck's body.

'I don't see many actually working vehicles,' I say.

'No?' she says. Frames it as a question, it's not a question. She knows how rare they are. 'You don't drive?'

'Too scared to. And my licence is long expired.'

'Huh,' she says. She stops winding the bandage. Tapes it, the tear of tape, the pressure of sticking it down. Pushing hard enough to get it to take. 'Your licence has expired, that's against the law to drive, then. And there are so many laws that they care about now,' she says. She smirks. 'Jeez, come on. The few cops who're left, they've given up, they don't care. I try to think of when I last saw police on the freeways. A long time, certainly. And I'm careful, anyway. Look, it's not like there's many other cars out here to cause an accident with, is there?'

'I suppose not,' I say.

'And if I wasn't driving, who would have saved your life? Shit, it's like I'm driving a goddamned ambulance here. I should paint this thing white and red, get a siren.' She helps me down. 'You stand okay?'

'I think so,' I say. She walks to my bag, picks it up, puts it on the flat-bed.

'Where are you headed?' she asks.

'England.'

'England? That where your voice is from?'

'Sort of. A long time ago.'

'Fancy, fancy. Get in. Let me drive you.'

'What?'

'I mean, not to England. But somewhere. You're headed east, I'm headed east. Unless you want to walk. Because night's coming, and night's really safe in the desert, so that'll be great for you. People are definitely more sane at night. Night's when Shawn and his winged monkeys really get methy. They make their own, you know, and they're just so shitty at it.'

'I was looking for the bus. I'm travelling.'

'The bus? You mean the Greyhound?'

'I think so,' I say. She tries to not smile, but can't help it. She's got one of those faces. 'What?' I ask her. 'What's funny?'

'It's been— Carlos, who drove it?'

'Carlos, yes.'

'Carlos gave it up, like, months ago. Scrapped it. I mean, literally, tore the fucking thing apart. He was so angry, this bridge collapsed on Highway One. He didn't die, but, I don't know. People did? Passengers, I mean. So he quit.'

'I need to get out,' I say. 'How long ago was this?'

'A year? I don't know.' She must see the disappointment on my face, disappointment I didn't feel crawling over it. We don't feel our reactions, I don't think. We rarely know when we're wearing our hearts on our sleeves. 'What's in England, anyway?'

'My wife, my ex-wife. She left here a long time ago, before I got to, I don't know. I wanted to say goodbye. And she didn't let me.'

'Maybe she didn't want to?' Rhonda says. 'Maybe that was, I don't know. It's not an accident to leave a whole country, you know.'

'I thought she was dead,' I say.

'Yeah, except you didn't. Nobody actually dies any more,' she tells me. 'You know that as well as anybody. Death's an obstacle. It's a sickness. Where were you when the Anomaly came?'

'Our home.'

'So if she died, she'd be right back there. You were in bed?'

'Yes.'

'So there she would be, however many years younger, wondering who the fuck this decrepit old man next to her was.' She walks to the driver's side, to the door. 'Get in. I'll take you as far as I can.'

'What?'

'Come on. Road trip. It'll be fun. The stereo works. I've got a glovebox full of albums from the last century. We can sing along. It'll be fun.'

'I don't have anything to trade,' I say.

'I didn't say you needed to,' she says. 'Look, I live here. In this thing. Doesn't matter to me where it is. As long as there's sunlight it'll keep going. And I don't think that sun's going anywhere anytime soon. Besides, I haven't been to the East Coast in, like, ten years. Apparently it's come a long way. So I'll take you. Road trip. Deal?'

'Yes,' I say. I feel like I could cry: the familiar welling, but I don't know if it's relief or pain, finally, coming through. But either way, she looks away, and I wipe my face with my hand; and when it comes away, there's still the trace of blood on it, still wet, from where she tried to clean it off.

I sit in the cab, and I peel my shoe from my left foot.

'Your foot hurt as well?' she asks.

'No,' I say. Beneath my foot, rows of pills, arranged into a blister pack I made myself from the unfolded body of an archaic plastic bottle: left to melt in the sun, then the tablets arranged, pressed tightly just before it sets. 'Keeps them hidden,' I say.

'Sensible,' she says.

She stares at the pack a little too long. But the engine is started, and we are moving; and it's too late now for me to get out.

6

I can hear music: songs about the road, about the sea, about trees and hearts and guitars and hotels. Rhonda clicks the tape to stop, and it jars me awake. The songs were there, somewhere, in the background: these radio hits I haven't heard in years, decades. Since my father, who was an avid listener of the rock stations that played the songs his father listened to. I remember them; I remember him remembering them.

'It's nearly morning,' Rhonda says.

'What? No,' I say, but I open my eyes and the deep indigo dusk has entirely given way to the curiously pale dawn we live with now. There's something incredible about the Anomaly's ability to dampen. The light is just as hot as it ever was, but not as bright; and some, I have heard, wonder if it's the thing keeping us alive, actually. If it's somehow our life support. Would we have overheated entirely, if it weren't making the sun's rays less potent? The West Coast of America basically baked, and yet: without the shield, would all life here be dead?

Ninety per cent of the world has gone. More than. Is it keeping the last ten per cent of us hanging on?

'You shouldn't have let me sleep,' I say.

'I couldn't wake you up. Sleeping like the dead. How docs it feel?' She's bent forward, close to the wheel, her driving position as if she's clinging on for dear life, somehow. Bent forward, squinting.

'Should we stop? Let you get some rest?'

'I've got speed,' she tells me. 'Found a stash a few years after this all started. Like, hundreds and hundreds of pills, you wouldn't believe it. There was this guy, he was making them, in a factory, or like, this abandoned warehouse. I found him, and you know—' She slows, looks at me. 'You know when you find a closed loop?'

'Yes,' I say.

'So, he was one. You can tell from before, I think, because everybody who knows, they've got these glassy looks in their eyes, you know? Because we know.' She's rambling. Her own eyes glassy in their own special way. 'I saw him, I was looking for somewhere to sleep, and I walk in, and he's there, making pills. I watched him: he had a tablet press, and he was waiting, staring at it. It finished doing what it does, he opened it. Turned the tablets out, and there's a pile of them, like, a mountain behind him. Not a mountain, because it slipped down, it flowed. An ocean. Like, how did he not notice it? But he was fucking tweaked. So he didn't look. He stood, and he didn't react, and then he fell down. Dropped dead, right there. Clutching his chest.'

'My God.'

'Yeah, it was, I mean. I don't think I could have done anything. If your heart's that fragile, you're going. Even if I stopped him—'

'And then he looped?'

'Then he looped. I blinked, or I turned away, I can't remember the first time. Then he's there, and I watched him load the press, turn it on, and then just stand there, like a mannequin. Then the press finished—'

'He died again.'

'Of course he did. Turned the pills out, added them to the pile behind him, died, came back. It was brutal, but not, like, the most brutal.' She doesn't elaborate. I don't push.

'And you took the pills.'

'Are you judging me?' She stops the truck, her foot slamming onto the brake. We skid, we screech, the tires burning their meat onto the tarmac. 'Don't you dare judge me.'

'I know,' I say. 'I wasn't. I mean, look: I wasn't.'

'He was fucking dead, okay? He was. He just was.'

'I know.'

'I tried to pull him out. Because you've got to try, don't you? I grabbed him, I pulled him out.' Part of the steering wheel is dug down to metal bone, the leather, the padding, torn open; her fingernails flicking, picking at it, even now as she speaks, the nail teasing the material, looking for what more there might be. 'I moved him on from the loop, and he screamed at me. He was all, like, What are you doing? What are you doing? I'm working, where did you come from, who sent you, that sort of thing. Then he died anyway.' She shrugs. Black leather clippings, strippings, particles, under her fingernails. 'Only then he died right in front of me, and it was like I was guilty.' She starts the engine, and we move again. 'So I left him. I took pills, I sold them, I used some. Whatever.'

'How long ago was this?' I ask, but she ignores it. I look

at the bag by her feet: pills, yes, but they're not dusty or dirty. Fresh, I would say. 'You've been back, haven't you?'

'I told you not to judge me,' she says.

'And I told you, I wasn't,' I reply.

The desert is wild. I remember driving across it with my father, when I was a child. We lived in Florida, for a while: my mother was an astronaut; or, rather, some sort of engineer, as my father reminded me, when I spoke about her. 'Don't put her above what she was,' he would say, bitter from their separation. We moved to Florida for her training, before she went to the space station, back in those last years before the Anomaly arrived. She was part of the last-ditch attempt to halt it, or to try and fathom it. Of course, she failed; she died. I think she died before she was in it, rather than being swallowed by it, dragged along in its wake. There were stories, in the early days, of the crafts that were in the Anomaly finally being able to return home: of crash landings, of fuel-less recoveries from our atmosphere, of inflatable life-rafts in the ocean laden with the crews of spacecraft that were never meant to see home. My mother was not one of them. And then, of course, the stories dried up; or, the means to tell those stories did. The national press replaced by the local, by printed materials, by home-made inkjet printers rescued from landfill to replace the lasers that simply had no way of working once the factories closed.

Regardless: my father and I drove through the desert back then, away from Florida, from my mother's family – desperates, my father called them, trying to cling to a past that's not a past worth clinging to, not when the future is so bright! – and we drove across every state we could in as near a straight line as he could muster. 'We should do this, like a holiday,' he said; but the reality was that he wanted to visit churches. All of them so strange, not like the churches I went to when I was even younger: instead, warehouses, old factories, spaces in houses, in the basements of homes; white walls, concrete floors, no distractions from the matter at hand. Rope, tied around the surfaces, so much that it reminded me of when we went to see a galleon, once, at a dock, the rope from the edge of it, running up for the sails, running everywhere, as if the whole thing was held together by it. Rope, when you entered; a length of it, run through everybody's hands, and we were told by the pastors to tie as we went, the ceremonies – their word – meant to be what would knot us together: in truth, in reality, in acceptance of the Knot.

They drew the Anomaly on their pamphlets, picturing it as this ball of twine, knotted up, perfect, with no beginning and no ending. When I left home, a friend showed me something from decades ago, this picture of something called the Flying Spaghetti Monster: a religion created as a joke on the internet, something for people to laugh about, to point out the fallacies of the religions that people accepted as somehow more valid. And the Spaghetti Monster, it was the Anomaly, as the worshippers of the Knot had it. Exactly the same aesthetic, the same sort of imagery, the same sort of drawing. The only difference was that the Spaghetti Monster had eyes, and meatballs; and the Knot was taken seriously. In those basements and town halls and closed-for-business local restaurants, my father drank in what they were selling, and I stood at the back and listened. He would leave there fizzing with energy, bouncing in the car seat as we drove to a motel, as he made me sleep on couch cushions under the car blanket while he took the bed, as he watched TV all night, his foot restlessly jiggering out of the end of the duvet. In the mornings, over eggs in IHOPs, he would jab his fork towards me, asking me why I wasn't with him; why I couldn't quite see what he could, the evident truth – a phrase that they used, the evident truth, a suggestion of evidence where they had none, of truth where there was none – that was staring me in the face. He would say, 'You're just like your mother,' shaking his head. And then we would be back into the car, back to driving: the desert stretching endlessly in those moments, as the Anomaly came closer and closer.

He said, I remember, when we were in Texas, leaving Austin – his experience there having dulled his enthusiasm, this bubbling anger in him that the people there weren't buying into the story; 'the goddamned liberal agenda', he said, and I remember spit-laughing, because what a thing, what a thing to believe, so ridiculous that it's burned itself into my memory, the way he said it, the delivery of the line – that time would prove them right. He said: 'That thing, up there, it's going to change the world. It saves, it saves, it absolutely saves; and we'll be saved by it.' The desert went on and on, and we drove into it. *No gas stations for one hundred miles*, said one sign, and the car told us we had 104 miles before the reserve; and he took his chances, grinning, as if this was actually life and death, not just a mistake that could lead to a sad trudge at the other end.

Rhonda stops driving, gets out of the cab, stands next to the door. Her hand on the frame, and she retches, gags, hawks up something and spits it to the ground. I imagine it scuttling away: a parasite, a dark mess of tissue and legs, a spider made of rank spittle. She doesn't look at me, but speaks through the opened window.

'You afraid? Of dying?'

'No,' I say.

'I am,' she says. 'Again.'

'How many times have you been around?'

'This is my third since I started counting. First two, they were quick, from what I can tell. Only four years total spent before this one, and I somehow managed to make this one stick. Probably a load before those, though. I was young, probably didn't make it far down many roads. Months, or weeks, whatever. Fucking dumbass that I am.' She rubs her chest, the bottom of her throat. 'I'm afraid I'm dying as well. I've got a lump. It's, I don't know. I haven't been to see anybody. I don't wanna know.'

'No,' I say. 'I can understand that.'

'Changes everything, really. I tried to stay alive, I wanted to make this one count. People liked it before, right? Having a life? Memories, that sort of thing. So I wanted it. I know people, I don't want to forget them. Jesus.' She's crying, I think. 'Hey, I get too sick, I could have you kill me,' she says.

'I'm not going to kill you,' I say.

'Spoilsport.' She hesitates, something to tell me. 'In my bag, there's a journal. I started a journal, because I thought— I mean, maybe it's useful. It's something that I can read, that I know I wrote for myself. So it's like a truth. An answer, because when I come back, I'll have questions. Tell the other version of me – the newer version of me – not to smoke. See if she'll listen. We're erased, right, but our impact on the world? That remains. Got to use that if we can, game the system.' She smiles. 'This fucking lump, let me tell you. Things sent to kill us. I don't want to die again, but I can feel it.'

I want to tell her: about how, when I'm lying in bed sometimes, I can feel every part of my body alert, inflamed and aflame; and I can feel my blood in my body, like some demented spirit level, settling and sloshing, and each movement of my body, each fractional gesture, makes it feel as if it's going to spill out, and over, flooding me. Drowning me inside; and after dying, and waking again, some thirty years younger, I would be relieved, probably, absolutely relieved, until I finally dredge up the strength to stand up, and find the book I have written for myself, in case of that happening, an emergency guide for me and nobody else, every detail, everything that has happened and will happen, to fill in the holes, to prevent the confusion I would absolutely feel. I would read that book, and it would ruin me. I want to tell Rhonda this, but I don't. She thinks she'll find comfort in knowing the future; who am I to tell her that she's wrong.

I say, instead, 'I am scared of dying most because when I come back, I know it'll just happen all over again.'

'You think it's better not to know?' she asks. I don't reply. 'Come on.' She pulls the keys from the ignition and starts to walk. 'Put your shoes on, we're finding food.'

'We're not taking the truck?'

'No vehicles allowed in town. Safer that way.' She starts to walk. I pack my pills into my backpack, swing it onto my back, and tighten the straps. I want to tuck them into my shoes again, but she knows all of my hiding places now.

Birdie would have told me to trust Rhonda now. She would have said, 'She's got as much as you to lose.' And I would have replied that that was what scared me.

7

A small town, this is, and I don't see a sign for its name, but instead road signs, all leading to places with names that are somehow absolutely ubiquitous and leave it impossible to pin down: Springfield, Clinton, Greenville, Salem. A number, also, written on a piece of card, planted into the ground at the side of the road: *Approx 35*, which I think must be the population. I wonder what happened here, beyond what happened everywhere. I wonder why they update the sign; who even cares any more.

'Down here,' Rhonda says, as if she's got some sixth sense for this. Past houses with boarded-up windows, past chain-link fences around desolate yards, past houses that are still tended to, still looked after.

'Have you been here before?' I ask.

'Yeah, yeah. Quite a lot. There's a cook every Friday, every Saturday, in the hall.' She points. 'See that?' A large red building, a barn of some sort, the doors thrown wide. 'They're all in there, and there's food. You go, they'll feed you. Of course, it's only—' She squints at the sky. 'What, maybe just before ten? So we've got waiting to do. I try and help out, do jobs some of the others aren't up to doing. Earn my dinner.' She steps towards a house that looks nice, actually: plants in planters that hang, a doormat that reads *Please Wipe Your Feet / After The Street!*, windows with a stained-glass effect stuck to them. Rhonda shouts: 'May? May, you in?'

A woman answers the front door. She's elderly: somewhere in her seventies, maybe her eighties. Hair like a cloud that she's walked through and taken with her, stolen in her wake, peeling away but fastened tight. 'Well,' she says, 'this is a delightful surprise. How long has it been?'

'A short while,' Rhonda says. 'This is my friend, Theo. Theo, May; May, Theo.'

'Good to meet you,' I say.

'You too. Been through the wars, I see.'

I touch the bandage lightly. Even that makes me wince. 'Is it that obvious?'

'There's blood soaked through,' she says. 'You should come inside and change the dressing on it. I have bandages, and ointment.' She turns and heads inside, expecting us to follow; and I turn to Rhonda, mouth the word *ointment*, so archaic, and I smile, and Rhonda laughs.

'She's a nice old coot, play nice.'

'I will,' I say. 'If it's still bleeding—'

'I won't let her touch it,' Rhonda says. 'She'll have gloves, but it'll have stopped by now. I'm sure.'

A house filled with marginalia and detritus: nothing but what May's collected over time, and it's clearly been a long time. So much stuff, and that's absolutely the correct word: as if it's not organized, not cared for, just possessions and belongings, anything that takes her fancy; a magpie for everything.

Rhonda leans close to me as May shows us to the bathroom. 'She's on a six-year loop, just FYI. Natural causes, she dies in her sleep, and she knows when it's coming, people tell her, she wants to know. We're a year or so away, I reckon. I've been here—'

'I'll just get the bandages,' May interrupts.

'Thank you,' I say.

Rhonda continues: 'I've been here the last two times she's needed me. She doesn't remember me, but I've got some old instant-print photos of us, so she knows I'm not bullshitting her. It's like dealing with somebody with, like, the longest, strangest dementia, something like that. Six-year Alzheimer's. I tell her what she needs to know, help her back on her feet. If I'm still here next time, I'll do it then as well.'

May's bathroom is pink and white, except the white has begun to almost somehow turn pink itself, as if one colour is bleeding into the other. I remember a *Cat in the Hat* from when I was a kid: the red whacked out of a stained bedsheet, turning the snow outside the house pink.

I sit on the edge of the bath, and she starts to unwind the bandage—

'Could you use gloves?' I ask.

'I don't have anything worth catching,' she says, annoyed at me.

'No,' I say. 'I didn't think that you did.'

'He's prone to infection,' Rhonda says. 'No big thing.'

'I've got Marigolds,' May says.

'That'll do.' May fetches them, from beneath the sink, and Rhonda takes them. 'I'll do it, don't trouble yourself. You can be my assistant,' she says, and May shakes her head.

'Assistant! I didn't work for as long as I did to be an assistant.'

'May was a nurse,' Rhonda tells me. I feel her unpeeling the bandage; the gentle tugging of it where the blood has caked it to my scalp. I can't see her face, but I can see her throat: and she swallows, in that way that people do when they need to pause, when they are confronted with something. She wipes my head with something, a wet flannel, the water running; and then she puts a new bandage on, and wraps it around. Not as tight. There, she says. All done.

'How is it?' I ask her.

'Fine,' she lies. 'Yeah, you're going to be fine.'

After a day of menial labour that feels genuinely good – hands in soil to pull weeds, regardless of whether they'll regrow; harvesting vegetables that immediately reappear, somehow, passed into the new world of the Anomaly at the perfect moment, an infinite source of rutabaga and yam and potato; painting a fence that needs painting, because it hasn't been done in this loop of hers, and she knows it won't be done before the next – May leads us from her house, down the street, to the red building that Rhonda pointed out earlier. 'Most of us are here,' she says. 'Don't know what's being cooked tonight, but it'll be what it'll be.'

What it is, we discover, is a barbecue: beef pulled apart with tongs, cooked for hours and hours; ribs where the meat has trouble remaining on the bones; chicken that's been smoked, tasting barely like the bird, but instead the dense, chalky darkness of the smoke itself. Potato salad, coleslaw. A spicy sauce that looks like salsa, but tastes thicker, sweet barbecue with corn and peppers and jalapeño. Plates piled high, eat as much as you like. Long tables, a feast. 'Sit wherever,' Rhonda says. 'I need to say hi to some people.'

I watch her as she goes around shaking hands. Her hand

on the shoulder of some of them, who didn't stand: older, or slightly more fragile. Hugging, kissing them. Rhonda, like a long-lost relative; or more, a conquering hero, returned to the place where everybody knows her name. Some old theme tune, and here she is, she is it.

Rhonda holds somebody, a woman whose face seems perpetually on the side of collapse, as if she's barely holding herself together. She holds her a while, and I think how nice it looks. How kind a gesture, from both of them. When they both clearly need it.

Rhonda looks at me, over the woman's shoulder. She mouths something: *go on, introduce yourself*. A prod.

So I do, I introduce myself. To Shep, the town's de facto mayor; to a man called William Wilson, who says his full name, his jovial face vibrating as he chuckles it out; to a younger man – younger than the apocalypse by a decade or so, but with the slightly grey eyes of somebody who isn't living it out just the first time – who tells me that the cows, the pigs, the chickens, this is game-changing, because it's truly humane now, to eat meat, they're not dying in order for us to eat them. He tells me that he was, once, vegetarian.

'I wouldn't even eat the ReMeat,' he says. 'Like, I was off it all. Veg only. And then the Anomaly, and—' He waves his hand; bone from rib in it, meat dangling. 'Look, if carrots die and come back, they're living. If cows die and come back, they're living too. Same rules. Same rules, same thing. No harm, no foul.' He grins. 'Except for chickens.'

'I tell him,' William Wilson says, a grin on his face, 'he should become one of them cannibals, out by Austin. Flesh of the flesh, all that.'

'It's not the same,' the ex-vegetarian says, 'it's not the same at all.'

'Why not? We're reborn. That's what they say, isn't it?'

'They're *murderers*.'

'Are they murderers, if there's no death? Ahh,' William Wilson says, 'and now we're into the eternal goddamned question, aren't we?'

'Don't listen to him,' Rhonda says to me, shouts to me, down the table. 'He does this. He loves this debate, it fuels him—'

'It's a worthwhile conversation, Rhonda,' William Wilson says. 'The only worthwhile conversation, if you ask me. We're past rules, we're past mortality, so doesn't it make sense we're past *morality* as well? Ethics? What ethics were founded on the new construct we find ourselves living in? Everything we have built is founded upon what we perceive to be right and wrong, where wrong, the worst wrong—'

'Here we go—'

'The worst wrong is, was, murder. Right? The killing of another person, that was the be-all and end-all. But we've all died—'

'Not all of us,' Shep says, looking at the younger man. Glancing at me, as if he can tell. The smell of me: a fresh life; or maybe a life gone stale.

'Most of us, then. Most of us have died. And we came back. Was death what I credited it with? Well, heck no! Of course it wasn't. There wasn't an afterlife, there wasn't judgement, there wasn't any river of Styx for us to cross, or purgatory for us to wait in, or reincarnation into a dung beetle or what-have-you. Instead, there was immediate rebirth, and reset. And if an action's reset, if it's forgotten and erased, is there actually any guilt to be felt for it? Is there actually any punishment that fits the crime? Because—' He bites from his chicken, mouth full of meat. 'Is there any crime, there? Really?'

but she lost her way. Went out there, to a church, and after the Anomaly came, she came home. Found us again.'

'For fuck's sake,' Rhonda says. 'She's not safe out there—'

'We don't know that,' Shep replies. But Rhonda's standing, eating the last of her food, drinking her drink. She looks at me.

'We're going,' she says. Then, to Shep: 'You knew I'd go, didn't you?'

'We didn't know anything,' Shep says.

'You did. You fucking knew I'd come back, and that I would go out to the factory to look for her. Bunch of goddamned cowards, all of you.' And then she walks, out of the red barn, and I follow her, thanking them for their hospitality as I move. We walk down the street, back the way we came, past May's house. 'God-fucking-damn it,' Rhonda says.

'What's the factory?' I ask, but Rhonda doesn't say anything, just mutters under her breath, kicks the dirt.

The road out of town is grown over, unattended to, uncared for. It's a minor road, leading, it looks, to nowhere at all. Weeds and plants and rocks, blown in; but they look as though they've been placed, and Rhonda swerves when she needs to, to avoid them.

'You should sleep,' I say to her, and she doesn't reply. So I let the silence be for a while, watching the headlamps illuminating the road in front of us.

She stops the car. Turns the headlamps off, and points into the darkness. 'Give it a moment,' she says. 'Let your eyes adjust.' So we wait, and listen to the clicking of the engine as it cools, and sure enough, there, in the distance, a series of structures. Towers, buildings, imposing. 'That's the factory,' she says.

'What is it?' I ask.

'An old silo,' she says. 'This is where they did one of their churches. Like a megachurch, you know? You remember them?'

'They? The Knot?'

'The Knot, sure, or whatever the fuck that bunch of maniacs morphed into. This was where they took all their people before the Anomaly came. All across the state, like Moses into the fucking desert. And this is where they ended up. All the ones from round here, anyway.' Pick, pick, her nails on the leather. It's a wonder it's held up, that there's enough for her to pick. 'Venda was one of them, or her family was. So she was there when, you know. Then she escaped, went to Shep and that lot, got taken in. Helped out. She's not, I don't know. She's special, you know? She needs help.'

'Of course,' I say.

'We can't go in now,' she tells me. 'I'm going to sleep.' And she takes herself to the back of the truck, to the bed; and she pulls back the tarpaulin, and there's a mattress there, covered in some sort of water-repellant sheet. 'There's a sleeping bag under the front passenger,' she says, 'seat goes back a good way.'

'Thank you,' I say. I find the bag, and by the time it's unravelled, Rhonda's already sleeping in the back, already snoring. But I can't sleep, so I get out again, walk around the truck. Look at the wilderness, the wildness. Eyes in the darkness. Somebody wrote, I forgot who – one of the nature writers who seemed to think that the Anomaly was in some way cleansing – they wrote about how it was a miracle that nature hadn't stolen back the planet from us. All of us, grabbed away, swallowed by elk and fox and brown bear. Eyes in the darkness now, and I wonder if there's more than there would have been before the Anomaly.

I turn back to the truck and I see something at the back, where Rhonda's moved the mattress. A glint of metal, curved, perfectly polished; and I reach for it, quietly, carefully, and pull it out. Circular, a perfect circle: a steering wheel. And not just one, but many, over and over, underneath this mattress, all peeled clean of their coverings.

8

I am woken by screams in the distance, carrying on the wind: different pitches, different tones, some male, some female. A pattern to them that I can't quite discern, a rhythm to them. I sit up, and see that Rhonda's already away, already cooking something on a small camping stone, attached to a miniature sol2r battery. The sizzle of something, the smell of bacon.

'What is that?' I ask.

'Breakfast,' she says.

'The sound,' I clarify.

'Oh,' she replies. 'From the factory. You know.' I go to stand, clambering out of the cab, when the pain hits. Through my head, through my skull: like a pulling at my skin, a tugging of every part of me. As if there's a seam, on my skull, and everything else is being hauled up from that point; and I'm being held by what little hair I've got left, yanked off my feet. I collapse, and she rushes over, helps me up. 'Easy,' she says. 'Easy now, okay, easy now.' She helps me to the ground, where I sit. I see myself, for a moment, as if I'm outside my own body: a confused toddler, seated on the ground, contrite.

Here:

'My head,' I say, and she's quiet. 'What is it?'

'I didn't say anything.'

'I should take the bandage off,' I say.

'I don't know. Okay, sure, yes.'

She unwinds it, and I remind her, 'Use gloves,' but she shakes her head.

'The blood's coming,' she says. 'What do I do?'

'Nothing,' I say, 'there's nothing you can do.' She hands me a towel, dirty, doesn't matter. I hold it up. 'It'll stop eventually,' I say, but then I see my hand, the blood on it. Not from the towel, not pulsing through and over, but from the hand itself. From the little nicks in the corners of my nails, from the scratch on my wrist where the watch was. Blood, coming, slow and thin; and then from the pores themselves, this strange pulsing. This seeping of it from me. My life, leaving. 'Stay back,' I say, and Rhonda does.

'This is what happens?'

'Yes,' I say. 'It's happened a few times before, but not for—' I would tell her more, but I taste the blood in my mouth. Gums, tongue, blood comes. I feel shaky, and everything gives way, and I'm on the floor on my hands and knees. I should be crawling: bloody handprint after bloody handprint, trail from my knees—

'What do I do?' she asks. She's terrified, I can hear it in her voice.

'Wait,' I try to say, spitting out blood, and I stay there and I feel myself heave, and I bleed; not to death, or at least not straight away.

A change of clothes from my bag; wet wipes to clean down every part of me. I feel so tired, so drained. Not that much blood lost, not really. It's more the action of pushing it out.

Expelling it. Rhonda still keeps her distance, until I'm dressed and wandering around, trying to make the aches go away, aches that set in and don't leave, but you have to try.

I watch her kick sand, dirt, over the blood. As it dries, baked into the ground.

'Have you seen anybody die of it before?' I ask her.

'When I was younger, sure. People in the loops of it. Or they lasted a few days, give or take, you know.'

'I know.'

'How are you still alive?' She seems incredulous. 'You're not lying to me?'

'Lying how?'

'Like, I don't know. Lying that you didn't just die and come back a couple of days ago. You're going to die, and this, I don't know. It's a short loop. Maybe you only just began.'

'I'm not lying. I told you.'

'But I didn't see it. Maybe you didn't even have it, you were paranoid or whatever. Now I've seen it. Everybody else with it has died. They died, they died so quickly. That was the whole thing with it.'

'You don't know that, we don't know that.'

'But you're alive.'

'Maybe not for long.'

'When was the last time?'

'A bleed like this?' I wring out my old clothes. I will wash them, if I get the chance. Until then, they're stained pink. 'Eight weeks, maybe.' She nods, taking it in. 'Before that, three and a half months. Before that, a little over six months.'

'So they're getting closer. It's coming closer.'

It. 'Yes. I think so,' I say. The world has seen so many people dead of it. Every case is different, of course, and there are no guarantees. There are no guarantees; except for one, that this will kill me, one way or another.

There were stories, way back, in the early days of what I've got, before the Anomaly, that people were treating themselves in the most extreme way: drinking chemicals that burned them from the inside; taking medication that made them lose their minds, their immune systems; flaying themselves, essentially, stripping their skin from their bones, suddenly unprotected but cleansed. Let the blood come, let it spill.

Birdie once said to me, 'You should try it. The worst case, you'll be in agony, and you'll die; but you'll come back.'

'I won't remember this time,' I told her, 'I won't know any of this.'

'So I'll fill you in.'

Four years, it had been. Four years that she would fill in. Four years; we were still kids, really. In the scale of things. She told me I should kill myself. Certain death, just to see what, exactly? She held me, and she said, 'It'll still be us,' but she was wrong. She would still be her, and she would know what would happen.

It would have still been her, and another version of me. Naive. Lost.

'Come on,' Rhonda says. 'We should make a move, if we're going to get there before they're finished.'

'Finished?'

'There's a ritual,' she says. 'Every day it's the same. They'll be distracted, that's probably going to make our lives easier. Venda won't be a part of it, I know that much.'

'Why not?' I ask. Rhonda's starting off, towards the factory; I bundle my squeezed clothes into my bag. Take the bandage, start to wrap it around my head.

'You don't need that any more', she says. She comes back, looks for something in the back of the truck. Finds it, holds it aloft: a hat, some old panama, dusty, stained. She beats the dust off, pours a little water from her cantina over it.

'I'm not a spy,' I say. 'I'm not on holiday.'

'British accent, thinks he's distinguished. Smells like a spy to me,' she says. 'It'll keep the sun off it, and it'll hide the wound. I don't care, but some people, they're not me. Fuck knows how they'll react to it in the factory.' She starts to walk again, but turns, and smiles. 'Maybe they'll make you their god: the last of the surviving bleeders.'

'Don't,' I say.

'It's not death,' she says. 'You said that yourself, for you, it's not a death sentence.'

'No,' I reply, 'it's worse.'

I follow her. I wear the hat.

Once, this was an enormous place, lit brightly at night, all manner of colours. The towers, the trolleys, the conveyors, the smelting furnaces, the silos, the storage units, the control rooms, the garages, the workers' areas, all humming with the same noise, the same clunk of industry and movement. We walk through the sheep – alternately scrawny and sheared or massive balls of wool, somewhere in their cycles; and I wonder, not for even close to the first time, if they're aware of their loops, if they have some concept of the familiarity of returning lives after they're culled – and the air gets warmer, the closer we are to the factory.

'You've been here before?' I ask, and Rhonda nods. She doesn't talk, so I go again: 'What are they actually like inside?'

'You've never been to a church?'

'Not one of these. Old churches, and the Knot churches, before, years before.'

She stops. 'Maybe you should wait out here.'

'I know what they do in them,' I say.

'You don't,' she says. 'I should've thought.'

'I've read the articles—'

'They're worse than the articles. Some of them are, at least. This one is.'

'I can cope with it.'

'Fuck off, you can cope with it. Fuck off, you don't know what it's like in there.' She's upset, and angry. Somewhere between the two. Bubbling.

I'm sweating under the hat. I can feel it: tingling, and I wonder, does it run dark? 'How bad can it be?' I ask her, and she shakes her head.

'They're desensitized, so they don't know. They don't realize how it even is. Like, you know Stockholm syndrome? It's that, that's all it is. That's why they don't leave.' She says the last bit quietly.

'So why would Venda come out here?'

'This is where she grew up,' Rhonda says. 'Before.'

'Oh.'

'Her loops, I don't know; she dies, and she wakes up, and usually, after a while, she finds her way back to the town. She saw stuff when it started, and she comes back to the town. She dies a few years later, some congenital heart thing. They looked into fixing it, but. The doctors, I don't know how they'd even find them now. People who would think it was worth trying to save her.'

'She's got parents?'

'No. I mean, yes, but: they die.'

'Oh,' I say.

'I can't stand this,' she says. 'Lollygagging. I'm going in. If you want to stay here, I get that, I won't be mad at you.'

'I'll come,' I say, and we walk. 'I wish I had better shoes,' I tell her, and she laughs.

'We can get you shoes. In there, there'll be shoes. They don't need them any more, you can take your pick.'

The sand gives way to tarmac, bubbled and cracked and risen and moved and shifted; small bushes, shrubbery, the plants that have managed to survive this heat, which makes them all thicker or more wiry, or somehow just with that look of the extreme weed. You can tell a plant's survivability from how unattractive it looks, I think, and these are all the most hardy of the species; thriving in a place that should, really, sustain nothing.

I say that to Rhonda as we walk, and she laughs.

'We're so fucking arrogant,' she says. 'I mean, Jesus, to think that this survival means anything!'

'I just meant, it's like us—'

'I know what you meant,' she says, 'I just find it so fucking funny. You read apocalypses?'

'What do you mean?'

'The apocalypse novels? Everybody did, I'm assuming you're not any different. You read them, right? *The Stand, Station Eleven, Canticle For Whatshisname,* the good ones. *The Death of Grass, Zone One, On The Beach,* all of them.'

'Yes,' I reply.

'So you know, then. Oh, here goes the Eastern Seaboard! Fucking rural pastoral England, here it is! How fucking— I mean, *The Road,* right? America got all blown up, and there's this man, and what a fucking miracle he survives.'

'He doesn't survive,' I say.

'Debatable.' A smile. 'This isn't literary theory class, Professor. This is about our arrogance. That we, the West, we're the be-all and end-all. And you, with your shrub, I mean.'

'It survived,' I say.

'Yeah, it did.'

'The heat, as well. This isn't just the loop, this is the collapse of the ecosystem—'

'No, it's an adaptation. You think there wasn't any grass in the desert before? There were plants that grew there, we just didn't get them here. I mean, actually, fuck it, we did, in the hottest parts. But they've spread, that's all it is. But we, all our stories, they're all about collapse because we lose the fucking internet, or how easy it is to drive to places or get on a plane. But there are towns, there are communities who don't even have the fucking phones, who haven't seen a fucking plane.'

'Of course,' I say.

'And in those stories, they're not affected. Or, you know, they're not mentioned. Easier to not mention them than to worry about if they're as broken as we are. This apocalypse, this real one, it's hit everybody. You ever think about that?'

'Sometimes,' I say, and it's true, I do, I have. 'Birdie and I used to discuss it: if you didn't know it was coming, if you were somehow naive to it all, what would it have felt like? If you didn't have the spread of the rot, if you didn't have the suicides, the cullings, the preppers, what was that like? To see this thing advancing, to see the blanket of dull night, and then nothing; until, of course, that first person died, and then came back? Wizardry, Birdie said. Witchcraft. Superstition or myth, something like that.'

Rhonda's dug her heels in. She knows this argument, this conversation. 'It's storytelling either way. If we didn't know anything about it before it happened, we'd be in Salem, dunking somebody who came back to life after being, I don't know, run over or whatever. Watching them come back, doing it all over again.'

'I mean, that would prove she was a witch, wouldn't it?'

'Wouldn't it just.' She's quiet for a little while. Something on her mind, and then finally: 'What's so special about Birdie?' she asks.

'What?'

'She left you twenty years ago, right?' Twenty-five, but I don't correct her. 'You've just been pining?'

'Not pining,' I say, 'but she left, I don't know why.'

'You do.'

'I don't. There wasn't a reason.'

'There's always a fucking reason!' She laughs. 'People say, oh we broke up, no reason, there's always a reason. You cheat on her?'

'No.'

'She cheat on you?' I think about the Pettersen book. She wasn't cheating; just distracted, maybe. In those moments, at least. 'No, you would blame her. You wouldn't say no reason if she cheated on you.'

'Our daughter, then,' I say. 'She died.'

'Oh,' Rhonda says. 'Before?' I nod. 'Maybe she couldn't get past it.'

Maybe, I think, all of the death in front of her – the death in me, waiting, bubbling under – reminded her of it too much.

'Okay, we're nearly there,' Rhonda says, breaking the moment. 'Sun's up, let's sit it out.'

'What are we waiting for?'

'The bells. You'll hear them, can't miss them.' She sits on the ground, pulls her knees up to her chin, rests her chin on them. Like a kid.

'You know their routines well,' I say.

'This is where I grew up,' she says. 'Or, shit, ha. Stupid thing to say. I didn't grow up here, I grew up in Atlanta. But my parents came here before, like a pilgrimage. This is where I came of age, that's what they said. Came of fucking age.'

'You knew Venda from here?'

'We lived here the few months before it happened. She was much younger than I was, a few years, so I took care of her, and she followed me around.'

'How old were you?'

'Fourteen. Venda was six.'

I sit next to her. 'But you left.'

'Yeah. After—' She stops herself from talking. Her tongue in her cheek, pushing, prodding; like it's a sore tooth, or a gobstopper. 'It was a long time ago,' she says.

'You said you'd died a few times,' I say to her.

'Yeah,' she replies, 'I did say that. I died a few times, until I got out. I think that's all I want to say about it, if you don't mind.'

'Of course,' I say. And then we're quiet, and we listen to the wind, which is nearly still and yet still finds a way to whistle through these buildings, past these towers, through the alleyways between these buildings.

'No,' a voice screams, on the wind. 'No, God, no—'

'Fuck,' Rhonda says. She rocks her head back, as far as it will go. I hear the small, subtle grinding of bone on bone in her neck. She rolls her head, her shoulders.

'Who is that?' I ask her, and she doesn't look at me. 'You don't recognize the voice?'

'Of course I recognize the voice,' she says. 'They don't change the fucking bells. They just don't, because routine, well, it's routine, isn't it. Routine's routine for a reason.

They're strung up when it arrived, they're not changing them, nobody's volunteering for that shit. Come on,' she says, standing up, 'this is it, let's go.'

'Hang on,' I say, 'that's the bells?' But Rhonda doesn't reply. By the time I'm standing, she's halfway across the courtyard between these buildings, heading for a doorway at one side, away from the largest building, the factory itself, between the towers, where the voice is coming from; and soon, joined by a cacophony of other voices; not losing any of their power, just faded, weakened, distant and yet so close.

'Please, please—'

'Save me, I'm a good girl—'

'Don't do this, you don't have to do this—'

'I accept this, I am here for it—'

'Blessed be the Knot, blessed be its glory—'

'Yes, yes! Yes! Do this! I am one with it, one with you all!'

'This will be glorious, we will all be glorious—'

Rhonda steps into the building, the door opening easily. No locks. And then she is inside, and I'm outside on my own for a moment, the sound of tears sobbing through the wind; but then I follow Rhonda, and everything is echoes, the crying so much louder, just so much louder.

9

She shows me the clothes, first, hanging on hooks or shoes stuffed into boxes, the furniture that stuff from Ikea that was everywhere, that everybody had, easy and useful and practical, those plastic boxes perfect for the sorting out of stuff; and I think of my records, perfectly slotting into those spaces themselves.

'What size are you?'

'Eleven,' I say. She looks through the boxes, finding some sneakers, and she throws them to me.

'Put them on.'

'They're somebody's,' I say, but she waves her hand; as if that's unimportant. As if they don't need them any more; so I sit down, and I pull my old shoes off, and I slide these new ones on. They aren't quite the fit, in that they fit better than the old ones, I think, but I'm so unused to them, I've lived out of the old pair for so long. It feels, as I stand, like I'm in my father's shoes. The roomy spaciousness of shoes somebody else has already worn in.

'Oh God, oh God, please don't make me, I've changed my mind—'

Rhonda stops and listens to the screaming, clearer in here, echoing around when it comes. The walls concrete except for where the concrete gives way to either moulded plastics or sheer metals, there's no glass in here, not even in the windows, at least not any more. And the voices have nowhere to go, funnelled through the corridor tunnels, bouncing around.

There's always screaming, I think. Everywhere, every place.

'What are they doing?' I ask her, but Rhonda shakes her head.

'Let's try and leave before you find out, okay? Let's just find Venda.'

'Okay,' I say.

'Through here,' and she leads me to what looks like it was once a dining room, cold metal counters on one wall, a kitchen off the side; but the floor is covered in thin camping mattresses and sleeping bags and possessions, divided into rows and rows. Like it used to be in the old internment facilities, when they showed them: people in hundreds of stacks of six foot by four foot personal spaces. Maybe a hundred bags in here, maybe even more; and to one side, another room, a long corridor, also full of bags. A pathway down the middle of it, for access.

'How many people are there here?' I ask her.

'A lot,' she says. 'A few hundred. A thousand, maybe. I never did a headcount. Or, if I did, I didn't the last time I was here. It was always in flux before,' she says. We go to another room, passing a bathroom. There's no door, and she says, 'Wait here'. Undoes her belt, pulls her trousers down, sits on the bowl, directly on the bowl, and the sound of her peeing echoes. 'What were the churches like before this all happened?'

'Curious,' I say. 'They tried to make them like gospel

churches, you know? With the singing, the persuasive happiness. Pettersen's rules, his instructions. His psalms, really. They turned them into songs, some of them. Made them catch, like pop music.'

'No shit?'

'My father was so dour and stoic, and then we went to church and he had this grin on his face; as if he'd finally found the thing he was looking for. He used to hold my hand and make me dance, and in the early days I loved it. I was a child.'

'Then in the not-early days?' She stands up, flushes.

'As soon as I had a choice, I didn't go. I went to London, to live with my— I called her my stepmother, she was my father's other wife. He had two families. One of them was a secret.'

'No shit!'

'She was good enough to take me in. I think she saw me as some part of him, maybe. Like, some connective tissue.'

'She treat you like shit? That's what they would do in books, old books.'

'She was very nice,' I said. 'Nicer than she needed to be. Anyway, she didn't worship anything, so I didn't worship either.'

'And your dad?'

'Dead,' I say. 'I mean, he abandoned me. He died later.'

'That fucking thing, making everybody grow up. You grow up. Anomaly or no Anomaly.'

'You do,' I say.

'Okay. Venda will be at the back of the church—'

'You're sure?'

'She always stood there. She wasn't one of the ringers or anything so she stayed back, she didn't like the noise.

Come on.' She grabs my cuff and leads me through. 'How's your head?'

'Fine,' I lie.

'How long do you think you've got?' The most casual way of asking the worst question.

'Weeks. Maybe months. I don't know when the next episode will be, but they're getting closer.'

'How long does the boat take?'

'The ferries are seven days, I think. Maybe six, with good wind. Is that how it works?' We are into a room that's full of computers and bright LED panelling that's all been pulled loose, replaced with vegetation in individual windows: plants, allowed to die, in various stages of death, allowed to be born again. One of the marvels of our current situation: there's no rotting any more; not in the dead, at least.

'Here we go, through here, be quiet,' she says.

A small corridor leads to a large hall, and I can see people through there, inside the room. The room opens up, what was once a factory floor, a processing area, enormous in scale, opened wide. And light coming in, from above; there are no windows, all gone with the time and the heat, I would think, so instead there are beams of sunlight, so bright they're almost inconceivable. Rhonda crouches, as if she's a soldier, and she creeps, and she holds her hand out to me, to stay back.

And we watch.

10

A woman takes to the stage, at the front. The stage is constructed from girders and wood, built here, for this purpose. Under it, the supports for it are old conveyor belts and their structures, large and grey and old and rusting in places – there was water here, once, and at night still it must get cold and damp during the winters – and the panels that were once used to control them; but this was long before the Anomaly, this place was closed long before that. Still: the bones are old, the bones haven't changed. The stage has been painted all manner of bright colours, and the swirl of them, some interlocking, intersected rainbow, strands of red intertwined with strands of blue, of purple, of green, of taupe. There's still wood showing through, and I can admire it: there's a skill of carpentry there, somebody who's taken care with their work, the nails deep-set, the boards unsplit. It's been varnished, sanded, a matte finish. A stage, not just a platform, and the woman walks across it as if she owns it, as if it was commissioned by her, and she understands the stability of it in exact terms. She is dressed friendly: jeans, a sweater from one of the old theme parks, a mascot dancing on it, sneakers that have been machine-washed or are never worn. Her hair behind her ears, pushed back with eager fingers; a rehearsed act, I can tell, rather than one that's actually easy and simple. And she smiles, laughs almost. A politician off-duty, greeting their potential constituents.

Rhonda steps forward, and I follow, and we see the people in front of the stage: hundreds of them. What is it that they say, a sea of people? I never understood it, as seas are moveable, constantly shifting, changing, where this is heads, static, standing in place. Not a sea so much as a lake, a calm, placid lake. So many of them, and they're staring at her, not all of them smiling, not all of them; but some of them, certainly, with grins spread cheekbone to cheekbone, teeth showing. Whiter than most in the current status quo; and they're not jaded. Hard to find anybody who isn't at least a little jaded.

'Who is she?' I ask Rhonda.

'She doesn't matter,' she says.

'She looks as if she does.'

'Hm.' Rhonda stares at her, steps forward again. There's a path down the side. We start down it, a thin corridor, an access tunnel, almost – there's bunting above, so I have to duck my head, scrunching it into my shoulders, neck tilted, the brush of the bunting against the panama – and to the back of the hall, as the woman starts talking.

'We're all here, aren't we?' She sounds happy. Jubilant, even. 'My gosh, we are all still here! I think that deserves a round of applause—' And the applause follows, scattered at first, but she makes whooping sounds, to swell the audience's noise. 'The instructions, as we understand them, are handed down to us from before, and we know, we have seen the chaos, the destruction; and we are back to order, to construction! We are reset, and we are complete: a part of the great Knot that we understand to be the path, the way to redemption. Humanity was born to die, and we will never! We are as we have been told we would be: immortal.'

Rhonda and I step to the back of the crowd. 'Venda'll be here,' Rhonda says, 'somewhere around here. She's small, red hair, I used to dye it for her. Red and curled, bundled up into a scarf? Like, floral, probably, I can't quite—'

'Everything is prepared, as it always is,' the woman on the stage says. She's holding a small bottle of something, the size of a hotel shampoo sample. 'We're all ready, I think, aren't we? Just think: this time tomorrow, we'll be here, doing this again.'

'Please don't,' a voice sobs. From one side, and I look, and I can't see who is speaking. The woman on stage ignores it, moves on.

'We're told, by every book, by every religion, every god, that we will have our chance at redemption. The prophet knew otherwise, he told us the truth: that nothing is fatal, nothing is ever truly over, and my gosh, aren't we just evidence of that? Because only hours ago we were all dying, all of us. And now we are alive! In this moment! Absolutely alive!'

'She's good at speaking,' I whisper, but Rhonda ignores me. She moves through the back of the hall, looking at the backs of the people.

'Everybody has their shot?' the woman on the stage asks.

'Please, please, let me go, I have changed my mind,' the other voice says; and I look in its direction, find it much easier now. I didn't see the bags: seven of them, hanging from the rafters of a high-up conveyor belt that stretches nearly the length of the entire hall, up at nearly roof level, from a hole in the roof where there's a pipe to deposit whatever it was they processed here; and the bags hang from it, wriggling, ropes tying them to the conveyor.

'What are they—'

'They're sacrifices,' Rhonda says. 'Don't worry about them, they die, they come back. They're like, I don't know. They chose this.'

'They don't want it.'

'Yeah, and they didn't want it the first time around. But they signed something. You know, this whole thing, it changes, it does, it shifts in subtle ways, and there have been times that she's even changed her mind, you believe that?' Rhonda's talking about the woman on the stage. 'They change their minds every time, some of them. Some of them are fucking gleeful about it, though. And they signed up, they signed it. What are you gonna do?'

I notice more of the small bottles in the hands of the people standing, watching. Some of them finger the lids; some of them fidget the bottles, manipulating them, or closing their fists on them, feeling their weight and shape against their palms; or holding them with their fingertips, not wanting them, wishing that they would drop. Regret in their clasp.

'There she is,' Rhonda says, and she moves off, fast, through the crowd, diagonally through them, not staying to the back, disturbing them, drawing attention to herself; but I stay back, I don't follow, I try to cut around, while looking to see Venda, to see if I can see her, which I can't; but Rhonda is driven, and fast.

The woman on stage notices, but she isn't fazed. She continues: 'It's time, I think? Time to understand what's meant for us, what's greater than even us. Because we are great, aren't we? We're human, we're humanity, and we find a way. That's the old phrase, life finds a way.' She says it as if it's not from a movie; as if it's philosophy. 'And it does,' she says, 'it really does. Here we are, at our most desperate: our land decimated, our people dead, or dying, our seas retreating, with food shortages, with temperatures we cannot control, with ice caps melting and belief – belief! – at an all-time low. As if there's ever been a time we didn't need to believe. So we believe. We believe in the Knot; in the glory of what it will deliver us to: our life, again, over, and over, in perfect worship, in perfect synchronicity with it. Raise your tinctures—' She lifts her bottle, undoes the lid. 'Raise your tinctures, and drink from them; and let the bells ring.'

The crowd raises their bottles, or most of them do; and I notice men and women at the sides of the room, dressed in black, staring at them, as the woman on the stage drinks; and as she raises her hand, having drained her bottle, something like a wave or a salute, and the crowd drinks; except for those who don't, which makes the black-clothes move towards them, to force them, that's immediately clear, a threat of this room. So some of the wayward drink then, or undo their bottles and go to drink.

'Wait,' one says, 'I'm doing it—'

The bells, then. The ropes holding the bodies in their bags from the conveyor are triggered, somehow, loosened, and the bodies fall, plunge—

The thick smack of ropes tightening; the gurgle of throats crushed on those same ropes. The crack of some bones, I don't know which.

The crowd watches as the bodies tremble and tremor, as they die, almost vibrating as they hang from their ropes, their faces hidden.

'We turn away from them,' the woman on the stage says.

'We turn from our dead, and we let them pass; knowing that they will return to us.'

She raises her hands, her palms, to her eyes, as everybody in the crowd follows suit. Many of them sobbing. The people in black, the enforcers, they come for me, then: they see me, and I see Rhonda and a young girl, the girl terrified, as Rhonda picks her up, throws her vial to the floor, and runs. Rhonda looks back to me.

'Get out,' she says, 'they will kill you. You need to run.'

I am staring at the twitching bodies; I turn, I run, as she told me to do, towards the corridor. The people in the crowd turning, looking as well. One man whispers at me: 'Go, get out.' I run, I move, I try, at least, even though I'm not what I was, and I wonder: when did I last run? Have I ever run as if my life depended on it?

My daughter, I suppose. Rebecca. Carrying her body in my arms, feeling the weight of her holding them down, and wanting only to stop, to lay her down, but my legs wouldn't let me, they went, they carried on regardless of my want or my need.

A scream, behind.

'Please, please—'

'Save me, I'm a good girl—'

I have heard the calls before. I glance back, as I turn a corner, to the corridor with the low ceiling, and I see them, in their bags, hanging from their hooks, moving, shunting. Chrysalises that will never split and materialize, destined to stay incubating. They have come back, their loops starting again. They were in the bags, suspended, when the Anomaly came; they died inside it; they came back, suspended again, as if nothing at all had changed. As if years, decades, hadn't passed; as if they weren't on what must be tens of thousands of awakenings after their own deaths, assuming they only died once a day, or twice.

I pass the space to the side of the stage, and the woman looks at me. She is familiar, in that moment, and I realize then that she must be related to Rhonda – the same eyes, the same chin, the same sadness – and she shakes her head at me, disappointed rather than anything else.

'Is this really how you would have it?' she asks. 'Defiant as this, when it has done so much for us?'

'It's frozen us in time,' I say, my breath lost, my lungs feeling as though they're about to give out, 'it's stopped us from moving forward, from growing, from grieving and moving past our tragedies.' My voice ragged, my breathing a rattle.

'Our tragedies are sins,' she replies, the most unnatural phrase, one of Pettersen's. 'They save us, they have saved us all.'

'You aren't saved,' I say, 'you're trapped.' And I move again, almost staggering through the room with the mattresses and the sleeping bags, and I see statements taped to the walls now, reminding them, when they wake up from their deaths: *This is the last day, it is always the last day, the days before do not matter, you are here to show the Knot that you appreciate it and understand it, and we will move forward and backwards in glorious synchronicity. You are a good person, who knows that death is not the end; it is simply a beginning you have encountered before.* More of Pettersen's words.

I tear them down. I should be running, the enforcers aren't far behind, but I don't. I need to do this, for when they wake up. Maybe save a life. I pull down each sign, tape that's been here for the longest time taking paint with it as it comes from the walls. I know, they can replace them, but maybe they'll not notice that I've done it. And the followers or believers or whatever they are, they'll lie down to sleep and die and wake up and they won't have the instruction; and maybe tomorrow will be different for them, in whatever way it can be.

That isn't what will happen; I need to hope it could be what will happen.

It's only when I'm outside that I realize I'm clutching the signs to my chest, crumpled tight, and I don't let go of them as I cross the facility, as I try to get away from this place and its towers and silos and concrete and steel; and when I get back towards the truck, I see Venda, kneeling on the floor in the dust, the dirt and sand, and she's crying. I ask, 'What's wrong?'

I see Rhonda, lying flat. She is dying, or dead; or dying, absolutely, because she is still here. Still with us, and I put her finger into my hand, and I squeeze it, to let her know I'm here, that there's somebody here with her.

I think I say that, as well; though I'm not sure, my mouth so dry, that any words at all come out.

Then I shut my eyes, and she pulls her finger away; and when I open them, she's gone, as if she's dissolved into air, to gas, to vapour.

11

Venda eats a rice cake in the passenger seat of the truck as I drive her back to the outskirts of the town. She doesn't talk much, which is fine by me – I don't know if I have the words to do pleasantries, or to even explain why she was saved, because she doesn't know, she's a child without the awareness of any of this – and I don't want to put on Rhonda's tapes, so we're in silence, listening to the sound of the tyres on the road or the engine when it seems to almost intermittently cough, throwing itself into another gear. And then we're back to the town itself, or the borders; and I park the truck where Rhonda parked before, and we get out. We walk slowly, Venda meandering, into the town; past May's house, and she peers through the windows and waves at us.

'Another day, good morning to you.' She doesn't ask where Rhonda is, and I don't offer the information.

'Where do you live?' I ask Venda, and she shrugs; because of course she doesn't know yet, not this loop. So we wander down the street, and she kicks a stone, and she eats another of the rice cakes, which must be stale past digestible, they're so flimsy and loose; and we pass houses that are boarded up, that I didn't notice the first time here, perhaps because I wasn't looking or I didn't want to look. Contamination tape on the front door, preventing anybody from entering, but that doesn't mean actual contamination, it means that there's a death here that cannot – or should not – be prevented. I remember one of the people on our street, he went to a neighbour and took a shotgun to the face, both of them dead there and then; and then minutes later, the same thing. Hard to stop, and the neighbour, he always died, he always did what he wanted to do, there was no talking him down. There's no stopping the inevitable, that was the lesson from that; and everything now feels curiously inevitable—

'What does inevitable mean?' Venda asks, and I stop walking.

'I didn't know I was talking,' I say.

'You were,' she says. 'Loud words.'

'I'm sorry,' I say. A slip: internal monologue overspilling. 'It's hard to know what's silence and what's not, in this quiet,' I say, which I don't expect her to understand or respond to.

We reach the red barn, and Shep's there, and his wife. He stands with his hands on his hips, craning his back.

'You found her,' he says. 'Venda, good to see you.'

'I don't know you,' she says.

'Okay, you will. People call me Shep,' he says. 'This is Cammy, my wife. You like the barn?'

'I do,' Venda says. 'It's so big.'

'We've got some toys, you want to come through?' Cammy takes Venda's hand and leads her through to the rear of the barn, where there's a play area. 'Her things,' Shep says. 'We keep them here, and she doesn't remember, but then, give it a short while, they're her things. She always comes back to them.'

'You look after her?' I ask him.

'We all do. All of us, we pull together. We don't have kids, or we didn't have kids. And we said, we can't bring them into this world. Because there are bad things that could happen, and God knows, we couldn't deal with that shit. And with her heart, I mean, can you imagine if it was your own kid?'

'I can,' I say. My words out on my breath, carried for me.

He nods at me. 'You been there?'

'Our daughter died before it came.'

'In many ways, that's a blessing, isn't it? My mom died the same way, days before. I think she even took herself, you know? Because she was worried, and we didn't know if the rumours were true, but you've got to wonder, right?' He looks behind me, at the door to the barn. 'Where's Rhonda?'

'They shot her,' I say.

'Fuck, no. She made it so far. So damned far, good God.' He smiles, something like consolation. 'Still: at least she's alive, right? She'll find us, we'll cross paths again. Nothing's ever truly gone. Hey: it's like those old horror movies, all pet cemeteries and burial grounds, *sometimes they come back*. Except, here, now, they always come back, and they're not dead. If ever we needed proof there's no such thing as ghosts,' he says. He looks over at Venda. 'She'll be okay here. We'll all take care of her, until we can't do anything for her. Good chance that Cammy and I'll be too old by then.'

'Maybe it'll be gone by then,' I say.

'The Anomaly? Ha! We'd be lucky. Very, very lucky,' he says. 'You want to stay for food? We're having eggs, so many eggs, can't even move for them.'

I thank him, and thank him kindly, but I have somewhere to be.

And then I'm back at the truck, and I'm driving, and May waves goodbye to me; 'I'll see you again,' she says, through her opened window, but I don't reply.

When I get to the factory, Rhonda's waiting outside. I recognize her firstly from her taste in clothes, which hasn't changed at all over the years, or won't change, doesn't change. All tenses operating at once. She's pacing, boots too big for her, treading into the dirt. She looks up at the truck, and she stares as I approach; as I park it, and get out, and walk towards her.

'What do you want?' she asks. I'm a stranger to her. 'If you're here for the church, they're all fucking dozy.'

'They've taken something.'

She chews on that. 'That wasn't meant to be until after.'

'It is after. Look up,' I say, and she does. 'You see how the sky's got that sheen? That haze?'

'Doesn't mean anything. Sky gets weird out here.'

'Look at the sun,' I say then, and she does. 'You can look at it. It's not quite as bright as it was.' The click of realization in her, and she moves, shifts on her feet, pacing.

'I hate them. I fucking hate them,' she says, the curse word so quiet it's almost ushered on her breath alone. 'You know what they're going to do?'

'They've done it,' I say. 'They've killed themselves already. It's just waiting to happen.'

'They told me I have to,' she says.

'You don't.'

'I was meant to.'

'There's a lot we were all meant to do.'

'You a creep?' she asks.

'A creep?'

'A pervert.'

'No,' I say.

She looks at the truck. 'That's neat,' she says.

'It's yours,' I say.

'What do you mean?'

'You're Rhonda,' I say. She steps back, immediately suspicious. 'We've met before.'

'The fuck we have, I would remember, stuffy-ass voice like yours.'

'You were older.' I grab her bag from the truck, rifle through it. A journal, just as she said. Her name printed on the front in thick pen. The volume of her life. Started when she was younger. Added to. Every page – thin-ruled, lots of them – filled with thick scrawl. I throw it to teenage Rhonda. 'The older version of you wanted you to read this,' I say.

Rhonda takes it from me with the hesitancy of somebody handling a stick of dynamite, about to go off in their hands. She takes it, turns, and she sits on the dusty ground, back against one of the tyres; and she reads. Flicks through some of it, reads other bits with an intensity that makes her start to tremble.

I sit in the truck. Shut my eyes. Time passes, some time. Hours. The sun lower in the sky, nearly night. Then I sense her, standing at the window. She squints at me. 'You're Theo, then.'

'Yes,' I say.

She reads: '*Nice-enough guy, looking for his wife, lonely, took pity on him. You can trust him.*'

'That's all it says about me?'

'And *Artist*. You're an artist?'

'Yes,' I say. 'I was.'

'Got a picture?'

I show her some of the sketches in my own notebook. Old sketches, of the house, of the small terrace garden. Of the immediate vicinity. That graffiti, out on the wall: retraced by me in soft pencils.

'You could have stolen that,' she says. 'You could have stolen the truck, killed old Rhonda, stolen all her shit, and now you're trying to paedo me.'

'What?'

'I've read a lot of books,' she says, 'I know what people are like when there's an apocalypse.' She stares at the notebook, at my hands. 'Okay, draw something.'

'I can't,' I say, so quickly, and she does this face, as if she's been proven right; so I say, 'I don't really, not any more. I sort of have it, in case.'

'So do something. I don't know: draw the factory.'

'It's not as simple as that,' I say.

'I did art at school, okay? Of course it's that simple.' She stares at the factory. 'I can wait, what else am I going to do?'

I find a rock large enough to sit on top of, and I take the notebook and the pencil. The pencil neat in my hand. There's a small groove, almost, in my skin, where the pencil is meant to fit. One specific type, a Palamino Blackwing 603: the *only* pencil, as far as I was concerned, as far as most artists were concerned. Certainly it was the one that spoke to me. That made me feel as if my hand were attached to it, as if we were one and the same. Birdie bought me a box once, before the Anomaly came; and then after, in the months after, when looting was basically just what happened, what everybody did, because the rules went, abandoned, that was how you ate or whatever, we scoured the city for them. Found boxes and boxes, because who wants pencils in an apocalypse?

I did. Even if, after Birdie left, I slowed; and then stopped, unable to hold the thing. Unwilling, maybe.

I don't think about the factory as I'm drawing. I don't think about the shape of it, the structure itself, or the landscape. I think about the bells, and I think about what Rhonda must have gone through. Those are the things I think about, and I draw, and I hear the scratch of the lead on the paper. That sound, so pure, impossible to replicate.

Then the sound stops, and my hand stops, and the picture's done.

Rhonda notices, and she walks over, and she climbs the rock next to me and leans over my shoulder. She looks at the picture for a long while, staring. Like it's caught her, somehow; and then she pulls away, and she smiles. 'Shit,' she says. 'Okay, we should go.' She climbs down the rock and gets into the car, into the driver's seat. 'This was my car, you said.'

'Yes,' I reply, climbing down after her. 'And you can drive?'

'No. But you can teach me.'

'I really don't like driving.'

'Then you've got no choice, have you. You want to go? I want to see what she can do.'

I get into the passenger side, and Rhonda rifles through the tapes, and her eyes go wide; and she pops a Springsteen into the player, and that's it, she's singing along. I tell her how to start the engine, and she does, first time, as if there's a knack to it and she's innately got it, and then suddenly we're on the freeway, and I don't even really know where we're going, except for east; and she hoots with joy, at the

We're silent. Those who know him smile, or don't react, or eat their food. They let the moment pass. I think about saying something, but he's a Pettersen follower. The little necklace dangling from his collar. Tucked in, but I can tell. He won't listen; won't even hear me.

Rhonda speaks, breaking the silence. 'Where's Venda, anyway? She's usually first to tell William he's lost it.' She looks around. Nobody answers her. What's happened?

'She's gone,' Shep says, finally.

'Gone where? She was—'

'We don't know. We just don't know.'

'Did she die?'

'Not that we saw. And if she has since, she hasn't made her way back here.'

'Who's Venda?' I ask.

'She's a friend,' Rhonda says. 'She's a good friend, lives here.'

'Lived here,' Shep corrects. 'Sometimes people move on.' He shrugs. Shep doesn't eat, I notice. No plate in front of him, just a glass of very pale beer. He's scrawny: all muscle and sinew. Our bodies are probably quite similar, except his is intentional where mine is involuntary, closer to atrophied. 'Sometimes, people leave, and they don't come back. You can't pigeonhole people these days, you know that.'

'She loved it here.'

'Things change.'

'Have you been to look for her?' Rhonda is slightly frantic, slightly askew. Her jaw tensing as she waits for a reply. 'None of you?'

'You know what it's like out there,' Shep says. 'We've always just waited for her to come home, to come and find us, and she always has.' He looks at me. 'She grew up here, driving, as I cling onto the edge of my seat, slightly terrified, but the terror giving way to something else. She yells, and I yell as well, and I put my hand out of the window, in the rush of the air, and I feel it there on my palm, and it feels good.

12

A floodgate has opened.

I'm sketching a view of the most peaceful place in the world. Nobody around. There's no tourism, nobody to maintain nature, so the parks are absolutely rewilded, given over to themselves. What used to be trails aren't any more, so there's no path, but you can see where somebody's boots might have pushed down overgrowth, squashing it into the dust; but then, it could be a coyote, lying there in the night, under the moon. Brambles and nettles and bushes with inch-long spikes jutting from their arms. I draw them all, my pencil carving out their shapes, their outlines. The vagaries of detail in the lead as Rhonda sleeps in the bed of the truck, still. She went out like a light, after a conversation about her parents: as if she was spilling everything she needed to spill, to empty herself before starting again. I showed her the notes, and I explained to her: this is hers, this truck, the tapes, this world, really; and she'll be safe with me, should she want to stay on our journey.

'Where are we going?' she asked me, and I said,

'I'm going to Europe, to England.'

'I've never been,' she said.

'You hadn't before, either. You were coming as far as you wanted to, that's all.'

'I want to see New York.'

'It's not like it was,' I tell her. 'It's not like you might remember from movies and stories, or from before, it's probably really changed. But we're going there, or we were.'

'Are we still?'

'That's up to you,' I said. 'I am, but it's your truck.'

'Yeah,' she says.

She stirs, now, and I go to the burner, to the frying pan. The preserved bacon pieces in the pan, starting to sizzle; but they take a long time, and the heat isn't what it could be, not retaining a charge, relying on the actual sun as it strikes. It's too early, but I toss them, let the fat sit a little. Finish my drawing; a new rule, that they're done when the moment is. Nothing like seizing that perfect second for drawing a line underneath them.

'What time is it?' she asks.

'A little after six,' I say. 'I don't sleep very well any more.'

'Oh,' she says. 'I do, I think? I mean, I sleep well. Do I, did I?'

'What you do now is all that matters,' I reply. She slides to the end of the truck bed, swings her legs off and starts to pull on her boots. The same boots, the exact same boots, I notice; or, likely just the same make, the same type, but still: it's unsettling. As if they didn't age with her. 'I'm cooking,' I say.

'Oh,' she replies. She stares at the pan. 'I'm vegan.'

'You're not,' I say, but what I mean is, You won't be.

'I think I know myself better than you do.' The spit of a teenager's affronted way.

'I'm sorry,' I say. 'Maybe there's something here?' And I rifle through Rhonda's – adult Rhonda's – tins, and I find tinned spinach, tinned mushroom slices, multiple tinned corns. She nods as I show them to her, and I peel one of the corn tins open, upend it into the pan—

'The fat,' she says, 'I won't eat the fat.'

'Of course,' I say. I tip the still-uncooked bacon into the scrub – foxes, snakes, mice, worms, coyotes, eagles; they'll scavenge it, I'm sure – and I start again. The vegetables all cook quickly, steaming more than frying, the liquid from the tins making everything too wet to do any more. She watches me, and then I tip the food onto plates, and I hand one to her. She devours hers, scooping the food to her mouth as if she's a toddler; and then she smiles.

'That was delicious,' she says.

'You were just very hungry.'

'That's as may be, doesn't change the taste.' She stands on the truck bed, looks around us. The road a few hundred yards away, a sliver of grey through the brush. Her body this smaller, slighter version of who she will one day be, but she holds herself exactly the same way: spreading her shoulders as wide as can be, this slight hunch to her. This leaden thump to her walk. It's not an affectation, it's just how she's built; how the synapses fire, how her body's meant to move. She bends down, finds the steering wheels. 'What are these?'

'Souvenirs,' I say, 'I think. Something like that. Mementos.' She shrugs. 'Driving lesson time?'

So eager, so willing to just do something. So quick to make a choice, and let that spur her on. Just as she was when I first met her. 'Sure,' I say.

* * *

She pushes down on the accelerator, and I don't notice for a moment. The radio louder than she used to have it, or will have it, and we're singing along – she knows every word, where I have the choruses down, some of the lines that have embedded themselves from ambience – and suddenly we're very fast indeed, suddenly we're faster than I realized, and I notice her fingers, picking at the wheel's material, and I say, 'Are you nervous?' And she takes her hands from the wheel, only for a moment, but it's long enough, and we wobble, start to spin, and I grab the wheel, righting us; but the hat, the panama, it flies off in the wind, in my sudden movement, flapping into the air. 'Stop the car,' I say, 'push the brake,' and she does, suddenly, and we jerk, turning, the immediate reek of burned rubber, just as the song finishes, perfect timing were it not so absolutely terrifying.

I get out, and I stand at the side of the road – sometimes you need stability underneath your feet; sometimes you need the feeling of stability, of not travelling, and sometimes control is all you need for that – and I breathe, deeply. The smell of the engine and the tyres still strong; the black rubber marks along the road, showing how much we were swerving.

'I'm sorry,' she says. She's still clutching the wheel, and she's looking down, not at me.

'It's okay,' I tell her. 'We all get carried away.'

She's crying, and she says, 'My dad said he would teach me, before he, you know.'

'It's okay.'

'Why did they have to listen to Pettersen?'

'I don't know,' I say. 'Lots of people did.'

'*Everybody* did. Were they all desperate or something?'

'Yes,' I say. 'That's exactly what they were. My father joined them as well.'

'Really?' She looks at me with the bleary eyes of somebody who needs that reassurance, who's ready to believe it even if it's not true. But it is, in my case. Into the car once more, I sit back. The memory comes easily: how he abandoned my mother, when she was doing work that she knew was necessary; how he abandoned me, or used me, the parents of some of my schoolfriends being a part of a local branch, brandishing their little knot necklaces; and how he persuaded me, only a child, to sign up to their cause, because I was missing my mother dreadfully, thousands of miles away from her in a situation where a climactic ending was a distinct possibility; and then, when that ending finally came true, dead up there on the space station, or out there in the vacuum, and he got the call from my mother's boss, telling him that she was dead, that she died in the line of duty, no higher honour than in trying to protect our planet, our people, our existence; and then how we became embedded in the Knot, and he lost his way with me almost entirely, and I pushed back, further and further; until finally he was a speck in the mirror, leaving me, not even a teenager, eleven or twelve or so, alone in the house, to fend for myself, to bring myself up, to act as if I wasn't abandoned and alone, as good as orphaned.

'Twelve?' Rhonda asks.

'Yeah.'

'Jesus. When I was twelve, I couldn't have even, I don't know. I didn't know how to cook an egg, even.'

'I had to learn,' I said. 'We owned the house, there was a payout when my mother died, so I didn't have to worry about that. We were a decade or so away from the Anomaly finally enveloping us all. It felt so close, but still: I had to live.' The tears are mostly gone, and she wipes what's left of them away with the back of her hand, and she smiles at me; and then she sees it. 'What's wrong with your head?' she asks.

My wound that won't heal. And the hat: it's somewhere down the road, tossed by the wind, rolling like a wheel, like a tumbleweed. I reach my hand to my scalp. It feels markedly worse: A strange friar's cap, my fingers finding moist flesh, the soft red dampness of the seep.

'You're sick?' she asks me.

'Yes. I'm dying.'

'So you've got the thing that they released—'

'A variant of it. When everything settled, there were three or four variants. There was one before, you remember that? You would have been ten or so. Lots of people died, mostly in Canada?'

'I think so.'

'So that was a trial, but they didn't know that at the time. Then the actual thing was released, the more fanatical sects of the Knot wanting to force everybody to die when it came. And those people died faster than intended, mostly. A lot of them, a lot of them. So many. It was meant to incubate for months, but it didn't. It tore through people.'

'How many people?'

'A lot.'

'How many?'

A number that seems unquantifiable to think it, to say it. 'Most people. Billions. Many billions died, and then more from the mutations of the virus. They started straight after it was released. Some weren't bad, they sort of neutered it. Some changed it in other ways.'

'And that's what you've got?' She moves her body back a little, as if she's making it smaller in the seat of the car; shifting her aura away from me.

'I think so. Don't worry, you can't catch it,' I say. 'Not from breathing or being near me or whatever. Not this variant. It's in my blood, nowhere else.'

'So how did *you* catch it?'

'I don't know. I just did. I had it, then they tested my blood once, and they found out. They made me sleep in this tent, like I was a threat; but then there was no shedding, not unless I bled, and I wasn't bleeding. So they let me go. I had it when the Anomaly came. No escape.'

'Holy shit.'

'Yeah.'

'So you've had it for – how long?'

'Since the enveloping. The whole time. Thirty years, give or take.' Her eyes widen. Maybe the realization of exactly how long she was alive before; what it means for her to have reset now. 'It's a long time. I don't know anybody else who's survived this long.'

'How'd you do it?'

'I don't know. The virus just took its time. And I've done what I could, I suppose, I've stayed safe. It's worse when you're injured, if you get a cut. There are things that stop the blood thickening, and you can just bleed out. From even a tiny cut, apparently. I haven't had many wounds, haven't been in many wars.'

'There's been wars?'

'No. Sorry. Figure of speech.'

'Oh.' She finds a bit of the steering wheel, pulls at it. A strip of black softness comes away, and I notice the edges, rough and worn. There's an unnatural desire in me: to reach up to my head, to take one of the skin tabs and pull it, let it unspool, let it unravel me entirely. This is the start of her own fascination with doing it, I'm sure. 'So I can't catch it?'

'No. Before, you helped me. That's how we met, I was hurt, and you used gloves when you touched me, and—'

'And that's not how I died?'

'What? No,' I say, and I'm shocked, but she's serious, deadly serious.

'Because I don't know. Maybe I caught it from you, maybe you're more contagious than you say. You said I was shot—'

'You were.'

'You said that, okay. But I don't know you. I don't know you, do I? My mom and dad, they wouldn't have shot me—'

'I didn't say it was them—'

'My mom runs the fucking place, so what are you saying, exactly? She doesn't know, she didn't know—'

'Maybe they didn't know who you were? You were older, and she wasn't, she wouldn't have recognized you, and you stole Venda, you took Venda.' I sound desperate, I think, even to my own ears, even with the distortion of hearing my own voice speaking. 'Maybe they just thought you were—'

'I get it.' She looks away from me, stares down the highway. 'Still doesn't mean it definitely happened.'

'I don't have any reason to lie to you,' I say.

'I need to think,' she says; and she starts the engine, and drives, forward, away from me; and I shout something ineffectual, something that feels like nothing more than a yelp made of words I don't even recognize; and then she's gone, she's the blip in the distance, and I'm in the sun, the heat of the day as I stand in the middle of a highway in the middle of a desert in the middle of a national park that goes on for so long, and there's nothing around me at all.

13

The gas-station forecourt is burned out, no fuel here at all – they were picked clean years ago, before people converted to sol2r panels or biogas – but there's at least an old freezer running off a set of panels that have been fastened to the roof, and a sign inside it, frozen over:

If there's food here and you need it, help yourself. Just remember this, come back and replenish, should you get the chance – Brett.

Inside, there are chicken nuggets, there are waffles, there are fishcakes and clear packets of freezer-burned shrimp, there are four tubs of ice cream where the lids have been demolished and contents frozen and defrosted, frozen again and defrosted again, a cycle that's left them a sludge of iced dairy. The waffles are the safest, I reason, and I find a small microwave behind the freezer, plugged into the same array, so I cook myself four of them – half the box, which feels greedy, but my stomach is growling so loudly it actually managed to surprise me – and I eat them, sitting there, cross-legged in between the scorch-marked aisles. There are magazines here, torn up and torn apart. The pages all with tell-tale staple holes in their creases. Some porn, some television, some political stuff. All from pre-Anomaly; the only representation of post is in the standee near the register, for the newsletters that this area evidently printed up and distributed. But I can't find one of them, so I settle on reading technology stories. *Wired* magazine, which I remember reading when I was a teenager; some article about what tech we'll be seeing over the next ten years, an end-of-year special that had to ignore the Anomaly, assume business as usual, assume the path we were following wasn't one we would stray from. But we did, our hands forced; and so it feels like science fiction, these glimpses of pathways we could have taken but obviously didn't. The tech companies pivoted, desperately trying to find a way to sell something to people who might die, who might not remember their purchases, who knew that you couldn't take it with you; and their factories closed, because the workers raged and rioted, the conditions too dangerous to even contemplate, the numbers of suicides potentially too deadly to keep on the books. And the tech never came to pass. Instead, we froze in time, in development. Maybe, if this all ends, maybe we'll pick up these balls and run with them; or maybe we'll go somewhere else. Maybe we will never have these handsets, these implants, these grafts, these biomes, these nanites. Maybe they'll just disappear.

I eat my waffles, and night comes, and I wait; and I rub my feet, and I cross my fingers that I'll see the headlamps of the truck on the road, coming to find me. I draw them, sketch them: bright orbs, in the darkness, even though they're not really there, even though they're only actually a fantasy.

There's a bathroom here – and a sign, *Customers ask for the key!*, that's been long ignored – with filthy walls and floors and no sign of any plumbing that works, and overflowing cisterns and cracked porcelain and no lights at all, the fluo-rescents stripped for materials, it seems; and yet, there's still a mirror on the wall, still pinned fast to the tiles that, all around it, have collapsed or chipped apart.

There's paper here, somehow, miraculously; so I use the facilities, even if they're this gone to seed, as I stand over the cracked porcelain and try to feel human again, for a moment, for this moment; not having to take it outside in a little bag and add it to the compost, but believing that some-body better than me has devised a way that I never have to think about it ever again.

I think about checking my head, but it's too dirty in here. The risk of infection too great. I will take risks, but not stupid ones. Better to ignore it, I think, for now.

Then I stand outside, and I watch morning coming up, over the mountains. And there's a moment where it's so beautiful that none of this, none of any of it, actually even matters any more.

The first sign of the commune that I notice is the smoke, some sort of dawn wafting that billows like a cartoon peace pipe, plumes of smoke in almost perfect clouds, rising one by one. I imagine somebody fanning a flame, waving a cloth over a fire. I walk to the crest of the small hill I am on – I wonder: when do hills become mountains? – and there it is, fifty or so tents around a larger canopy in the middle, the canopy stretched across poles jammed into the ground, pulled taut. There's a smell in the air – fresh food, vegetables and meat – and something happening there. Women and men, topless, dancing. Some sort of bacchanalia, even this early in the morning; and I sit on the rocks and I watch: as they drink wine from goblets, the red spilling over the barrels, while others tread grapes that have come from God-knows-where because there's nowhere to grow them here in this desert; and some of them dance, and others kiss, or more, hands down inside their underwear, rubbing and massaging; and others eat, tending this grill over massive flames that prickle and spit as the fat from the tray drips onto them. They are all young, or younger than I am at least. Lithe, sun-baked. Like some sort of hippie desert festival, that presumably never ends.

'This isn't for me,' I say, out loud, surprising myself; at the timbre of my voice, which echoes, but doesn't reach them. This is not a movie.

Once, Birdie and I would have gone down there. We would have loved it. Once.

I walk back to the road, and I think how pleased I am: that somebody, at least, has found the peace to be here, doing what they are doing. I assume that there's something I don't understand, some hidden death or suicidal urges, but it's not mine, or for me. I get a snapshot only, just that perfect moment.

The walk is long, but there's nothing else to do. A second gas station, and a shelf-box of Twinkies, though it feels utterly improbable that they would still be here, these strange, still-wrapped bars, the radioactive-white cream in the middle of them tasting exactly as it always has; and then I walk again, and the day turns to night, and I take the wrappers with me, to keep count of how many I have eaten. My gut tells me, though, turning in on itself, and I sit at the edge of the road, cramping, drinking the last of the water that Rhonda left me with, which I have eked out like I've never eked before.

As I am sitting, a car approaches, the silent glide of a modern-before-the-Anomaly vehicle. Sleek lines, silver finish. The click of the battery as it stops not far from me. Out of the front door, a man steps, and I see sandals, toes yoked by fabric, and a towel around his waist. His hair a knotted mess of rat-tails.

'Hey,' he says. 'I don't want to assume—'

'Hello.'

'You need some help? Like I say, don't want to assume, but you're looking pretty banged-up, there.'

I don't know what to say. 'Yes,' I eventually stammer, 'I could use a hand.'

'Get up, get in. Plenty of room, and there's enough battery for air-con, you want a blast.' He opens the passenger door, and extends a hand to me, pulling me to my feet. 'I'm Nasim,' he says. His accent suddenly clear to me. Australian? Or New Zealand, or maybe somewhere else entirely.

'Theo. Good to meet you, Nasim.' I get into the car. He has a good face, I think, the sort of face you want to draw: enough angles, but still with the jowly softness that might let you be looser around the edges. As the light is on between us, before it dies, he glances at my hatless head.

'Nasty wound.'

'Yes,' I say.

'It's not healing, I'm guessing.'

'No.'

'You got it? You're sick?'

'Yes.'

'How many times you gone around?'

'This is my first,' I say.

'Oh shit, okay. And you've got it?'

'Yes,' I say again.

'My God, you should be dead!'

'Shouldn't I just.'

'But you're not. So that's good news, for all involved. We've got a couple of firsts at the camp. I mean, they were kids, so there's been some keeping them safe. I adopted one when she was only three months, you believe that? She's older than me, now.' He grins. 'She doesn't want to try again, which makes sense. Imagine going back to being a ruddy baby! You're an adult, and then you're shitting yourself again, waiting for somebody to wipe it up. Madness.'

'Yes,' I say.

'Bad enough when *I* go back. I was thirty when it hit—'

'How old are you now?'

'Thirty-two, forty-fifth go-around. This body's only a week old.' He starts the engine, the soft purr of it vibrating through my shoes. 'I leave myself notes and videos and the others all tell me. Trust is a circle, we all trust each other, we know how it works.' His grin is infectious. 'Hey, you ever see that movie once where a guy had a thing with his memory, and he tattooed his skin, to let himself know?'

'I think so,' I say.

'There's some dude in Seattle, that happens to him. He's on a short cycle, like a couple of months, cancer, terrible. But his skin remembers.'

'I don't think that's true,' I say.

'You calling me a liar?' The smile never breaks. 'True as the fucking morning, my friend. His skin remembers. He's an anomaly inside the Anomaly, how much of a trip is that? Anyway, I did this.' He shows me the inside of his forearm. *Trust yourself* tattooed on the skin in thick black ink. 'I dunno, maybe I'll slip the net, I reckon. Get myself some skin that sticks with me. Fuck me, I've done this enough.' He turns away from me, looks at the road for a moment. 'You need a ride? Where you headed?'

'England,' I say, and he laughs.

'Fucking joker,' he says. 'British people, always fucking joking! You can go there tomorrow, maybe. You want to come to the camp today? Get some food, rest up, start fresh tomorrow? I can likely drive you as far as . . . Well, depends on how far the sun gets us. Doesn't charge as fast as it drives, I'm afraid to say. You drive?'

'Sort of,' I say.

'So we can take it in turns. Might even get as far as the Big Easy, something like that, I'm happy to put in the work, a few days of this stuff. If you fancy it, I mean otherwise we can try and get to a hotel or something tonight, there's one in Springfield I know is still open, if you've got trade—'

'Is the camp the one I saw? With the smoke?'

'Yeah, that's nothing. Ignore that. Drunk pissheads. When your body doesn't need to be kept pure, they really push things to the limit, you know?'

I don't want to go there, but I want the lift. One night, I tell myself: how bad can it be? They're drunk and foolish, so head down, get some sleep. Tomorrow, move on.

'I've got a friend as well,' I say. 'She's run off, could we maybe look for her?'

'You don't ask much, do you? Sure, we can look for her. Hey, you're settled, maybe she'll find you. You saw the smoke, that's what it's there for.'

I get into the car, and he starts the engine, and he drives us down the road, and off-road, and he sings rather than plays the radio, this song I don't know that's aimless and formless, built around this one repeating melody: da da, da dum, da da.

* * *

'Everybody, this is Theo. Say hi—'

'Hi, Theo,' they all say, smiling; and I think, well, this is a cult, but of course it is. A cult is a gathering of like-minded people in a situation. Aren't we all in a cult, really? Haven't we all always been in a cult? Their polished bodies, their muscles that take on the definition of ash-blasted mannequins. One of them hands me a beaker of something, the sweet waft of home-made wine; and I taste it, because I'm thirsty, but the tannin almost immediately dries my mouth and throat.

'It's been a while since I drank,' I say.

'Then, it's probably time to make up for it,' another one of them says.

Nasim shows me around, and it is as I suspected: tents, mattresses arranged inside them. Many of the tents connected by small tunnels, as if this is some giant pillow fort, and this is all playtime; and beds that spill over to each other, a chaos of sex and rest amid them. We sit around a smaller campfire, and he tells me about the place:

'Started a few weeks before the enveloping, all of this. Everybody here came from Vegas. Not natives, but performers and staff, and there was an exodus—'

'I heard,' I say.

'Nobody was coming, there were redundancies . . .' He grins. 'Seems insane, now, to think we even gave a shit? We came here, got the fuck out of that hellhole. You been there?'

'Not since,' I say. 'I've heard stories.'

'It's a *crazy* place. Dead eyes, everybody there. Dead eyes, dead eyes. Like, before, where you lost all sense of time because everything was open and it was just, you know, whatever you wanted whenever you wanted it? It's like that but worse, because there's no sense of life, either. No danger, because you're there. All the guests just in this perpetual circle-jerk of life, killing themselves for soft resets, starting again. Nutso place. But we came here, and we haven't been back. Easier out here, because we've got everything we need, you know? There's cattle, there's fish in the river—'

'There's a river?'

'Sure, few miles to the mountains. Salmon in it, you believe that? I figure there's not many, but we take them, kill them, whoomph, there's more. Obviously. Then we eat, all of us, and we do whatever we like. The brakes are off here, you know what I'm saying?'

'Yes,' I say, but I think back on my own brakes, and I'm not sure that I do. The craziest I have been: some drugs, dabbling rather than embracing; and I slept with a couple of my friends before I met Birdie, but those were teenage fumblings, practising for the real thing; and I've thought sexually about women since she left, about what I would do to them if we crossed lines from acquaintance to friend to romantic: soft skin in the sunshine, both of us with sweaty bodies, but I never had the gumption to make a real move, let alone explain the rot, and tell them about the precautions we would have to take. To even hold hands, if she was worried that there might be a wound. It wasn't visible, obviously, but I knew it was there, my body staving it off. My will staving it off.

'We're supportive of each other, that's the crucial thing. That's the most important facet of our new reality,' he says. He reaches for a rib, from the barbecue. A rack of them, nestled next to five fish, the skin on the salmon crackling. I wonder what meat it is: there aren't any cows here that I can see or hear. 'I've done this enough times that I'm kind of bored, so I push myself. And we are here for each other to do that.'

'How many times did you say?'

'Forty-five. Some people here— Hey, Janet! Janet!' He shouts to a woman who trots towards us, her feet padding on the sand, delicate on top, henna swirls and toe-rings hiding calloused skin beneath that you can only see as she gets close enough. 'Tell him your number.'

'Coming up to a thousand,' she says. A thousand. I do the maths, that's one every ten days or so. She sees me working it out, and she laughs. 'It doesn't hurt, and I get to be pure so often. I get to run myself down, give myself up, for the betterment of our little community. And then I get to be new again. It's beautiful. I don't ever need to worry about anything. I'm free,' she says.

Nasim stabs the air with the bone from the rib he's picked clean. 'That's what this is all about, the freedom of understanding that you don't need to worry any more. Do you worry?'

'Of course I worry,' I say. More honest than I expected, as my brain parsed the question, but it's out there, and Nasim hoots, hurls the bone into the brush. 'What about animals?' I ask him. 'Won't they smell that? Come looking for it?'

'We've been killed before,' he says, 'when that happened, but really, who gives a shit? Who cares, that's the whole . . . It's nature. There's a loop, nature's on a loop. The food chain is a loop.'

'It's a ladder,' I say.

'You think a chain's a ladder?'

'It's connected pieces. So, yes.'

'Nah, mate. It's a loop. A chain, it's a loop. You pull all the links apart, put them together, that's just one fuck-off massive loop.' He pulls another rib from the barbecue and holds it out to me. 'Go on,' he says. The bone is long, curved. Meat charred, but slightly pink still.

'What animal is it?' I ask him. 'I know, I know, I'm not complaining—'

'It's Paul,' he says. 'This is Paul's flesh, which has given up to you.' I put the rib down, or I drop it, into the sand. 'What a waste', he says. 'Don't be freaked out—'

'You're cannibals—'

'We are not,' he tells me. 'We are absolutely not. Jesus, we're not animals. The rules have changed but the morals haven't. One of us did this, and when it's gone, they'll come back. This is Paul, he is a good guy, really good guy. Clean-living, but husky, you know? Like, a big lad. A unit. He makes really good meat, great meat. The right amount of fat to flesh. He gave it up, it's his offering. And he knows he'll be back! This isn't some bullshit thing where we're killing somebody for food. This is a gift. All of us, we share in it: meat with no victim, no crime. No record of the death, because he's not dead, give him an hour, he'll be back. No effect on our ecosystem, even: a presence that was here, that existed, and then it still exists, but food is created. It's quite incredible, when you think about it. It's basically perpetual motion, *infinite* energy. And eating it, it's no different than anything else. It's meat. It's food, it's protein.'

Most post-apocalyptic stories have their own cannibals. Most have reasoned with the logic behind it, the new truth giving them the ability to do the thing that they do, to justify their choices. Nasim, the rest of this camp, they're no different.

'It's the circle of life,' Janet says; and she sings a song about it, softly hushed, like some singer from the last century, one of those old folkies, Joan Baez or Judee Sill, that my mother used to like. Her voice pretty, reaching for notes. 'It's the wheel of fortune.'

'I can't eat that,' I say. I think about running, but I'm not sure what they would do. They're peaceful; and there's no sign that they mean me harm. But still, people are people. Nothing changes their people-ness. 'I'm sorry, Nasim—'

'I don't take real offence, but I do think you're closed-minded,' he says. 'Come on, Theo. How trapped were we before? How fucked up were we? And now . . .' He puts his hand on Janet's belly. 'Janet's eight weeks pregnant. And, wait—' He whistles, shouts to a teenager standing near us. The boy's beard growing in in a way that suggests he's been told it'll get there, in the end. 'This is Jacob, Janet's son. And inside there,' Nasim says, his hand still on the belly, 'is also Jacob. Fucking mind-bending. She dies, she comes back, and she's pregnant again! So he exists, he's here, she birthed him once, and now, what's in there? A goddamned clone! There's no rules to killing clones. Janet used to be anti-abortion, didn't you?'

'Pro-choice,' she corrects him. A hint of who she used to be, maybe: a flash of digging her heels in, of spitting venom.

'And now, she's not. Because there's no abortion, there's, I don't know, what even is it? Another facet of Jacob entirely. And here's the kicker: you remember they used to say that souls happened at the moment of conception? That can't be true. Birthing him is a change of state, that's how there's the clone of him. It's such a fucking trip, I can't even tell you.'

The boy, Jacob, waves, and Janet waves back. I sit, and I stare, and I don't talk for a little while; until Nasim gets up, and says, 'I'll sort out a bed for you,' and I thank him, but I know I won't be staying here tonight.

I hear them having sex, through the fabric of the tent that they've vacated for me; thick grunting, moans, gurgles, trills. Noises that seem extreme for the sake of making them, really, rather than actually having truth to them. Or maybe they are absolute truth? Maybe they're what we would do if we were this uninhibited? Because they are, they truly are free, I think?

I don't know if Birdie and I were ever that free. If we were ever that uninhibited. I think we always loved each other. I think, or I thought; but then she left.

So maybe I was wrong.

The couple now are not distracted as I sneak out, as I take the few things I can truly call mine – my backpack, my sketchbook, my pencils, my bottle, my Twinkies, my photographs and memories – and make my way to the edge of the camp.

I see the back of somebody, and I think I might have to avoid them, but they turn, look at me as I'm contemplating my approach. It's Jacob, Janet's son.

'Hey,' he says.

'Hello,' I reply.

'You leaving?'

'Yes.' He's smoking weed, the thick smell hanging in the air at throat-level.

'Makes sense,' he says, offering me the joint. 'You want?'

'I'm sick,' I say. 'We shouldn't share that.'

'I'm done,' he says, 'you finish it.'

I hesitate; and then I think of Rhonda, so willing to just embrace the moment. I take the joint, and I take a drag, deep. I hold it for a beat, then exhale—

I choke on the smoke.

'How does it feel?'

'It's strong,' I say.

'No, I mean: dying.'

'We're all dying,' I say. 'I thought you were into this?'

'They killed me,' he says. 'Only one time.' He smiles. 'Unless you count my mom's pregnancy, which I don't, not all the time. So sure, we're all dying, but you're dying dying. You're, like, it's out of your control. You don't have a choice.'

'They killed you?' I ask, and he nods. 'You didn't have a choice then.' He shrugs. 'How did they kill you?'

'I don't know, nobody'll tell me. But I know how long we've been in here, and I know the first go-round, that's how my mom had me. She died giving birth to me. I'm her first notch, that's what she says. So, she dies, giving birth, every time.' He takes the joint back, drags deeply. 'I would leave.'

'Why don't you?' I ask.

'Because she's dying. Over and over, and I want to, I don't know. Make sure she's okay, all that sort of thing. In case, I don't know. In case something happens.' He passes it back; I take it. 'You think . . .' He looks down. He's a child, really. 'You think the Anomaly'll ever go?'

'Yes,' I say.

'When?'

'I don't know.'

'Because—'

'I know,' I say, but he says it anyway.

'I don't want her dying if it's gone. Like, I don't want her gone for good. And I was thinking: like, what if I die right before? And then she'll have me, as a baby, and we can go through this, you know: normal.'

'I don't think we'll ever be normal again,' I tell him. 'I think, after this, normal means something else. Or I hope it does.' I pat him on the shoulder, because it feels like what I should do, and I walk away from him, down to the road, feeling the rubble and grit give way to the relative smoothness of it under foot, and I walk, just as the sun starts to crane on the horizon.

* * *

130

I recognize the sound of the engine before I see the truck; because there are no other trucks, not on this stretch, and because it's such a distinctive barrel-chested cough and wheeze, the dying choking of man at his last, packed into a tin box and made to turn wheels. I stand still, to see where she's coming from: further down the road, towards me. Only hitting forty, maybe, holding back, relative restraint there. And then she's in front of me, and she stops maybe sixty feet down the road, the engine cooling with a tick, tick; and I see Rhonda staring at me, over the steering wheel she's a little too short for, doing this thing with her mouth, pursing her lips and then relaxing them, over and over, as if she's about to say something but the words feel wrong on their way out. 'Are you okay?' I ask her, shout at her, over the distance.

'I'm fine,' she says.

'You heading back to the factory?'

She shakes her head. 'I came to ask if you still wanted to go to England.'

'Yes,' I say.

'Okay then, I'll take you to New York. Get in.'

'You're sure?'

'I just said, didn't I?'

'Your driving is really coming along,' I say.

'Yeah,' she says.

'You didn't even need me to teach you.'

'I got better when I didn't have to listen to you worrying about it,' she says. She does a tiny hint of a smile. Tiny.

I climb into the cab. She's in different clothes, and there's blood on the dashboard. I imagine where a head was pushed against it? Or smashed into it? But not hers, her side is fine, her face isn't marked.

131

She sees me looking at the blood. 'Don't ask,' she says, 'I won't tell you.'

'Okay,' I say.

I don't ask.

PART TWO

'Memory likes to play hide-and-seek, to crawl away. It tends to hold forth, to dress up, often needlessly. Memory contradicts itself; pedant that it is, it will have its way.'
Günter Grass, *Peeling the Onion*

14

The drive takes days, weeks, in which we sit in that truck, and we see so much of America; or, so much of the little lane of America that the road trip takes us on. We stop at a sandwich shop just outside Phoenix, called *Sierra*, and it's still open, still serving, a bastion of taste; and I eat the best sandwich I have ever eaten, this green goddess and chicken sub that is so incredible I can't even really speak for a moment; and Rhonda finds it hysterical, that I should be so wowed by something like that. Then she tries it, and she says, 'Holy shit, holy shit!' and we order another, and we eat them silently, reverently. We drive through New Mexico, through the actual desert, and the truck clicks constantly, as if it can't quite cool down enough, as if the sun might be too hot for the sol2r panels; and we're forced to pour drinking water into the engine, just to keep going. We worry we'll die, and we pass a person sitting there, dying himself. A loop of about fifteen minutes, as he quietly sits at the side of the freeway, and then slumps over; and then he's back, sitting upright. His mouth cracked-dry, and Rhonda asks to help him, but there's nothing we can do. He is dying whatever happens. We go through Texas, which for whole expanses seems as if it's a literal war zone, or the remains of one, the land torn up, archaic and aged and seemingly somehow time-slipped from another era entirely. Nooses hanging from a tree, but they're empty. They were waiting for people, and they're empty, which means that there's a loop somewhere that's hopefully been broken. Through countryside that turns green, even as it's still baking hot, but there's more green pushing through, a lot more. The sun being so slightly dampened having an effect; and Rhonda says, 'Well, maybe the Anomaly is a good thing,' and I don't really know how to reply to that, because maybe it is, maybe she's right. Through Atlanta, and past the Center for Disease Control buildings, like a pilgrimage: it's burned-out, taped up, *Do Not Enter* over everything.

'Is this where the virus started?' Rhonda asks, and I tell her that that's one of the theories. A weapon in a vault, then somebody working there realized that they could use it. Some Knot fan, some lame horror in thrall to Pettersen. The rumour was, they set fire to the building, stole the virus in the chaos of sprinklers and alarms and emergency-lock doors. The burned part is true, at the very least: it's barely anything but hollow concrete now. Then we're in Virginia, and we drive up a mountain, and we stay at a lodge that's long abandoned, but there's ski gear there, and it's sort of snowing on one of the peaks, so we snowboard for the first time in Rhonda's life, the first time in mine since the Anomaly. And maybe I'm too cautious, clinging to trees, falling to my back rather than going too fast, feeling the thin layer of snow puff around me, soaking my clothes. We drive down that same mountain, to Washington DC, nothing but security gates and armed patrols that don't look official, but maybe they've just given up. Telling us to all move on, to get lost. Nothing to see here: just an off-white building, a blur that exists behind fence after fence after fence.

The signs on the road start to say *New York*. We don't stop driving after that.

Rhonda's got a tape, a cassette tape, that she found in some old secondhand record store which had already been ransacked but which, she tells me, had everything good left behind in it. Because they've got no fucking taste, she says. She's used to swearing now, and you can hear it in her use: every word with the power of knowing that there's something gently forbidden to its use. She shows me the cassette, still in its box: Frank Sinatra, *In the Wee Small Hours*. 'This is the "New York, New York" guy, right?' she asks.

'Yes,' I say.

'Good then.' She puts it in and presses play, and we listen for a while, as we approach the city, as the towers start to loom, and the road turns into overpass, diving above run-down beige buildings. And we listen, and she says, after a while, 'Jesus, he's depressing,' and she ejects it, and puts Springsteen back on.

'I think he came from here anyway,' I tell her. 'Or near here. Jersey.'

'Well, of course he did,' she says. 'Everything good happens in New York.'

The city is startlingly populated; not like Los Angeles is populated, with pockets of people living in communities with each other's backs, but an actual population, actual work, actual lives. I visited here a few times before the Anomaly arrived, before the enveloping, before any number of ridiculous capital letters that somehow signify important events: the Great War, the War On Terror, the Pandemic, the Collapse. And we gave them to ours, because that's how we define the power of a thing, through its name. The Anomaly. The definite article. Regardless: I came here, and there were crowds everywhere, every street in Manhattan feeling absolutely populated. I was smaller, then, a child and a teenager and a young adult, and each time I was overwhelmed: because there wasn't respite in any direction, only inside, and sometimes not even then. I remember the museums, and how early we got there; my mother, holding my hand, pulling me through to look at the dinosaurs; and then she had to lift me up, to hold me, because there were people in front of us who wouldn't move, who wouldn't let me see. And now, there are people here, and shops, and what might even be tourists, families clinging together, holding hands. Not quite the same crowds, but a mass, certainly.

Rhonda stops walking. 'Oh,' she says, just that little exclamation, quiet and soft.

'Have you been here before?' I ask. She shakes her head. 'This is Times Square—'

'I know what it is.'

'Of course. I was just—'

'Don't worry about it. This is where the theatres are?'

'Somewhere near here, sure.'

'Are they still working? My mom used to talk about how she was in a musical once.'

'I don't know. Was she here?'

'I don't know.' Quiet sadness; a question she won't get an answer to.

We walk past these people, who don't stare at us, unalarmed to see others; and we see shops open, restaurants serving. An old McDonald's, and there's the smell of meat;

and inside, a sign, *Only Protein Macs and ReMeat Big Macs*, twenty dollars, served with fries and drink, above the counter, and people serving out of uniform, but the smell, it's pervasive. I remember it, I remember eating it, tasting it.

'What is this?' Rhonda asks.

'You never had one?' She shakes her head. 'Come on,' I say, and I join the queue, behind other people who seem almost nervous about this as an experience, holding their indestructible plastic banknotes in their hands, worrying the translucent protective covering of them with their thumbs. 'Which one do you want?'

'What's the difference?'

'One's meat, one's not.'

'Then the not real one.'

I step up to order, and the man behind the counter sticks a sticker over the *Protein Mac* option. 'Sorry,' I say to Rhonda. 'You want the other?'

'I don't eat meat.'

'The meat's not actually real,' I say. 'That's ReMeat's thing, it's grown. Or developed. Something.'

'So it's from a lab? It's not from cows?'

'I don't think so.' I picture cows dying, being reborn, dying, being reborn. Like Nasim suggested, back at the commune: a zero-sum operation. Maybe ReMeat's whole operation is a lie. Maybe it's only as real as you think it is; as you want to think it is.

'I don't know if I've had meat,' she says. 'I've always been vegan.'

'We ate it together,' I remind her, 'in the red barn—'

'That wasn't me.'

The person in front of me receives their burger and steps to one side, and I step up. The man asks, 'What'll it be?'

'Two Big Macs,' I say, and he shouts it, repeats the order—
'Fries and Fountain?'

'Fountain—'

'We've got a batch of Coke-mix, if you want it. Five dollars extra.'

'Yes,' I say, 'we'll, yes, absolutely we'll have that. Real Coca-Cola?'

'The real thing.' He smiles, this somehow languid smile that takes what feels like forever to draw itself across his face. 'Couldn't believe it when we got it, head office said they're starting to roll it out again—'

'There's a head office?'

'Hell yeah. This isn't some bullshit small-time knock-off, this is McDonald's. You haven't been in the city for a while?'

'I live on the West Coast.'

'Oh,' he says, and that same slow smile stretches, cheek to cheek. 'There's nothing out there, right? I've heard it's like a desert.'

'It's a little quiet.'

'A little quiet.' He hands me a tray, and I haven't even noticed him arranging the items on it. Two wrapped burgers, in branded paper; and those cartons of fries, and drinks, soft drinks, Coca-Cola served in self-clean beakers. 'Enjoy your food, bro.' I hand over the money, tell him to keep the change, and we retreat to the front of the restaurant, near the entrance, two seats at the window; and we sit, and we look at the world. I give Rhonda her meal, and she sips from the drink—

'What is this?'

'The recipe's a mystery,' I say. 'It was very popular way back, when I was your age.'

'It's so goddamned sweet.'

'You get used to it. My dad said it used to be even worse. Or better.' I plonk my cup against hers. 'Cheers,' I say, and she laughs.

'You're so weird,' she says.

'I feel alive,' I tell her. 'You can't imagine, but this is—'

I bite into the burger. I taste blood. And I know that McDonalds doesn't cook burgers rare, so this is wrong, something is wrong; and then I notice that my hands are wet, and Rhonda's eyes widen, terrified, petrified—

'Get the fuck out of here,' a man behind me says, his voice shaking, quivering; so I turn to see who he's talking to, and he's talking to me. He's standing behind me, and he's holding his burger tight to his chest, his hands shaking. 'Your back's bleeding, get the fuck out of here, I don't want any trouble.'

'Please,' I say, and I feel the blood coming, soaking through the back of my shirt, my hands, my feet – my feet are wet, my shoes *filling* – I feel it coming—

'You shouldn't be here,' he screams, and Rhonda grabs me. 'I'll fucking kill you, you're near my family, you fucking freak, you sick fucking freak—' He turns to Rhonda, as she's helping me up, because I can feel it: beneath my clothes, as if my insides are bubbling to the surface. A pocket of air in water, the bubbles rising. Blood, rising. 'You get your father out of here!' he screams at Rhonda, and she's panicked, terrified—

Rebecca, right there, on the tip of my brain, a memory half-formed, half-magical, barely there and yet absolutely present—

Rhonda gets me outside, as the man keeps shouting, as the people around start throwing things; and she takes me down an alleyway, behind the restaurant, where there are trash cans and loose paving slabs and graffiti on the walls:

141

We will both be dead! one reads, and I stare at it as I bleed, as I heave up, as I shake. It's worse than last time. Worse.

I shiver, and I curl up, and she says, 'Are you going to die?'

'Not now,' I manage, 'I don't think,' but that's all I can say; as my blood pools, and she stands back, to stay out of it.

She takes money from my bag, and she leaves. 'I'll get water,' she says. I sit, and nobody else comes. I wait, and I am alone. The blood dries. Hours, I sit there, hours I wait.

As I recover.

Then Rhonda comes back, and she's holding wrapped items. 'I found these,' she says, and she holds them out: clothes, from a branch of Old Navy that somehow still exists. A packet of wet wipes that she throws to me. She helps me to stand, and I clean myself off again, and get dressed. The clothes hanging off me a little too much. Doesn't matter. She slaps a navy blue *I Heart New York!* cap on my head. 'There,' she says, 'much better.'

15

The bleeding was a mystery for minutes, and then it wasn't, because the truth leaked as truth always does, and suddenly we were terrified. A bio-engineered thing, and everybody assumed an enemy at first – until it became clear that maybe the enemy was within. The enemy was the Knot, doing what it was always going to do: condemn us all. They released the virus – they didn't give it a name, to keep it casual, to stop it being something bigger than themselves – they released it because they wanted us all to die when it arrived. A tribute, a sacrifice: like drinking Kool-Aid, just on a scale of the massive and the involuntary. They planned global extinction; they nearly got it. It was thirty years ago, near as damn it, and they killed so many people, so many, only before it arrived, because it was so potent; and more after, trapped in their awful condemned death loops. And then, because we were terrified – of the enveloping, of the change in our sky because suddenly there was a quality to it that we didn't understand, of the virus – because we were terrified, we didn't huddle and we didn't get together, and the bleeding, the virus as it was, simply died out. But that version, the one that nearly caused our extinction, that was the second version. The first incubated, for an undetermined amount of time. It sat, waiting, like a predator; and then it made its move. It didn't spread nearly as powerfully or as wide; and most of the people who caught that first version died of the second anyway.

I have, at times, wondered if I'm the last one left.

It creeps across and prickles my skin, as if my skin is on fire, except not with flames; but with myself.

16

We find a hotel open: a blue awning stretching out to the sidewalk, and a blue carpet, and polished glass, and a valet in a suit as if nothing's happened at all, as if everything is exactly the way that it once was. Inside, a woman behind the desk asks us if we're tourists, and Rhonda laughs as she might have done before she reset, the comedy of finding this all so funny, acting normal and getting on with life here.

'We are,' I say.

'Well, welcome to New York City,' she says. 'Would you like a room?'

'Two,' I say, 'please,' and I open my bag, find the clip of money that I brought with me. She tells us the price, and I flip out notes, and I hand them to her.

'How come you work?' Rhonda asks her.

'What do you mean?'

'I mean, when there's, like, this? All of this, the chaos and the Anomaly.'

'What else are you going to do?' she replies.

'But what do you—'

145

'I get paid. This is my hotel, I get paid.'

'And what do you spend the cash on?'

'Food. Nice food. I go out. And clothes, and I collect old things. I like old things.'

'And this is your hotel?' Rhonda asks.

'Indeed it is. I always wanted to run one,' the woman says, 'and look at me.' She hands me a keycard, another to Rhonda. 'Two rooms, on the seventh floor. The elevator works, if you want to ride that up.'

'No way. No way!' Rhonda runs to the back of the room, presses the button, and there's a ding. The elevator's insides are mirrored, and Rhonda giggles as she presses the button, and holds her hands to her belly as we ascend, and there's that feeling – of the floor leaving you, of being slightly other for a moment – and then the ding of our arrival, and the sliding open of the doors. I step out, but Rhonda waits behind. I grin, because it's so nice to see: somebody taking so much pleasure from something so simple.

'Maybe we could?' she asks, and I nod, step back in. She presses the button for the top floor, and the door shuts, and we ride it, up and down, up and down, until she gets bored, or tired, I don't know which.

Then into the rooms, which are adjacent, mirrors of each other. Incredible, really, and Rhonda throws herself onto the bed as if she's never seen one before. And she looks at the window, which itself looks out onto the city: onto the lights, neon, blaring, buildings with lights in them in deco styles, rooftop parties, people and life—

And cars, down in the street. The beeping of horns, a memory that floats, lands, sits.

We stare for a while. This is a lot. Maybe I say that, as well. Maybe, I don't know.

We leave, heading downstairs – down in the elevator – to the lobby, to find food. The owner asks us how the rooms are; we grin.

'How does it work?' Rhonda asks.

'What, sweetie?' the owner replies.

'All of this.'

'She means, where does all the power come from,' I clarify.

'Niagara and St Lawrence hydro are both up and running, and there's the world's biggest solar field upstate that's taking us through most of what we use. Of course, the authorities say that'll be harder as we scale up, as the city becomes more like it was. You know, before.'

'It's amazing,' Rhonda interrupts.

'Thank you,' the woman says, genuinely proud.

'What happens tomorrow?' Rhonda asks me, through mouthfuls of pasta. A restaurant that advertises itself as *The Oldest Italian Restaurant in New York That Never Closed!* and which the waiter – waistcoat, white shirt, Italian accent that feels forced to breaking point – tells us does the best meatballs we'll ever eat, bullies us almost into ordering them, though we don't need much bullying.

'Real meat,' he says, 'real cow and real pig, and then herbs, and we grow the herbs, a lot of these places, they don't make their own, there's no provenance, but we're proud, this is Grandmama's recipe!' And then he brings them, and they're incredible, or at least they are to us, and Rhonda says that she doesn't think she's a vegan any more; and then she asks me what happens tomorrow.

'I need to find a boat,' I say. 'I need to get to Europe, and then—'

'So you're leaving me?'

'I'm not leaving you,' I say, but I am, I absolutely am. 'You can come if you want?'

It's off the cuff. I don't expect her to, or to even reply. 'Sure,' she says. She stuffs pasta into her mouth, and chews with her mouth open, and looks happy, this beamish grin. 'Sure, I'll come. I always wanted to travel.'

'Okay then,' I say. I want to tell her how pleased I am; but also, I wanted to give her the space to change her mind, to leave me alone here. I don't want her feeling guilt-tripped into staying, so I'm quiet.

But she looks happy, as well.

We are, neither of us, alone.

We're walking past a theatre on the way back to the hotel when we hear singing from inside. 'Come on,' Rhonda says, walking through the unlocked doors, and making her way to an auditorium, where two men and two women stand on the stage, dressed in white and cream and beige, and they sing these songs from this musical about one of the founding fathers, doing all the parts themselves, collapsing in laughter when they mess it up, getting the words tangled around themselves and each other; and we watch, Rhonda and myself, and eventually we know the lyrics a little, the tunes and melodies, and Rhonda sings along under her breath. And then we leave the theatre, and we're out onto the street again. We eat from a cart, hot dogs that taste exactly like I remember them tasting. And then we're at the hotel, and we say good-night.

I shut my door, and I hear Rhonda creep past; and I hear the ding of the elevator, and the swish of the doors shutting.

I realize, suddenly, that my face, my cheeks, hurt from smiling. I still don't stop.

In the night, sometime bleary, with the skyscrapers that are still standing twinkling their few lit rooms like low-hanging stars, I'm woken by tapping on the door that connects our rooms. I get out of bed and sit next to it. 'You okay?' I ask.

'I can't sleep,' she says. 'I'm thinking: what if Europe's not like here? What if they're different?'

'They're not.'

'Yeah, but. It's a long way.'

'You want to go back to your parents?'

'No.'

'It'll be fine,' I tell her.

'You promise?'

'I promise,' I say.

'When are you going to die?' she asks. 'What happens when you die?' And I don't know what to say, just as I didn't know what to say when Rebecca died, and Birdie asked me then, this sad voice in the darkness of our bedroom, begging me to tell her where our daughter had gone.

I sit quietly; and after a while, I hear Rhonda snoring, soft purrs; and I sleep there, on the floor, listening to the sounds of her, a white noise machine drowning out the world outside, the blare of horns, the muttering of the city.

17

The ship's horns blare so loudly that Rhonda jumps, an actual jump like you'd see in an old cartoon, exaggerated and ridiculous and so inducing of shock that she collapses with teary laughter. 'Oh my God,' she says, and she sits on a bollard and stares at them. 'I've never seen them before.' Maybe you did, I think, but you just don't remember it. 'I think, I don't know. Did I know that they were this big? Look at all those things, what are they?'

'Shipping crates.'

'What's in them?'

'Stuff, 'I say. 'Food, I think, and, and, I don't know. Whatever's being made. And people, I think. There used to be smuggling—'

'Smuggling?'

'People, and— Slavery, and prostitutes. It was terrible. A lot of people used to die in them.'

'Okay.' She shuts me down. I was blabbering. 'So how do we get on one of them?'

'We ask,' I say. 'I think we just ask.'

* * *

Rhonda asks questions in a way that I find impossible to do myself. I'm blustering, certainly, and I don't like to get to the point, because rejection feels too inevitable and hard to cope with; but Rhonda doesn't care. 'Screw you,' she says, when one captain laughs at her, after she asks him for passage; and she drops her voice, to explain why she's travelling with an older man when a female captain asks her if she needs help; and then, when there are three men loading a crate, and they say something to her that – again – I don't hear, she looks visibly shaken, returning to me, taking a tiny bit of the hem of my shirt in her fingertips and saying, 'We should try further down, I think?' but it's not really a question, I can tell from her voice. More a desperate instruction, pleading. So we do, we move on: as far as we can, down the length of the dock, and then past, to where there's a temporary dock, boats and ships moored just off-shore, waiting for slots. I wonder aloud if there's any structure to them, any real order; if somebody's taken up the mantle of overseeing the coming in and going out again, if they're taking cash or trade for slots, if there's a commerce to this again. And: are there customs? Is anything allowed in? Does anything have to be paid? If there are customs, then taxes will follow. Is that when we know we're back on our feet? When there's a way of collecting money from us all again for infrastructure?

We find a bar in what used to be a tourist shop, and there are still the remnants of the things that they sold there: a plastic Statue of Liberty as big as a toddler, inflatables mounted on the walls – NYC lettering, an apple, Lady Liberty again – and then clothes, framed and mounted like the proudest of memorabilia. A baseball shirt, a basketball. An

151

old photograph of firefighters on the ground of what was once the Twin Towers. This is the industry starting again, and the barman knows it: he greets us with a 'Howdy!' and we sit at barstools with picked-leather seats, and he says, shouting a little over the playlist of quintessential New York music, 'What'll you have?'

'What's good?' I ask.

'We've got some Brooklyn just in this morning.'

'The beer?'

'Very same. Brewed local, they drive it across themselves.'

'Please,' I say. 'I haven't had one in God knows how long.'

'I'll have a Coke,' Rhonda says, and the barman doffs an imaginary cap at us before retreating behind his makeshift bar.

'I thought it was too sweet?'

'Sure,' she says, 'but now I've got a taste for it. Look what's happened, you've created a monster. What's the plan?'

'I don't know. We go and ask again later, or tomorrow. Somebody will turn up.'

'Where are we going when we get there?'

'Depends where we land. Europe's one mass, really. Or, most of it's connected, until we get to the UK, that's drifting off a little from France—'

'So we drive?'

'If we can find a car. We can try and buy one—'

'You've got enough money?'

'Dollars enough for something terrible. I don't know if they'll take them, if they're worth anything. I don't know much of that.' I stare over Rhonda's shoulder: a man, sitting with something, unfolding it, reading it. A masthead. The *New York Times*. 'A newspaper,' I say aloud. Rhonda looks.

'So?'

'I didn't know that they still made them.'

'You didn't get them in LA?'

'No,' I say. 'I didn't. Maybe some did.' The man stands up, leaves the newspaper where he was sitting. I get up, rush to it, in case somebody else swoops and steals it; and I'm almost expecting vintage, expecting it to be part of the bar's schtick, but it's fresh, new folds, still that smell of print that fades to must so fast, but for now is still absolutely fresh.

But it's recent. I ask the barman, 'When's this from?'

'That's today's, pal,' he says. And that's overwhelming, almost: to have a sense of actual linear time here. Time continuing.

I cry. That's what does it, that's what ticks me over, that moment; holding something that I thought was dead, but it's not, it's come back, just like everything does now.

Rhonda eats chicken wings and I read the entire newspaper, end to end. I learn so much about the world that had sort of passed me by: because California's dead, according to the paper, a forgotten state, abandoned, and the way that they talk about it is like a joke, Remember California? There's a nascent movie scene rising out of Vermont, studios established there instead—

Everything east and south of Colorado is all-but vacant as well, it seems: graphs on page sixteen putting the population very low indeed. The population graphs are, I gather from the date, from the comparative data presented beneath them, published every month; the newspaper on a weekly print run. I am lucky to have caught it, I think, lucky the man was there. Places where it's harder to live are all but vacant; if they're too hot, or too remote. Almost everybody crammed onto the East Coast now.

There is no obituaries section, no announcements. Advertisements are few and far between, and all have the slightly podunk feel of local community information to them: *Refrigeration systems mended! Electricals rerouted, call Jeff! We buy any old media!* And there are stories about the government that give names to those in office, that talk about elections and senators and policies, but all of them in this veiled way that I don't recognize. *The Oversecretary for Recommencing said, in an interview Thursday—* Words that mean nothing to me, really. There's mention of the President, a sensible man, from the few sentences presented about him: a placeholder, a steady hand, there to guide the great nation back to something resembling its former self. There's no mention of his party. It isn't until the letters page that there's more insight:

This 'President' calls himself a great man, every President should be a great man, but he's hiding! Why are we keeping him safe? If he dies, the same rule as before should apply: he can run for his own job when he's reset, but it'll pass to somebody else! Why are we keeping him alive for the sake of continuity? This country was built on change, on a desire to change, to grow! What makes him so special?

An arts section, somewhere in the middle. A movie reviewed, and I wonder: is this like in the days of Technicolor, or 3D? Where the existence of something meant it should be lauded? Because the critic loves the movie, and I wonder if it's simply because it exists. And books, three of them: one historical text, about what we have endured, a sort-of potted history of the past hundred years; one biography, of the Hyvönen twins, and their discovery of the Anomaly; and a novel, about somebody who finds this old device in the rubble of a building that allows them to steal memories, who makes somebody forget that the Anomaly ever happened in the first place. And then, below them, there's a review – my hands shake as I read the word – a review of an art gallery show. A new artist, a new viewpoint. The world carrying on, and people wanting their work. Wanting their voice, their ideas, their soul on paper.

I want to draw, I want to contribute to the world in that way again; and my hand trembles over my pocket, over my notebook and pencil; and I feel the weight of it.

At the back of the newspaper, sports. I never cared before about baseball, but now, reading about the teams, a league of ten teams, players from all over the country, reading about the fact that they even are, I am fascinated.

'Hey, listen,' Rhonda says. She's eavesdropping on another table: a woman in a pressed blue suit, the smartest-dressed person I have seen in years, maybe; certainly outside those who wore suits to end the world, and have been forced to revisit their choice repeatedly.

'What are they—'

'Shh. Listen.' So I do, trying to tune into the frequency of their voices. The woman is talking to a man who doesn't seem particularly happy, whose face droops a little as she speaks. A good twenty years younger than her, I think.

'I'm sorry,' she says, in a tone that suggests she's already said it hundreds of times. 'It's not like I want to go.'

'So don't.'

'I have to. There are people relying—'

'I'm relying on you. Jesus, Madeline! Jesus!'

'And you're okay.'

'I'm sick. I'm fucking sick, you get that?'

'I do. And I know how long you've—' She stops herself.

'Oh, that's real fucking nice. How long I've got? Just because you've done this, doesn't mean I'm not feeling it. Doesn't mean I don't want to go through it all with you.'

'And you will. It's only a week, and then I'll be back.'

'What if something happens?'

'Nothing will happen. I know. You've got months, Dean. A year, nearly.'

'I could kill myself.'

'You could.' She says it sadly, because he's done it before, that's clear; but also because she's testing, pushing. 'But you know,' she says, 'there's only so much one person can take. We've had this conversation so many times—'

'You have. You have, I haven't, I'm fucking new to this. You,' he says, with this tone of understanding or realization, 'you could do it with me. What about: we kill ourselves, together. And then we'll be back together, and you won't have this job—'

'We're not Romeo and Juliet,' she says. 'This isn't high school. I'm going, okay? That's it. I'm flying tonight, and if you want to come—'

'I'm scared, you know that,' he says, his voice pleading, desperate.

'You're scared because you're new. I am not fucking new. Not to you, not to this.' She stands up, starts putting a coat on, a pilot's jacket, a pilot's hat.

'So, what, you're just going to fly somewhere I can't even reach you—'

'That's what I do. And then I'll come back.'

'Flying,' Rhonda says, quietly, conspiratorially.

'Yes,' I say.

'She's flying. You know where?

'She didn't—'

156

'Don't forget to make a note of what's happened this loop,' the woman says. 'You'll want to remember that I did this, I'm sure, give yourself something else to hold against me.' A sigh, and then: 'I'll call you from Barcelona.'

'Barcelona, where's Barcelona?' Rhonda asks.

'Europe,' I reply.

'Europe's England, right? Ask her!' Rhonda snaps. The woman leans in to kiss the man, and he shies away; so she walks, to the door, out of the door— 'Follow her, ask her!' Rhonda urges, and I stand, and I run, because she's right, why am I hesitating?

'Excuse me,' I say, and the woman stops, and she's crying a little but she listens and I feel terrible interrupting her in this moment. I explain what I'm after, what I'm hoping for. And I'm expecting her to tell me to leave her alone, but she listens, and then she says,

'Of course,' and then I cry as well, in the relief, in that moment.

Hers is a cargo plane: a massive green thing that was, I would guess, once a military transport of some sort, only it's been repurposed now. On the side, a branding: five symbols that I don't recognize, like hieroglyphs. Hundreds of people, I'd estimate, queuing to get on; and crates of produce, belongings; and a larger crate of livestock, two cows, two sheep, two chickens. It starts to rain as we wait on the tarmac of what used to be JFK airport, from the signs, and now seems to be just runways and storage sheds; but the rain is quite nice, in its way, cooling as it smacks onto the tarmac, which seems to be radiating its own stored heat. That smell of it, I forget the name, but people used to fixate on how beautiful it was, a word, until it lost all meaning.

'You ever been on an aeroplane?' Rhonda asks.

'Yes,' I say, 'a few times. When I was little, we moved from Europe to America, then I moved back to England.'

'That's a lot,' Rhonda says.

'It wasn't the easiest. My mother was an engineer, on the space station. So she was an astronaut, and then she died up there. But we moved for her work, and then after she was gone, everything was less . . . anchored.' I picture my mother: our final conversations, screen to screen, her up there, worried about how long she would be until she got home. I can remember them, just about. Just about. We could have recorded them, but didn't; there would have been something nice about having them on a drive somewhere, this evidence that she existed, that we spoke. 'It was hard,' I say. But Rhonda turns, suddenly, full of teenage spite, of anger.

'At least your parents didn't try and kill you,' she says. But she doesn't shift away from me. She huddles closer as the rain picks up, pushed against my coat, my hand on her head, sheltering her as best I can.

On the plane, we're not fastened in. Instead, we're all packed into the space, but we don't complain. We sit on the floor; or curl up, in Rhonda's case. And the plane rumbles and rumbles, and then we're moving, and there's that flooring of your gut that I remember, that rush of movement, as everything shifts, it feels like; and we're in the air, and Rhonda's scared, holding my hand. Through turbulence, and above a city I remember as being twinkling once, a long time ago; but out of the small windows here, I can see it much darker, just those few lights of somewhere picking itself up, dusting itself off, starting anew. The plane rattles, and I hate it: I imagine dying, I imagine crashing, what a terrible way to end this life. But it's what we've got.

'It's okay,' I say to Rhonda, hoping I sound convincing, 'it'll all be okay.'

And it is: the turbulence moves on, or we move past it, and Rhonda relaxes a little.

When she feels like speaking, she says, quietly: 'I remind you of somebody.'

'My daughter,' I tell her. 'She died before she was your age, before the Anomaly came.'

'Oh,' she says. 'But I'm like she was?'

'No,' I say, 'she didn't get to be old enough for me to know. Not really. But I wanted her to be strong, and happy, and to be free. I think you're those things, or you could be.'

She doesn't reply.

She sits quietly. Then, suddenly, she reaches into her bag, and hands me a book: her journal, her diary. The one that she writes for herself for when she comes back each time; her own personal history.

'Read it,' she says.

'It's fine,' I say, 'I don't need to, it's yours.'

'Read it, I don't know. Might as well. It's easier than talking through it, right? You should read it.' And then she lies down again, and I stroke her hair, and I think about my daughter's hair, so soft against my fingers, this thing I used to do when it was wet and there were knots and Birdie would tell me, 'Get the knots out,' so I would, even though I hated that word, can't we call them tangles?; and I read Rhonda's story.

18

She starts with a thing I heard in an old folk song, the words singsonging their way around my head as I parse them: I was born at half past twelve, almost one in the morning. Like an epigraph, but unattributed. And: *Abandon Hope, All Ye Who Read This Thing*. And: *This is not for you*. She's funny, her tone dry, droll. She talks about what she remembers first. This is, she writes, to prove that I'm you, and that you're me. These are things that only we could know. Like, these are the secrets that bind us together. And then she writes the secrets, and I read the first, but then skip the rest, because I don't need to know them, and even that one secret feels like an intrusion, like I'm somewhere I shouldn't be. If they're private, better that they stay that way. Then she writes about her mother and father, who seem like terrible people. Not even in that way that you can pretend there's goodness in them, but more the way that you can smell the stink of evil on their breath, and it's pervasive and perverse, and makes you know that they are not people you would trust.

* * *

They were part of the first wave of believers in the Knot; like my father, I suppose. People who felt that the existence of something bigger than they were meant that they owed nothing to the reality around them, and everything to their beliefs. Something immense excusing their actions, their guilt. She talks about them: a potted history of their lives, here's why they are the way that they are; but it all amounts to: they're bad people. There's nothing about their parents, no sins of the father bullshit. Which is, I suppose, easier. Rhonda doesn't want to use that excuse for herself, so why should they be allowed to? Her parents, her mother and father, they were obsessed with the idea that humans could ascend to something else, some other plane. That the Knot, the Anomaly, whatever you call it – Rhonda shortens it to A, like *The Scarlet Letter*, this repeated A: A arrived and we were doomed; A ensured that life would never be the same again; A destroyed everything and we were left with only picking up the pieces.

She writes nicely, for a teenager, a good sense of control and style. It's easy to see that she reads, that her education meant something to her. When her parents – J for Joan, I think, and D but I don't know what for – removed her education, her schooling, she was furious. There's a passage early in the journal that recounts the moment that they told her, written as a play: dialogue tags, stage directions, performance hints for the actors. This is my life, the actor playing Rhonda would say; Only as long as the A allows it to be, her mother's actor would reply. Then, they bring Pettersen to dinner, and Rhonda ignores him, shuns him. A deus ex machina: A leaves them, and Pettersen kills himself at the crucial moment, thinking he will begin anew, but of course, he doesn't; and as he bleeds out, Rhonda crouches next to him and tells him that she hopes he understands what's happening to him. That his life is nothing more than fluid, and fluid goes where it will. Fluid fills all space that it's allowed to. It's very poetic, at least to me, in the moment of reading it.

Then she goes on, and she writes that she knows it will end – it being her life, I suppose, but all she ever calls it is It – so this is her document. Her past, as much as she remembers it; her future. Every moment. A potted history, for herself. Because, and this is her teenaged hand writing it, she says that she won't make it. She'll either get out or she'll die, and she wants this as her proof to herself that she did as she said she would. If A never leaves, she writes, then I want to know how I began, or where I left off. I'll write this until the day that I die, and then I'll have it back, so it'll be there for me: spoilers about what's to come. It's naive, I think, but then we all were. We didn't know how it would play out. How jarring and interruptive and interrogative the loops would be; how unsettling, that they didn't play out with order or structure, that instead you were left flailing, alone and terrified. In those early days, when we wondered if everybody might be on the same loop, say; but discovering the chaos that actually occurred. There's a page in Rhonda's journal taken from a magazine, ripped out and stuck in with tape, about the astronauts who tried to stop this thing from happening. A quote: 'They must have been so alone up there, in the darkness, not knowing what was happening to them. Dying, slowly or quickly, but dying; and then not dead at all, but alive, at the point they entered the Anomaly, unaware and blind to how to save themselves; still, always, running out of air; still, always, alone.' It's unattributed, but she's drawn stars around it, and a moon, and then figures: small, bloated stick figures of astronauts, tethered to the article, drifting off towards the edges of the page.

I wonder if she read about my mother as part of her interest; if she knew about her, what she gave up, what she lost. My mother's name isn't mentioned. They never seem to remember the dead. I tell myself to tell to Rhonda, as I read. A mental note, scrawled on her pages. She is back, then: her voice so strong in the words, spilling out in her scrawl. The way that the lettering becomes looser with her passion, the speed of her writing. I imagine her: her wrist curled over at the nape of the page, the pen almost bent back on itself, the way that Rebecca's hand used to, the way that her pen used to. This is as much about me as it is about Rhonda; I am stealing her pages from under her nose. Her descriptions of her life, playing out as with Rebecca's, except they are entirely different. Her parents were, are, will always be monsters. Their grip on her, their desire to control her before the Anomaly even reached us. Their insistence on who she becomes: one with their way of thought, without her own freedom of thought. They caught her too late, she writes. Astute of her. If I had been a few years younger . . . and that's the fact of it, if she had, she would never have questioned anything. She would have woken to the Sacrifice of the Knot, and she would have died, and come back, and died, and come back; and because of her reset, she would have been programmed into her loop, unable to break, unable to find herself. Instead, and she writes this in large lettering, gone over a few times with the pen to make the impression of it on the page somehow more indelible, I suppose: I did not die, and I will not die now. A list, after that, of everything she has discovered: the people, the places, what she has done, how the loops work. You live, and the point you were at when the Anomaly swallowed you, that's the point you reset. The world carries on; you do not. Bullets run out of guns; the desire to die never leaves. There are pages where she's taken technical data, articles, explanations, but the truth of it is the same in each: you live, you die. So much of this feels private: her relationships, her life lived. I do not read the details: her privacy, her loves and losses. Another story, not mine to read; and a story which no longer happened. All the protagonists are dead, reset; until I come along. She writes a little about me, the stuff she told me before. And then she dies. Then she is dead, and she begins again.

She should be furious with me. She should be incandescent with rage, because if she hadn't met me . . . But she doesn't remember. Perhaps that's the benefit, not the curse; because if we carried the memories with us, we would never be able to move on.

19

The wall of heat when the plane doors open, and we walk down the ramp to the tarmac. It's startling, and immediately gets into your lungs. I remember being a very young child, one of the few memories I actually have that are mine, rather than that I was told about, received memories from photographs or stories: of getting off the plane in Florida that first time, of feeling that wall of dense, damp air, cloying in its heat, heat that stuck to your mouth, your throat.

Rhonda says, 'Tell me about myself.' We walk across the empty runway, towards the terminal. A long walk, but there are no planes landing as we do it. No danger.

'I read the same book as you,' I say.

'But she – I – she's so dry. You know? What was she like? What am I like? Am I happy, sad, do I mope around, am I excitable, what?'

I say, instinctively, 'You seemed content.'

'Content! Fucking content? That's all I get?'

'I mean, you seemed happy. Content, happy. You saved my life.'

'No shit?'

'You did. It was incredible.' Her eyes light up. We are at the doors to the terminal, ready for the empty concrete, for the quiet solitude of a place that should once have been bustling. She didn't know it, this will mean nothing to her. She didn't write this bit down, and I wonder why. Not wanting to boost her own ego, perhaps? But now, I spin the story, wanting it to hit harder. 'I would have been killed, it was literally touch and go.' We stop walking, letting the other passengers – or cargo, are we cargo? – go in before us. 'There were three of them, absolutely deadly, weapons, willing to kill me; and you came along and saw them off.'

'Shit, okay. Was I, like, dangerous?'

'You had that air about you,' I reply. She looks pleased with that. I bend the truth, or maybe I don't: 'They saw you, and they legged it.'

'Legged it, what's legged it?'

'They ran off.'

'What were they doing to you?'

'They were beating me,' I say, 'stealing from me.'

'Shit!'

'It was,' I say. 'That's how I hurt my head.'

'I wondered.'

'That's how. You patched it up.'

'She did, she patched it up. And then, what, you told her: you needed to find Birdie, right?'

'Yes,' I say, but as soon as I say it, I can feel the logic unpick itself; a seam ripper, down the line of my quest. Why am I searching for Birdie? What can she offer me? Rhonda then, she had asked me why I was looking for Birdie. What I wanted to get out of it.

She left. She left me, and I say I want to see her, but really: is this about me? Not her?

'And she helped you. A fucking quest, she accepted a fucking quest! Badass.'

'Yes,' I say. I want to know why Birdie left. But more than that: I want to know why she left *me*. I have never reasoned with it before, because it felt without reason. It felt like nothing to me.

I walk, almost on autopilot – I pace when I think, that's the only way that the cogs can turn, Birdie used to say, the only way for them to find their teeth – and suddenly I am through the doors, to an abandoned passport booth, a vacant baggage claim. People holding cards, with the names of loved ones or simply – in the cases of the men in dark suits, electronic tablets held out in front of them with an assortment of names printed on them – drivers, chauffeurs, here to collect their charges. And beyond the small crowd at the barrier, there are shops, and stalls, and people sitting eating, drinking at a restaurant. A larger crowd. More people in once place than I have seen in a very, very long time.

'Holy shit,' Rhonda says.

'Yes,' I say. Or stammer, because it takes longer to leave my lips than I expected.

I want to cry. I feel a welling—

'Have you got any cash?'

'I don't know the currency any more. They used to use the euro.'

'Dumb name. That's like, calling it the amer. Or, I don't know, the canad.'

'I suppose so,' I say. I root in my bag, give a ten dollar bill to Rhonda. She rushes to one of the stands, selling churros. I ate them with my mother, at Disneyland, I remember. That is where I ate them, with her. Sitting on a bench, my grandfather – a blur, really, of both his face and his form and his words, his general presence – but he was sitting next to me, the other side of me. The last time I saw him. The churro, that trip to Disney, the last time I saw him.

Rhonda tries to pay, and the woman says, in perfectly accented English, 'Don't be ridiculous, you've had a long trip, enjoy your treats.'

So we do. We sit outside, at the fringes of a car park that has actual cars in it; and on the street adjacent, a bus rumbles, and a plane flies overhead, just a small one, a Cessna, but the buzz of it in the sky is so comforting; and the taste of the sugar, of the cinnamon, of the puffed, sticky dough, its sharp edges.

'I never heard planes in LA,' I say.

'Well, I certainly didn't hear them out in Bumfuck,' she says.

'Bumfuck?'

'My friends and I used to call it that. Bumfuck, USA. Nothing ever happens in Bumfuck, USA. We didn't hear planes, didn't see people that didn't know we were out there.'

'Even before?'

'Before, yeah. All I've got is before.' She looks suddenly saddened by that. A life not lived, or something. 'What was before like for you?'

'A lot of planes,' I say. 'A lot of planes, a lot of traffic. A lot of people, and noise, all sorts of sound, and light. It was overwhelming, a lot of the time. I was younger, and I had anxiety—'

'But you don't any more.' She's joking, she's grinning, a small laugh on her lips. 'You're a picture of not-anxiety.'

'I am better, sometimes, believe it or not,' I say.

'What made you better?'

'Starting to die,' I tell her.

'You didn't tell me how you got it,' she says.

'I did,' I reply.

'The other me.' A sad smile; the her that she's yet to be.

So I tell her now: about how, after we knew the Anomaly was coming, the cults and the gangs and the maniacs and even, if you believe the rumours, the leaders, how they all released their weapons, desperate and terrified. How the world was swarmed and sickened and diseased. How we were forced to hide, how we were forced to fight. Hospitals overwhelmed, then shut, because there was no escape from catching it. The most potent of the weaponized sicknesses, it lay dormant in many. They didn't know that they had it; they spread it unwillingly. The second was terrible, and terrifying, pustules and sickening and sallow skin that at least let you know who was sick. And there was no cure, there was never going to be a cure. A year at best, I remember a scientist saying, a year at absolute best; but we don't have a year, that was his punchline. His quiet, small voice, before they cut him off: If you have it, if you're symptomatic, kill yourself. Do it now, save the rest of us. That's how you can do your bit for humanity. And I didn't know, so Birdie and I stayed inside, we hoarded and did as we were told; and then how Rebecca got sick, and needed blood, and we tried, but then in the hospital they freaked out, panicked, locked me down; and we waited for results from them, clutching hands. Waiting, waiting, just as we had once for the results from a pregnancy stick, waiting for that smiley face or that sad-for-you frown; and then the doctor came in, in full PPE, and I could see that frown over the mask, through the glasses.

I don't tell her about Birdie's face when the result came

through; her panic, that I had given it to her. Her flinch, as I reached for her, in my desperation, in my want for an embrace, because of my sentence. How she took herself off, as she would have put it. Found somewhere warm, and quiet, away from me. How she did a test of her own, the doctors checking her out, and then only returned to me when it was negative. Then, she could give me sympathy. Then, she could touch me, her hand on my shirt. Not on my skin after that, so rarely ever on my skin; even if it wasn't damaged, even if there was no blood. The doctors telling me that it would be better if I stayed at home, until it happened.

It.

So we stayed there, the two of us, rarely going out. Waiting. Suffering a bleed, my first; then my second, eventually, years later. Still never touching me; she let me clean myself up. Not even gloves, just this look on her face: that, somehow, I was being selfish by having this thing that I didn't ask for.

It's only as I'm saying it that I realize: she wasn't scared for me, so much as she was scared for herself. I think I was only scared for us. Me, her. Both of us, all of us.

Rhonda is quiet for a while when I have finished telling her the story. Eventually, with her churro tissue scrunched in her hand, she sits forward. 'This place is insane,' she says.

'It is,' I reply.

'I didn't think I'd ever see a city like this.'

'And you've seen New York as well. Ticking them off.'

'Yeah, but all of my friends before had seen New York. Who's been to Spain?'

'You have,' I say. 'You have now.'

'Damn right,' she says. She stands, and she stretches herself into a yawn, and I think of my own daughter, of who she might have been, stretching into a yawn just like this one at

170

the end of an arduous journey, or at the close of long day. She must notice something on my face about it, the look of that yearning for a life that didn't exist, that could never have existed, that was destroyed by death, and time, and the universe in which we live. 'What's next?' she asks, to move us on. It's apparent, but I appreciate it.

'Well, next we go north,' I say. 'We see if there's a car, or a bus?' I turn, to see that there's a car rental place up and running, one of the old booths manned, a tray of car keys for vintage vehicles hanging behind them.

But then there's a horn. A race of something: the roar of metal on metal, as a train wallops past in the distance, a rocket on rails.

I haven't seen a train in decades. Rhonda's mouth hangs wide.

'Mother *fucker*,' she says. 'We're getting that, right?'

'Yes,' I say.

Inside the carriages, there are a lot of empty seats. A conductor, who roams, and who takes money – my European notes, absolutely good enough for him – and who sits opposite us for a few minutes, and asks in exceptional English where we have come from, and where we are going; not because he is prying, but because we look American, he says, and there aren't many Americans. ('Here?' I ask, and he does a small shy shrug, that I take to mean, in general, and I have no idea how to respond to that.) He asks about America, and I tell him: the west is lost, the middle is vacant, the east is recuperating. Or, at least, that is my experience of it. I ask him about Spain, about Europe, and he says, 'It is not so bad. We are all staying alive, unless we are not.' Which seems philosophical, in the moment, and makes me smile, and he smiles. He is about my age, I think, and it's nice, for a moment: to feel like I have made another friend.

Then he moves on, jolly, jovial, full of smiles as he takes money from other people. Rhonda watches him.

'Nice guy,' she says.

'Yes,' I say.

'It's a scam.'

'What is?' Something about her naysaying makes me instantly weary. A reminder of Birdie's inherent suspicions of anybody who didn't immediately have an aura she could read clearly. One of her little things. Rhonda sits on the chair the wrong way, looking over the top of it, watching him.

'He's not from the train.'

'Not from the train?'

'Don't be dumb,' she says. 'He's working the carriage. This thing's free. Look.' She points to a sign on the wall. Handwritten, but in a beautiful hand; a drawing of a train beneath it, delicate ink lines committed by that same calligraphy pen. '*La donación*, right? That's donation. As in, you don't have to pay unless you want to. That's what it means, right?'

'Yes,' I say. I watch as the conductor – the man – steps through to another carriage; as he continues talking to people, sitting, mopping his brow from the sweat. His affable requesting money for passage, and people handing it to him.

'You want to go get it back?' she asks. But she doesn't move, just as I don't move.

'It's fine,' I say. 'I quite like it, I think? I'm pleased that there are still these things happening. People trying to scam.'

She laughs. A teenager's laugh, slightly hysterical, absolutely at me, and at the absurdity of the situation, fuelled by her tiredness, her weariness. 'You like it.'

'It's reassuring,' I say. I think about the grifter who coerced me out of my father's watch; the fact that they're everywhere, there's something unified about us. People, experiences: the same the world over, still.

The train slows, the tell-tale creaking of the brakes. We are in the countryside, somewhere with fields that are green enough that there are crops here, irrigated to allow the growing of something. Mountains in the distance, and I think of the flow: of water, from snow, down into rivers, then here, to allow whatever they are growing to feed them, to nourish them. We stop, a train station that seems to be in the middle of nowhere, and I watch, through the door between carriages, as the faux-ticket master steps off the train and onto the platform. A waiting lover; a kiss between them, as if he has been away for a while.

When I turn back, Rhonda is asleep, sprawled across seats next to me. I leave her be; her head lolls as the train starts, against my arm, and I shut my own eyes in the comfort of feeling it there; a sense that, in this moment, I am not alone.

As Rhonda sleeps, I examine myself in the small mirror in the train bathroom. Steady myself with one hand as the train shifts and moves. The mirror is cracked, and a piece has been taken from it, a sliver of the corner. There is something written on the wood beneath: *esto no eres tu.* In my reflection, I see my skin as it sags. I wet toilet paper, and I clean myself: pits, crotch.

I think how pointless it is; because when it comes, it will come, and it will be relentless. I will bleed, and no amount of cleaning – of preparing – no amount of anything will stop it.

'What is the best way to die,' I say, quietly; and I see the cracked mirror corner, *esto no eres tu.* I open the door, and Rhonda is standing there, waiting for me.

173

'I was worried,' she says. 'You were gone a while.'
'I'm fine,' I tell her. 'Can you read this?'
She leans in, peers at the mirror. 'This is not you,' she says.
'Oh,' I reply.

I remember wondering, with Birdie, what would happen. Talking through the scenarios, night after night – because we rarely spoke about them in the day, when we were ostensibly working, or acting as if we were working, pretending to make progress – and working them through, start to end. My end, and then my start again. I said to her, This feels so unnaturally cruel. To make you endure this more than once.

I'll know what's coming, she said, that feels like something.

We assumed I had months. Months became years. Years became me wondering if my body had built some immunity, perhaps, or if the virus had petered out. Because I was afraid of the hospital – the closest working one was a long way off, and even then, the stories we heard from the community made it sound horrific, made it sound like it was safer to avoid – and the tests all expired. So when it told me, Positive, you still have the sickness, that was hard to believe.

Birdie even said, once, Maybe it wasn't real at all. Just like Pettersen's lot, believing that it wasn't real, or that it was all part of some plan, or that we were meant to catch it, meant to throw ourselves into the maw because of the Anomaly. Kissing open-mouthed as some sort of public service announcement, breathing and coughing. Find the smallest shared space, inhabit it, share the wealth. The bounty. And Birdie had thought them all insane, of course, she had assumed that it was some mass delusion; but then, four years in, when I was well past what could reasonably have been expected of me, only one bleed down, waiting for the second, she said, suddenly, 'Maybe you're not ill at all.'

'What do you mean?' I asked, and she waved it off.

'Don't worry, I'm being silly,' she said, but I pestered until she told me. 'Well, look, you've been ill for a long time, and it doesn't really affect us. So what if that was all a lie? A way of making people kill themselves, like some people said.'

My jaw hung, I remember. I remember thinking, This is what they mean, slackened jaws, jaw hit the floor. The words unable to form, because she was quoting a tenet of their belief, unformed, uninformed. Pettersen removing himself from the radicals who created the virus, who distributed, even if they did it under his gaze, reading his books, listening to his sermons. But he removed himself, and he said that he never directly told people to kill themselves. He said that maybe it was all just groupthink: that nobody really died. Not from that.

'I told you, I'm being silly,' she said, 'you've got that look now.'

'No, no,' I said, 'there could be false positives. They said, false positives, false negatives, those are both entirely possible. So maybe I am one of those?'

I could feel a sense of disbelief deep inside me. The desire to keep the conversation moving, and not just moving but speeding, past us, away from us. That we were linked, and I discovered how she felt about it then; in this couched way, slipped out, almost. Maybe you won't die, that's what her mouth was saying; but I knew that, deeper, it meant she wondered about everything.

I think, maybe, that right then was the moment that we lost each other.

20

We sit and play a game: Spelling Bee, where seven letters are drawn in the rough shape of a hive, and one must make words from them, always including the letter in the middle. Rhonda is remarkably good at it: she finds the longer words I search for so quickly, snatching them while I'm still dealing with three- or four-letter runs.

'It's the brain,' she says, 'it slows with age. That's right, isn't it?'

'Probably,' I say.

We thump on something, then: as if the train is running over something.

A woman nearby makes the sign of the cross and whispers a prayer. She looks to me, watching her. 'He cannot be saved,' she says. 'This happens.'

A man has gone under the train. He must have been there as the Anomaly arrived, and this is what happens, now: he lies there perpetually, waiting for the train.

I see the realization land on Rhonda. 'What if the trains didn't run?' she asks. 'I mean, then he'd be okay, wouldn't he?'

'My dear, he is already dead in his heart and in his mind,' the woman says. 'Let him have the satisfaction of his physical death.'

Our game ends, then. Her words an anvil, destroying anything that came before. There is no way to continue. We sit, and we feel every rumble of the wheels on the rails beneath us; every stone, every lump of turf, every judder in the steel.

Rhonda stares out of the window. All through the night, she's there, practically pressed against it. Her cheek a face at a window, eager for the return of a loved one, or a toy that she's lusting for; but she's simply looking at a place she's never even dreamed of.

'The trees here are different,' she says, at one point. 'And the grass.' Patches of it here: rain-soaked, still cared for. 'Why is this place like this?'

'Like what?'

'Like all of this. America wasn't like this.'

'Well, no,' I say.

'So why?' She turns back to me, and she's a child. I think of my daughter: but why? Every question, But why?

And of myself, in the hospital, as they told us. I asked them that same question; maybe because she could not.

'Sometimes, there is no why,' I say. The same as the doctor. A response I cannot help but find when I search for anything else. So I try details, plucked from nothing: 'America was ruined by sickness, and in the wake of it, by fear. It's very hard to right yourself when you've been upended. And the weather didn't help, but the spread of it started there. It went east, and it got better, in its way.' I stare out of the window with her. A small town: and there are people here, walking, going to their jobs. The train slowing as we approach a station.

'What about here?'

'Well, here they're out of the cities. And maybe they listened more. Maybe the Knot wasn't this far out. I haven't seen any of the iconography, the markings or the symbols or anything.'

'I liked the symbol,' she says. 'When I was a little kid, I really liked it. It's weird, like a corn doll or something.'

'I liked it too,' I say. I feel myself scratching at my chest, at the skin there where it must have hung: the necklace that my father made me wear, that he told me would guarantee me something. A path somewhere else. And I nearly keep this secret, except: the words rush from my mouth, a rock moved to allow the water passage. 'My father was a follower,' I tell her. 'Not like your parents, of course, I do not wish to steal your thunder. But he was a believer, he thought that Pettersen and the Knot were going to save us. He thought that we would ascend, that was the word. Ascension.' She looks sad. 'If you want to talk about your mother and father,' I start, but she interrupts me.

'They were crazy. Don't even,' she says, 'they don't need defending. Crazy people following a crazy thing.'

'My father wasn't crazy,' I say. 'At least, not at the start. I think that's what scared me. He was rational.'

'When you were a kid, sure. How old were you?'

'Five or six,' I reply. 'Five, when my mother left, and he started taking me to the church.'

'That's when she went to space?'

'To the space station, yeah. It was in orbit. Maybe it still is? But it was. It was there, and they could see the Anomaly coming. It was, like, fifteen years away then, still. A really long time. It got slower, I think. I don't know. It didn't move with uniformity, that's what the man who told my dad she died said. It didn't move predictably, so there was nothing that they could have done.'

'And she died up there?'

'Yeah.'

'What happened?'

'Nobody ever told me. Not exactly. She died up there. One of her friends came down, though, somebody she worked with. And she was furious at my dad, she went mental at him. I remember watching them fight, she said it was all my dad's fault. What happened. She couldn't stop crying, though. She hated it, it was hard for her. Then she died, and they couldn't tell us how, or why. They danced around it, all these explanations that weren't explanations. She hated it up there, and then she died.'

'I'm sorry,' Rhonda says.

'She wanted to do good. That's all she wanted, she wanted to help people. I remember that: she went because she hoped it could help. Like she could save the world or something.'

The train slows more, coming to a stop. A station, but then a dinging, an alarm: the manual ringing of a bell. We look down the carriage, where a woman in her twenties – young enough that I wonder if she was born in this, or if she's going around again – says to us, 'There is a wait, six hours or more. The driver will have a meal and a rest, and then we will continue again.'

'Six hours? So we wait here?'

'Go, walk. Come back. Your bags will still be here,' she says, and then she moves to the doors, as everybody does; and she's out onto the platform, wandering off with others. A café across the way, full of people; more on the street,

179

drinking, waiting. Smiling, and one woman greets this other as if they're old friends.

'Should we go?' Rhonda asks.

'Probably,' I say.

We find a shop that's exchanging currency, and I take some of my dollars to the counter, hand them over to a large man whose moustache covers most of his mouth as if it's some sort of curtain to his teeth; and when he talks, the hairs slip against his lips. I want to ask him how he can handle it, if it's not the most uncomfortable thing in the world. The irritation makes me want to scratch at my own skin, to rub my own face.

'Where did all of this come from?' he asks.

'America,' I say, and he laughs, as if that's a fantastic joke, the best he's heard in a long, long time. 'I don't need any of it any more.'

'No,' he says. He flicks through a notebook in front of him, lists of numbers and names. Looking for something, and he finds one, a dollar sign next to a name. 'I don't want this, but I know a woman who will.' He tears the page out: Sylvia, written at the top, and an address underneath it. 'You go to her, she will buy it from you.'

'We're not from here,' I say. 'I don't know the way.' So he draws me a little map, smiling the entire time, streets as tubes—

'Then you stop,' he says, and he draws a little house. I thank him, and Rhonda takes a little boiled sweet from a bowl at the till, and we leave. We follow the map, turning the paper until it makes some sense; matching his scrappy handwriting to the street names posted up high on the corners of buildings; down a street that's cobbled, that makes Rhonda gasp, because it's so quaint and old.

'How old?' she asks.

'Hundreds of years. Thousands, some of this place. These walls.'

'How is it still here?' she asks.

'It just is,' I say. 'They wanted to maintain it, so they did.' I think of fabribuilds they made in the deserts outside Los Angeles, of the new favelas along the border states, of the north-eastern undergrounds, of Telosa and the other imagined cities that they tried to persuade people to move to. I think of how they were emergency solutions to crises, thrown together, or just there, and then these buildings – with their leaning that's not problematic, not a reason for destruction, just a sign of their weathered age, their need for brickwork patching, for repointing or plasterwork, cracking wooden sills and doorway arches that look to be on the verge of imminent collapse, and have no doubt looked that way for decades now – these buildings that simply stand, that weather the time and the climate. Baking heat, torrential rains, the heat again, the rain again. 'The people have made them last.'

We find Sylvia's street, and her house. It is painted in this hue that seems to flit between orange and pink depending on the light, next door to a plain-looking house that seems only to make Sylvia's shine all the more. I ignore the plain house until Rhonda grabs my arm. 'Look,' she says, her voice a little hushed. It's not just plain: it is concreted, it is sealed shut. The doors and windows closed to the world, no way in, no way out. A face without eyes, a mouth; like some old horror story. And at the base, flowers, cards, notices: all in this muted greyscale, dyed or painted, seemingly to match the palette of the wall itself. As if they are a part of it, melded to it. 'What happened?' she asks.

'The woman inside there is dead,' a woman says. She's standing in the doorway to Sylvia's house. My age, or there-abouts, and dressed in a way that suggests that only she cares what she thinks.

'You're Sylvia?' I ask, and she nods. 'I was sent to find you, by a man – he had a moustache,' and she laughs. Of course she knows him.

'Hang on, so she's dead, but why is it—'

'She cannot be saved. She placed the knife onto herself before the Anomaly came, and she waited and waited. She felt the air change and she knew, that is what people say. The incision here—' She draws a line up her forearm with her finger, from palm to the soft flesh of the inside elbow, her fingernail pressing down on her own skin so hard that it makes an indent. 'So deep. We have tried to save her, of course. There is nothing to be placed between the skin and the blade. We have tried knocking her over, one time we tried shooting her, nothing worked.'

'You shot her?' Rhonda doesn't know whether to be shocked or impressed. The smile threatening its way through on her mouth.

'In her shoulder. To knock her hand away. But the incision has already been made. Her timing was exceptional. She was exact, perfect with it. To the very second. I have never seen anybody more absolutely perfectly on time.'

'Did you know her?'

'I remember her. And you know the great irony?' She smiles. 'She was always rushing, from her house, because she was late for something or other.' Sylvia points to the flowers with her foot. A kick that doesn't connect. 'We do this for her. A tribute.'

'Like flowers on a grave.'

182

'Not like, this is the very same. This place she dies, the place she inhabits, it is a grave and yet not a grave. Everything in stasis, in flux. So we lay flowers, and sometimes we paint pictures.'

'You paint pictures?' I ask.

'I am an artist, sometimes,' she says.

'So am I,' I reply.

She stares at me, eyes me up and down. As if she's trying to work out whether I'm any good based entirely on how I comport myself. 'What did Albert send you to me for?'

'Dollars,' I say. 'I have some I want to sell, and he said you might – you would – be interested.' She doesn't really react. Her face somehow static. I wonder if it's a tactic, a trader's lack of tells.

'Where are you from?' she asks.

'California,' I say. 'Before that, London, before that, Florida.'

'But recently America.'

'Yes,' I tell her, 'and she,' Rhonda looks up, 'is from Nevada.'

'Is it bad out there? It's hot, yes?'

'Very,' I say. 'There aren't many people left.'

'Another irony: your country's ancestors left here to find that place, to claim that they discovered it, eh? And now look at you, back here again. Wanting nothing to do with it.' She looks at my bag. 'How many dollars have you got?' I show her. She nods. 'More than I need, I suspect. I will make you an offer, come in, come in.'

She leads us into her home. I am struck: the walls covered in writing. Not unfocused, but delicate, deliberate. A neat cursive, black Sharpie over the surfaces. She has moved the paintings before writing, the walls with tell-tale rich-paint squares, less sun-damaged. There is a large *Start* at the top left wall, above the staircase – where the eye is naturally drawn to – and then, from there, her name, a number that I presume to be her age, then words.

'You cannot read it?' she asks.

'No,' I say. 'Not really.'

But Rhonda can. She translates it slowly, steadily, only tripping over the occasional word, and even then I wonder if it's the handwriting or placement rather than the knowledge. 'You were born—' She looks to me. 'It says that. *You were born,* that's not me changing the words or anything.'

'Okay,' I say. And I feel myself smile, at her insistence on the detail.

'I address it to myself,' Sylvia says.

'You were born on a Tuesday, the child of Marta and Julio, in the town of Ronda—' She stops. 'That's my name.'

Sylvia smiles. She seems very happy with that. 'Ah! It's fate, then! Fate, that we should meet! Rhonda, do you know of Ronda?' She moves to a cabinet, to a book of photographs, and opens it to a page of a bridge, a creek, rocks. Sundrenched, so bright that the glare almost seems to shine off the paper. 'This is me, when I was a child. A teenager, probably your age, I think?'

'Maybe,' Rhonda says. 'It looks nice.'

'It is,' Sylvia replies. 'It's beautiful. The people there, they are so friendly.'

'The bridge is in the town?'

Sylvia describes it: a bridge that runs right through the heart of the place, as tall as ten trees. People abseil down the sides of it, they stand there and stare at the canyon, and they're glad to be there, grateful for the view, for the place itself. 'A place of true beauty.'

'I want to go,' Rhonda says. 'I feel like I should go. We have the same name, how often does that happen?' Sylvia smiles, but it's sad, curious. Not the smile she had before. She puts the photographs away, takes out another box, opens that. A pile of plastic notes suddenly in her hand, and she flicks through them with the trained fingers of somebody who has handled a lot of banknotes in their life. She folds a bundle over.

'This is what your dollars are worth to me,' she says. There's no haggling, and I'm grateful for that: I would not even know where to begin. 'Nobody wants to go to America, nobody wants American money. You are lucky you found me.'

'Do you have a bathroom?' Rhonda asks, and Sylvia shows her to it; then we stand, the two of us, in her room of writing.

'I am dying,' she says, apropos of nothing but the silence and the words surrounding us. 'I am going to America because I want to see it now. I will write up here that I went, and then I will wake up here, and it will be as if I went, nearly the same. I send to myself letters from places, postcards to myself, and photographs. This money will pay the postage, because I will die there.'

'When do you go?' I ask.

'My next life. I am dying, very soon I am dying.' She leans close to me, as if we are together in this, two old friends, I will understand her words. 'Do you know, I always die the same way, the same day. The sickness for me has no compunction, is that the word? I cannot sway it. It is far enough along that when I die, it is no surprise. Always the forty-third night I am alive. This section—' She points to a part of her wall. Neat words, but written over multiple times, for emphasis or clarity. 'This is the moment where I die. Sometimes, you know, it is the same hour. These . . .' notches, marks, like pencil dashes '. . . are the hours counted down. To see if it is exact, and to learn that it is.'

'What is it?' I ask, but I know, I already know.

She smiles. 'I think it is the same as you,' she says.

'I think so too,' I say.

'And how long do you have?'

'I don't know,' I say.

'How can you not know? Is it not the same each time?'

I lie to her. I don't want to tell somebody who only lives weeks that I have done thirty years. 'Yes,' I say, 'it varies, I don't know why.'

'My word,' she says. 'To have the chaos of not knowing, that's a gift in its way, I think?' I don't correct her. That the chaos is, in its own way, a curse. Whoever would have thought that life was something to rally against? It isn't life, I want to say; it's waiting. And when coming back, to endure again; when I think, sometimes, that if it could be over, then I would find peace, maybe. Perhaps. 'I have found a peace, a comfort in the knowledge of what is to come,' she says. I wonder if I paused, perhaps a little too long. 'There is something substantial about forty-three days, when you know that is your allotted window of time. A lot can be achieved in forty-three days.'

'I can't imagine,' I say. I have sat in my house, afraid to go out, waiting to die. I cannot count the days. I do not own a calendar that could accurately tell me. I have no real idea. Years, yes, probably. Months? Days?

What have I achieved? What have I lost?

The sound of the cistern; then Rhonda comes downstairs. 'Your house is lovely,' she says. Sylvia smiles.

'I always spend my forty-third day cleaning,' she says. 'There is always a lot of blood, and I want that the house is as nice as it can be.' She looks at a clock. 'You came on the train?'

'Yes,' I say.

'You have an hour until it will leave again, maybe. Maybe a little more, maybe a little less. You should go to the café, get some food. It is a long journey from here. Where are you terminating?'

Her word is so on the nose I nearly laugh, I nearly burst with laughing. 'As far north as we can get. We want to go to London.'

'London? What is in London?'

'My ex-wife,' I say. 'Or, my wife. She's still my wife, I think, we didn't divorce.'

'Why are you looking for her?' she asks.

'Because I am,' I say. 'She left, and I don't know to where, and so I'm looking for her.'

'Does she want you to find her?'

'I don't know,' I say.

'Maybe you should think about that, uh? You tell your father to not look for somebody if they don't want to be found.'

I wait for Rhonda to correct her, but she doesn't. She stares at Sylvia, and she shrugs. 'It's his life,' she says.

'As it is hers.'

'He just wants to know why she left.'

'Maybe because he is chasing her, maybe that is why?' Sylvia is suddenly serious, but then the seriousness breaks; and she smiles, laughs. We are all friends here. 'Your lives are your own,' she says, 'who am I to judge?'

We are leaving, then; and on the back of her front door I see a square, carved with pen. Crude, this, not like the penmanship of the other writing. This is scratched in: notches, for every day she's had. Counting down. All exactly the same. The latest box with forty-two of those delicate scratches, on a quick count. I notice a spray bottle of bleach; a rag. She is preparing. And I think, as she waves us off, as she bids us farewell, that I should probably start to prepare as well.

We eat little custard pastries, and sandwiches with cured ham and the richest butter, and we watch the other people as they wait for the train – faces we recognize, and nod at, we are all on this journey together. Rhonda listens to Spanish, floating in the air, and she occasionally looks at me, tells me quietly what she's heard. This couple is headed for France, she says; or, this man's got a dead mother to visit, she's just come back again and wants to see him; or, he's a musician, he's got a concert, he's really nervous. Life pushing through death, in little ways.

Then the train driver returns. He doesn't have a uniform, but some of the others waiting recognize him, shout hello, start to follow him up to the train. We all reboard, back in the seats we had before.

I think it is only moments before Rhonda is asleep. Minutes later until I follow her.

I dream of my house, in California. Of the walls, open and yet closed; of the elements outside, but in the dream, there's rain that I never really saw in truth: thunderously heavy yet silent, pooling outside the doors, around the walls, rising higher and higher; and the house rocks on its foundations, lifting at the corners like pages, threatening to take me and the walls away from there entirely.

21

Checkpoints are quiet; they are rarely policed, and when they are, it's people making sure that nothing illegal is being smuggled. A man on one train, as we travelled up through the northern areas of Spain, into France's Provence region, told us a story about gun smugglers, how they were especially vigilant here. Smelting factories to turn old weapons into reusable metal, and to keep them away. He said, 'The hope among the French and Germans is that they will have no more weapons. That this is a reset, in its way! Imagine that, starting again?' He told us about his life – we didn't ask, as others didn't ask us; but he spoke, just as we did, because that was how the time was passed it seemed, like some *Canterbury Tales* of the post-apocalyptic train journey – and how he hadn't died, how he hadn't even really been touched by the Anomaly, by the virus, by the collapse of everywhere else. He said, 'You're born in a village, you live in a village, you die in a village. Some people have died, and they come back. That is normal now, just as they died before and did not come back, that was the normal then.' Rhonda was fascinated by him: her experience running so short, and he had lived through it all. I did not say, Well, so have I; his experience was, to her, something individual to him.

'What do you think will happen when the Anomaly leaves?' she asked him. And he laughed, as if the concept was so strange, so alien.

'We do not know it will leave,' he said.

'We don't know that it won't,' she replied.

'If it leaves, and death resumes, as it did before? Then we will find that as normal, suddenly. Suddenly, that will be all we know, and we'll come to forget this time. Remember when we couldn't die for good? Remember?' He laughs at that, then. 'Children,' he says, 'what it would be to have the hope of the children.'

When he's gone, Rhonda turns to me. 'Prick,' she says. 'Always thinking people younger than them don't know anything. He's pretended this whole thing isn't happening because it doesn't affect his little fucking world.'

'That's what people do,' I say.

France brings a night staying in what was once the house attached to a vineyard, a hotel we saw advertised at the station between trains; and the vines are incredible, overgrown to a degree that I can barely fathom, like some old-fashioned concept of nature reclaiming the urban from mankind: sprawling, untethered, loose from whatever structures once held them, now knotted together, grown on each other, using the branches and stems and trunks of other vines as their struts. We drink wine – Rhonda says that she's already had it, but I'm not sure, because after her second glass she starts losing words, or fragments of words. The wine is made by a couple who live here, who don't know what they're doing – they have a book from a shop, they say, but they only found the vineyard a few years ago, abandoned and needy, and they let the grapes grow as they will. That's the wine we get: and it's sharp and sweet at the same time. Seven of us staying here, and the two of them; the guests all passengers, all heading north. We don't share names, for whatever reason. As if it's cleaner; we simply act as if we have known each other for decades, as if shared experience levels us absolutely.

'There's a thing about wine,' the male owner says, 'it's only meant to get better with age. But, Jesus, who doesn't want to drink fresh wine? Now, when there's none really being made, all I want is fresh wine!'

We get into a conversation about grapes, and whether they're coming back, or if they're new grapes. How to even tell. Vegetation: the life cycle so fickle, and it takes so long to die, and so long to grow, so would we even notice?

'A seed is rebirth, is it not? Plants, flowers, they make their own spawn, we never thought anything of that. That was natural to us, and this . . .' He shrugs, as if there's no answer, or difference.

'So do grapes die?' I ask. 'Has anybody even seen a raisin?'

There is a moment of pause, where that lands; and then laughter, tremendous gulps of laughter from all of us. Collapsing, like it never really happens until it does.

'A raisin!' the female owner says, and she keeps saying it. 'A raisin! A raisin!', before rushing to their kitchen and rummaging, then running back—

A box of classic California Raisins in her hand, God only knows how old. The contents one solid mass of dark, shrivelled fruit, plopped out onto the table in the middle of us all, and that only makes us laugh harder. Rhonda, asleep now in the corner, wakes up, and asks what's so funny; and that only makes us laugh more, as one of my new friends tries to relay the story in broken English – they are Peruvian, their accent blunt and rounded on the translated words – and Rhonda stares, like she doesn't understand at all.

Finally, she says, a little slurry: 'My mom used to force me to eat those when I was a kid.' And that's it, we are finished, all of us; even Rhonda, though she doesn't quite know what she's laughing at.

I am drinking my wine, and Rhonda is talking to the one of the other travellers, a teenager travelling with her mother. This other girl is slightly older than Rhonda. Sixteen, maybe. She is neat and tidy, not a hair out of place; and she and Rhonda speak closely, and I watch out of the corner of my eye at how happy Rhonda looks in this moment; that she is not where she was, back in the factory, and we are still for a moment, and her life – her actual life – is continuing here, even if it's only briefly. I drink more, and I watch as Rhonda and the young lady's hands entwine each other, fingers interlocked. She is German, her English basic. Does that matter? Birdie would say it doesn't matter. Attraction transcends so many things, language, identity, the past, the future. I drink once more, and one of our hosts is talking about something – something about a douche, and I laugh, and they explain that the word is different in French, then one of them says, 'Oui!' and we laugh at the baseness of that, at how basic it is, that joke; another thing that transcends. One of them points to me: 'You are bleeding, I think?' and I say that it must be the wine, but then I feel it: warm, thick, on my chin. The laughter stops. I look around, Rhonda and the German girl are gone, and I stand—

'That way, end of the hall,' one of the hosts says, for the bathroom, and I run, and I see myself in the mirror: as blood spills from my mouth, spurting over my teeth, my tongue, into the surface-cracked white porcelain of the sink, and it doesn't stop. I close my mouth, hoping that will somehow stop it, but instead it flows down, back, into my throat. A gagging, a retching. There is so much blood; and I wonder, how can a body make so much blood? I cling to the sink, and I hear my voice—

'Not now,' I say, but then the seeping begins anew: from every pore, every hole. I feel myself shedding. As if I am becoming something else entirely, transforming. Becoming.

I strip, sodden clothes peeled from my skin, which feels so hypersensitive that it's agony; every single follicle exhuming a pittance of blood from it, but that pittance combining to become a flood. I feel every brush of the wet fabric on my skin; every inch of it.

There is a shower here, run-off water, everything recycled. I stand under the faucet and let the water rush down onto me, the warmth of the night the only heat in it, a cold-tepid that hurts, aches along every inch of me. And I sob, I cry; my tears blood—

'Are you okay?' Rhonda asks, through the door.

This is how she finds me: on the other side of doors, asking if I am hurt, ailing, maybe dead or alive, depending on which way you look at it. She is my minder.

'Has it happened again?'

'Yes,' I say. I spit the blood of that solitary syllable. That tiny word.

'Do you need me to help?'

No. No. No, I don't. Birdie telling me to leave her alone. That my hand on her was a reminder of the hands that were not; my fingers on her shoulder, because I needed contact, I needed that, I needed to feel her skin, the warmth of her body to let me know that I wasn't alone in there, even as she acted as if I were.

Rhonda doesn't wait for the answer. She comes in, and she takes a towel from the side, and she wraps it around me. She is so old; like she remembers what it is to be not young, to have to care for others. She helps me from the bath, and I dry myself. I hear – distanced, almost: as if there is glass between us, or a wall, and I am hiding inside it, away from the house itself, away from these people, protected and secretive – I hear Rhonda shout for the hosts, and she asks them for clothes. Of course, of course, is he okay? She doesn't reply. 'He needs to get dressed,' she says, 'he needs clothes and some privacy. A bit of decency,' and then there's a voice, one of the French voices, repeating her: 'Donnez à l'homme de la décence!'

'You're going to be okay,' she says, in the tone of somebody who knows that I will not be; that there is an end to what is happening to me, that it is coming.

The clothes arrive: white. Nothing to spare, no shame to hide. White trousers, white shirt, in linen. A uniform, yes, but not mine: the uniform of a Jesus, a modern prophet. Her eyes as she hands them to me: apologetic, but this is what there is.

'Has it stopped?' she asks. I nod. I wipe myself down, clean myself. My skin tingling, as if in the afterglow of some drug when I was young; those moments of heightened touch, of fingertip electricity. She holds the shirt for me, passes me the trousers, the socks, the undergarments. I put them on; my skin still damp from the shower, the wetness still there on these clothes. A patch at the small of my back that I can feel. A glimpse, a little reminder.

We leave the bathroom – she puts her hand on my arm, to reassure me – and the others stop talking. Their voices were a murmur, and now they're silenced. They look at me.

'Are you sick?' one of the hosts asks.

'Yes,' I say.

'You're dying?'

'Yes,' I say.

'Are we at risk? Are you a risk, I mean?'

'No,' I say. 'I don't believe so.'

'You will sleep in the barn?' she says, posed as a question; it's not a question.

I am there, and Rhonda is in the corner, watching me as I shiver under a blanket, in those clothes that I know, ultimately, will be ruined; will run red with my blood, like a costume change in theatre, a production trick. I sleep on an old mattress here, and I hear the crackle of a fire from outside, and the smell of fabric burning; and as Rhonda sneaks out, thinking I'm asleep, I shoot a glance and watch as they all stand around a fire in a trash can, and they hold my clothes out on a stick before dipping them into the flames and burning them.

It's early morning, a rooster in the distance. Crowing, crowing, and I wake up, and Rhonda isn't anywhere near, and I am alone. I stand, shake off the sleep, the muscle pain from the old mattress and the cold. I feel my mouth, almost on instinct – remembering last night – but my chin is dry. The taste of blood still lingers; and at the door to the barn, I look out, to see the sun craning the sky; the beautiful pinks and blues of a place that feels almost otherworldly. Where I come from, this isn't what the world is like: vineyards and greenery and irrigation systems. The ashes on the ground, the bonfire extinguished, the land blackened by the flames; the tangle of the vines clearer in the daylight.

I could go. I could, in this moment, leave. Rhonda won't be awake for hours yet, and she won't know; and there are people here she can travel with, people she can live a life with. I can go on my journey alone, which feels like the way, if there is one. It's my journey, not hers; and who am I to drag her along with this? I think of a life she could have: meeting people, adventuring. Exploring who she is, and who doesn't want to be an explorer? To have that sense in your bones of: I was there first, I found that thing. I made it, I discovered it. I created it, I destroyed it; whatever it is, the sense that it is yours, and yours alone. That could be her story. With me, I am dragging her, or she is caught in my wake; with me, this is my story, not hers. I think: I could say these things to her, explain. Hold her hands, as close as we are in this time – both of us a proxy for something else, for somebody else, and both of us knowing that, I am sure – I could hold her hands in mine, and I could say, 'This is what you have to do, and what I have to do. You are not my carer; you are your own life, and that is all you should be.'

I would – in the past, when Rebecca was sleeping on my chest, or sleeping on my arm, or in that restful moment between wake and sleep of a morning, in bed with myself and Birdie, lolloping as we did – I would wonder what she would be, who she would become. And I would think about what I would say to her, the words I would use to let her know that it was okay: that she was her own person, no longer attached to us, but free to do what she wanted. We prayed the Anomaly would be gone; we prayed the virus would leave; we prayed for normality, for a return to the truth of the mundane. So she would get older, and school first, then university; then marriage, or a stream of partners first, and some travel, a job she doesn't like until she finds her way. And of course I wanted for her to be creative, to find a thing she loves that she could make money from. Follow in footsteps, without feeling the shape of my footprints, of the shoes, without – as when she was a toddler, laughing, clinging to my hands – without standing on my feet themselves, as I paraded her around. No choice where she should go; only the promise we would get there.

I would get there.

I collect myself, and I think about that phrase to do so: what am I collecting? A fragmented whole that is rapidly collapsing. Shoes on, and these clothes that were so crisp and white and now have creases down every part of themselves. I leave the barn, trying to orientate myself – the passageway here through the vines, not easy to see. And from inside, it looks like perhaps a ringed fort, closed off to the rest of the world. Impossible to penetrate. But there: the light, and the soil trodden into a roughshod path. I make for it—

A cough, from behind, like a parent warning that they're watching you.

A girl stands there, smoking a cigarette. Her hair shorn so close to her head that it's fuzz, really, little more; and she's in Rhonda's clothes, so I wonder, is this the girl from last night? Did they swap their outfits?

'Where are you going?' she asks, and I hear that she has Rhonda's voice, that she's Rhonda. I didn't recognize her, her head shaven like that.

'You look older,' I say, blurting it out. She looks momentarily satisfied with that, rising a little in her own body.

'This is what I looked like when you met me?'

'Yes,' I say. 'I mean, older still, even older. But yes, this sort of style. Like, this is a nascent version of who you'll be.'

'Okay,' she says. 'I don't know if that's a compliment.'

'It is,' I say. 'But also, that doesn't mean you need to do it,' I say. I feel as though I'm telling her off. A hint of reproach to my voice.

'I'm her, though.'

'Yes.'

'So, you know. This is me. This is how I have my hair.'

'In one future, maybe—'

'It's not fucking time travel.'

'No. I mean, maybe it is, of a sort—'

'Anyway, it doesn't matter. I got Freja to do it for me.'

'Freja,' I say, and Rhonda shrugs. A Gallic shrug, I remember. Something my father once said. A Gallic shrug.

'Where were you going?' she asks, and her voice is smaller now. Not quieter, but smaller, definitely. She knows the answer, of course. I don't lie.

'I was leaving,' I say. 'I thought maybe I could go before you woke up, and this would be better for you. To be here, or somewhere else. But not with me.'

'Why?'

'I told you. Because it would be better for you.'

'Why not with you, though? You don't get to decide that.'

'What do you mean?'

'I mean: you don't get to decide what I do, or what I don't do. I want to come with you, you ever think about that?'

'I don't understand why,' I say.

'Because! Fucking, because! Like, your wife, you're chasing her—'

'I'm not chasing her.'

'But she's gone! She didn't ask you to follow her.'

'I'm not asking you to follow me.'

'So you'll just leave me here.' Her lip trembling. Her whole body following it, as if the lip is the origin, and it spreads down her flesh. Gooseflesh, vibrating at a higher frequency.

'I'm not abandoning you,' I say.

'Fuck you.'

'You're better off without me.'

'Fuck you.'

'I'm dying,' I say, and I expect it to have weight; finality. And it does; but for me. Because I feel myself sag, I feel the weight of gravity pulling me, dragging me to the ground. Gravel under my hands, in my palms, the sharp edges digging into my skin. I am snivelling, suddenly, tears and mucus, and I feel Rhonda's arm around my neck, her hand rubbing the back of my head. There's no hesitancy; she just wants me to feel better. 'I'm dying,' I repeat, I feel myself repeat, the words out of my control.

'We're all dying,' she says. 'I've died since you knew me, even. You're not the king of dying, you know. Fucking get over it.'

She's joking, she's trying to make light, but it makes me cry harder, harder. She holds onto my neck as if I might rear up, roaring, and she's clinging on, and laughing, and I would stomp around the room as a dinosaur, growling and snarling while Birdie takes photographs; and neither of would know, in that moment, that she was sick, that she was going to leave us.

Rhonda brings me TCP, an aged bottle that I think probably predates any of us. She pours some onto cotton wool and cleans my hands for me. The smell is so distinct. It drags me back.

'Wait,' Rhonda says, and she rushes off, comes back with a needle. Holds it over the flame of a cheap disposable lighter for a few moments, then takes my hand again. 'Don't move,' she says. She uses the needle to dig into the small cuts, to fish out pieces of gravel from inside me. It stings, and I flinch, so she grabs my hand tighter. 'I said to stay still,' she says.

I watch her as she works. Along the line that cuts right across my palm. When I was a child, before she left, my mother had her palms read. Afterwards, the lady read mine, and she said, 'Oh, the line is broken here. Perhaps a broken heart, or perhaps sickness.' My mother explained that it wasn't real: that it's something people lie about, for money, stories told as entertainment. Really, how it's no different to a book or a television show. But I look at the line now, and a break in it: where it branches, and wildly. I know this is just the way that the flesh moves, defined by bones and muscle more than any pagan witchery or mystical power. And yet: there's the divide.

It doesn't loop. There's no curlicued fracture to the skin lines.

'There,' Rhonda says. 'You get a sticker.' There are no stickers, just a thing she says. There's a clattering behind her. The others, starting to wake up. 'We should get going,' she says. 'While it's still early.'

'What about the girl? The other girl.'

'Freja. She left in the middle of the night. She doesn't sleep, she said. I don't know.'

'Okay.' We walk to the doors to the main house, to the kitchen. They – the hosts – notice us, and they look me up and down, eyes moving in perfect synchronicity. Checking me for signs. 'We're leaving,' I say. The smell of bacon; the sizzle of fat in a pan. 'Thank you for your hospitality, and for your clothes.'

'It's nothing,' one of the hosts says.

'It is something,' I return. 'I'll remember it,' and then we turn, and we're walking away, towards the vines when one of them shouts after us. I turn, and they're standing a little way back, a small wrapped parcel in their hands.

'Sandwiches for you,' they say, 'for your journey.' They put them onto the floor between us, and stand back. 'You should take them.'

'Thank you,' I say, and Rhonda steps up, scoops them from the ground. I bow my head, and we turn, and leave, through the vineyard. In the light of the morning, it's remarkable; these knotted tangles of grapes and stalks, perpetually growing, and this path being held back from them, just by dint of people walking it.

We sit on the outskirts, and we eat the bacon sandwiches, so rich and salty and with homemade jam in them, grape and tomato it tastes like, and we stare at the vineyard, and can't see the houses contained within its fortress walls at all.

22

Towns and cities, they are the worst part. They are the part where you remember what exactly is missing. Because the countryside, it's always empty, and in the moments you spend in cities, they feel like they're abuzz again; but the reality is you're in a sectioned-off area. You're in Soho, or Manhattan, or the Marais. The outskirts of Paris are cold and abandoned, and it's here you remember that we went through an apocalypse, or an event that could be counted as one; but actually, we aren't even yet post-, we're mid-, we're embedded. I've seen some of the old films that spoke to events like this. They had empty dystopias, masked policemen, cannibal ravagers or feral creatures that lived in the darkness. They didn't speak to this: the Marie Celesting of square miles of conurbation, the boarding up of the things we can't change and the hoarding of things we don't want to. They didn't speak to seeing nobody and finding that unsettling. Not that there could be something lurking, but more: knowing that there isn't anything lurking. The attackers, the maniacs – I think back to the people who assaulted me as I left Los Angeles, how long ago that feels, and how Rhonda was there for me – they are few and far between. They're in the counties and states that have been forgotten. They're not where people live.

Now, people live in the houses of the dead, assuming that they were left vacant. An elderly man – keeping his distance, wary of anything, having seen this through, a first-timer like myself – an elderly man on the train spoke to us about what Paris is like now. He is in the apartment he grew up in – 'And where I will die, I hope!' – and those around him all came after the Anomaly arrived. In the wake of it, as the city shrank, they came, and the city got smaller and smaller. Kept getting smaller and smaller. His hands demonstrating: open palm, closing to a fist, then gone. 'Kaput,' he says. 'Now, it is the Marais. Outside the Marais, ahh, that is for the tourists.'

And that's borne out as we travel through the city. We came here, once. Years ago, my father and I. He brought me here, and we went to EuroDisney, an attempt to win me over after the loss of my mother. She had taken me to Disney in Florida, it was one of my happiest times; with my grandparents, and before she knew that she was leaving. Before any of us knew how bad the world was – the galaxy, I have to remind myself to think bigger, always – before then, we had time that meant nothing other than the moment it existed in.

My mother, sitting with me on a rollercoaster made for small children, holding my hand as I screamed with joy.

My father, holding the knot on his necklace in his hand, pulling on it so hard that the skin around his neck creased into leylines. Asking me why I wasn't having fun, asking me what he had to do. Telling me, in a rage, in a hotel room of gaudy pastel colours, designed to feel like it was ripped straight from a movie, that I was a waste of time and energy; and that the sooner we were swallowed – engulfed, his word – the sooner we were engulfed, the better for us all. Maybe then you'll see.

The old man, Claude, asks us if we need somewhere to stay. We thank him, but we are just passing through. He smiles, and nods, and – because he has the air of the mystical to him, and who is he to let us down – and he says, 'Aren't we all,' with a smile.

When he is gone, Rhonda whispers to me, impishly: 'Was he Santa Claus?' and we both laugh at that. Leaving the train station, and walking up through the 1st arrondissement, through the 8th, along the Champs-Élysées. There are only a few other people here, and we do not see them up close. Instead, they're always in the distance, always further away than allows for details.

'This used to be heaving,' I say, 'so busy with people. I remember it a little, it was so busy that my father had to take us away. He said it was too much.'

'Why?'

'Because it was famous. People are drawn to things that are already busy. Like moths to a flame that's already absolutely engulfed by millions of other moths.'

'You should sketch it,' Rhonda says.

'There are enough pictures of it,' I say.

'Maybe,' she says. 'But how many of them are from the goddamned apocalypse?'

'Not many, probably.'

'So, then. Be a pioneer or whatever. Do it, draw the street. The chans-whatever.'

'Champs-Élysées.'

'Yeah, that. Come on.' She leads me to a bench at one

204

side, and she sits. 'There's no immediate rush, right? No train to catch or whatever.'

'No,' I say.

'So you sit here and draw, and I'll go find us some food.' She doesn't let me say no. She reaches into my bag and she takes money, and she looks around her. 'Maybe some clothes, as well. I stink,' she says, but she doesn't, I do, she's just too polite to tell me so.

I hold my sketchbook, and I take the pencil up, and I start to draw. I find a base shape, first: the lines of the street, the intersecting angles with the buildings at the sides. The Arc de Triomphe at the end, like a gateway. Was that always the point? I wonder. I do not know why it was built. I do not know why it stands, beyond the fact that it does.

I have lost time, because suddenly the picture is complete, or nearly: everything in its place, and Rhonda is back. A bag in one hand with clothes, a bag of food in the other.

'That looks good,' she says.

'I don't know,' I say, and she laughs.

'Of course you don't. Jesus, we'd all be fucked if we thought we weren't useless.' She sits next to me and hands me a salad in a cardboard box, a hunk of bread on the side. 'There was this writer at the factory, he used to say, If you think you're good, you're not. The minute you think you're good at something, that's the point when you've stopped trying.'

'I suppose,' I say.

'So, you don't think you're good?' I shake my head. 'There you go. You're probably a fucking master warlock of art.'

'I don't think that's a real title,' I say.

'I've made it one,' she says. We eat our salads in silence for a while. Wooden forks into lettuce and egg and tomato and tuna, I think; and I notice a young man standing near us. Looking confused. Rhonda notices him as well, and we both half watch as he scratches his head, as he stumbles towards us. 'Is he drunk?' Rhonda asks. He looks it, certainly.

I feel my hand reach for my bag, a movement I make on instinct. Keep it close. Notebook and pencil back inside, people still want to steal. The looters took everything worth taking from the places we abandoned; this place has been left to dry itself out, a rot of dust and baked tarmac.

I see, in his hand, a gun.

'Don't say anything to him,' I say to Rhonda. She opens her mouth, as if her own muscle memory prevents that from happening. 'Don't. His hand—' She looks, and she sees. A moment as she tries to understand what it is, and then that look shifts, and she tenses her entire body. I feel it through the bench.

'What does he want?' she asks, but I don't reply.

I held my daughter tight to me as she was afraid in the night. She did not know what she was scared of, and neither did I; but I could tell her that everything would be okay, and I believed it, and so she believed it.

'It'll be all right,' I say to Rhonda. I feel her hand on my back as I turn myself more towards the young man. My body a shield, and she is using it.

The young man looks at us. 'Quel jour est-il?'

'Quel jour – what day,' I mutter. 'C'est—' I run them through in my head. Lundi? Mardi? Mercredi? Is that right? 'Mercredi,' I say.

He nods, as if understanding something. Then: 'You are American?'

'Sort of,' I say. 'British. A bit of everything.' Blabbering. I think I heard that, once; engage the shooter, they will see

206

you as a person. They will be less likely to shoot you if they relate to you. 'I have lived all over, but I spent the past few years in America. Decades, really.'

'Decades, okay. Decades,' he says. His tongue finding the word clumsily.

'We were just leaving,' I say.

'Where are you going?'

'England,' I reply. 'My sister – my half-sister – is there.' A pause, as he stares at me. His eyes are not sunken as you might imagine. They are the opposite: absolute clarity in them, of their form, the light inside them, the skin perfect around them. They are eyes that haven't seen enough yet. 'Where are you from?'

'Here,' he says, quick as a snap. 'I am from here.'

'Okay,' I say. I look behind him, at the wall: a graffiti of words, in black marker. Nothing artistic to them. *Il vient de cette ruelle.* Arrows accompanying the words. I didn't notice this before, I was so intent on looking forward – at the quiet, the arch. Would I have noticed them otherwise? A symbol: a gun, stencilled, as if this is art. *Le sien est dangereux, il est toujours dangereux.* Markings on the floor, I realize now. Lines, painted in yellow. A path for him, or that he will follow. Dangereux, I understand that. Toujours, the next? Tomorrow? I forget. Il est toujours dangereux; he is toujours dangerous. Doesn't matter what it means. This is the man, his toes on the edge of the yellow demarcations. He paces, and stays within his box. The gun loose in his hands, as if it could drop at any moment. 'Do you need help?' I ask him. I feel Rhonda's hand pressing to my back.

'I do not,' he says. He looks behind him, at the writing on the wall. 'Do you know what this says?'

'I didn't notice it,' I say.

'I am a dangerous man. It is me that it is speaking of, I think. Come.' He indicates behind him, to the alleyway he evidently came from. 'Come, I will show you,' he says, and he beckons me with the hand that's not holding the gun.

'Don't,' Rhonda says, but I have to, because I think somebody always dies here, if they can. I look to the ground, where the pavement is stained with spatters of something: darkened, like mud, but I know that it isn't mud. It is ingrained.

'Don't worry,' I say. I stand, and I walk towards the young man.

'My name is Theo,' I say, 'what's yours?'

'Alain. Come, through here, I want to show you the writing about me.' I follow him, around the corner, into this small space. Barely an alley at all. More a place between buildings, as if they forgot to fill it in, somewhere that shouldn't exist. It leads through to an adjacent street, in the distance. A couple of doors, which I can barely believe have the space to open out into here. And writing: as if somebody famous lived here, or we are in a museum, a curator's card on the wall next to one of the doors.

'You see?' he asks. And I try to read it, but it's dense, tightly packed French that seems impenetrable.

'I don't read French,' I say, so he puts his finger beneath one of the words, and he translates.

'This man who lives here always comes from this door, and he is always armed. The cycle, the loop, I think?' An aside, he looks at me to agree to his translation, which I do with a nod 'The loop means that he is with the gun, and he will always shoot it, because he wants to, he has got that into his head. He is a murderer—' Alain looks to me as he says it, his eyes somehow even wider. 'I am a murderer,' he says. 'I did not know this, until I left here. Until I saw it, you see? Every time.'

'You have a gun,' I say.

'For myself. The Knot, it is coming, yes?'

'It is here,' I say.

'Well, then. I am going to kill myself. For its glory.' I see his skin, on his neck: a tattoo of the symbol. Curled in on itself. 'But now I see, I am a murderer?'

'You weren't going to kill other people.'

'I have never hurt anybody, why would I begin now?' He jabs at the words. 'But this says I am a murderer. So I am, I have been.'

'Maybe it's not you,' I say.

'I live alone. The man who lives here – it is me, it is very direct.' Now, finally, as if we have both been waiting for this, he lifts the gun. A snub-nosed thing, that seems to almost disappear in his hands, his long fingers uncomfortable on its shape.

'Why did you have the gun?' I ask.

'For myself,' he says. 'The Knot said, That is the day. It is the day and—' He raises his voice, some dramatic display of his own lack of power. 'I wanted to be heard! Heard!' The echo of his voice around this small alleyway, in this space. Reverberating off every wall. 'But they were correct, yes?'

'Correct about what?'

'That we go around again. That the Knot is not the end. It is a knot, yes? We can unpick it, and tie it again, and again.'

'You can't take back what you have done.'

'It is not permanent. That is the word?'

'The world is permanent. Your actions might be forgotten by you, but for everybody else they have consequences.'

'Consequences.' As if he's trying on the word.

'The world continues. It is simply your time that does not.'

'But I get to do it again.'

'You get to repeat mistakes.'

'Or successes. Maybe I am meant to kill you. Maybe you are a bad person, a bad, bad man.' He smiles, the thought tickling him. He does not believe it. He is broken; I wonder how long before this it was that he broke. On his timeline, his sense of linear time: days, weeks, months, years. Was he born broken? Waiting for something like the Knot to give him purpose? 'Maybe I kill you, and I have completed my, what is it? Mission. Maybe we are all on a mission, maybe then I will be allowed to live.'

This cannot be the first time it's happened. We are destined to rally against the things we are told are inevitable, I think. I wonder: is that why I have lived so long? To be given a lifeline with such finality, and yet here I am still. Not for much longer, admittedly, but regardless. Perhaps that's why I am still here. So has this man—

'Alain,' I say, his name loud on my lips. And he stares at me. He nods, as if to pre-emptively say that whatever question I would ask him, I am correct, I am on the right path.

'Get back from him!' a voice shouts, and I turn, and I see a group of people, six or seven of them, pushing through from the avenue. Elderly people, for the most, and one pregnant woman, standing at the back, shielding herself behind the others. All wearing the telltale near-neon orange armbands of the Police Nationale. The speaker, an older man, walrus moustache and combed-over hair, stands at the very front, preceded by his rifle: this almost comically massive hunting thing, I am sure. I wonder if it is a blunderbuss, even; try to picture what such a thing might look like. 'He will kill you, you see.'

'We were talking,' Alain says.

'Alain Patrice, tu sais comment ça se termine,' the older man, the Walrus, says, but Alain just smiles at him.

'Do not smile,' the pregnant woman says, then she looks to me. 'He always smiles, it is very unpleasant.'

'Unpleasant,' I repeat.

'Venez avec nous, maintenant,' the Walrus says, but Alain doesn't move, doesn't flinch.

I realize, in this moment, that I could die now. Right now. The group are sweating this moment, worrying for their safety – and mine. Behind them all, Rhonda. The pregnant woman telling her to stay back, ushering her with her hands.

Alain keeps the gun pointed at me.

He is not trembling, not even a little.

'He needs help,' I say, to Walrus, to the group, but Alain laughs, and—

The blunderbuss roars, a shot that is so loud in this alleyway, and that echoes so much, it feels as if it never ends, pinging off the walls, a message to the streets, the city, the sky. I crouch, instinctively, hands over my head. And I gasp, and I laugh, because I can't help that, I can't help the noise coming out; and I watch as Alain slumps, feet away from where he was standing, I'm sure. The walls peppered with red pockmarks, bloodshot shot dug into hard old stone. Alain is barely there, barely intact.

Walrus reaches his hand to me, even though I am only cowering. A gesture, and he says, 'You're American,' with the disdain that suggests I am not the first American he's had to save from this situation.

'Of a sort,' I say.

'Ahh, you are all American. You live there for any time, you're American. France is blood, eh? America adopts, even if you do not want it to.'

'Well, thank you. You saved my life.'

'We saved many lives. He goes on a—'

'It is a spree, if he escapes,' the pregnant woman says. 'So many people die, or as many people until his bullets are run out.'

'So you kill him.'

'Yes.'

'What about restraining him?' I look to the house he comes out of. Noise from inside there: of thumping around, of grumbling. Murmuring under breath. 'He's awake,' I say. I mean: alive.

'He has his gun in his hand. We have tried, you think we haven't tried? We stand there, we wait, we blink, he is there, and he is holding the gun. We have been shot.' Walrus looks to the others. 'We have died, and come back, to protect the city from him. He kills himself, or he kills us, some of us, or he escapes and he kills strangers, and he causes them to lose where they have gained up to. You see?'

'Like a video game,' Rhonda says.

'Yes,' Walrus replies. 'Like a video game, you see? There is no winning, you only keep defending, you keep defeating the big boss, and then it comes back. Like a video game, or a horror film.'

'It's not like that,' Rhonda says.

'It has become like that,' Walrus says. He turns to me. 'We saved your life, eh? You are lucky, American.' More clunking around from the house. 'We were having lunch, we got the timing incorrect. Maybe we are complacent.' He smiles at me, a big shit-eating grin, his moustache trailing in his mouth. 'I do not know, whatever happens, you are lucky.'

'So what happens now?' I ask him.

'He will stay in there for two hours and four minutes, and

then he will leave. We try to finish him here, it's kinder. In his house, it is . . . It is not right.'

'I could reason with him,' I say. 'Try and save his life.'

'He has killed so many people,' Walrus says, 'what about his life, exactly, is worth saving? No, he is better dead. This is our job, we protect this part of the city.'

'You do this every day?'

'We have shifts,' one of the others says, 'we take turns.'

'As I have said already: this is our job,' Walrus says. His face suddenly serious. 'Do not try to stop us doing our job, American. We are the Police Nationale, you understand? Do not stop us from doing what we are here to do.' His gun, which has been limp, at his side, twitches a little. The nearly imperceptible lift of its heft. A gesture. I understand it, Walrus understands it. I look to Rhonda, and she's scared; even she understands it. 'You should leave now,' Walrus says. The gun stays where it is: hovering, almost, held in a way that is surely less comfortable than hanging loose, or than actually being aimed.

I push through the group, to Rhonda, out of the alleyway and onto the avenue; where the air feels, suddenly, fresher, cleaner. 'We have to leave,' I say. Rhonda doesn't reply. She follows me as I walk to the bags, as I gather them up. Our food only half-eaten, but I have no appetite. 'Quickly,' I say, because men like that are liable to change their minds, I think, liable to backtrack on their words.

We are walking away, down the avenue, towards the arch. Rhonda looks at me, and she says, 'Behind us,' because there are footsteps behind us, a distance off but quickening. 'What do we do?' she asks, hisses.

I breathe, as deep as I can; and I stop, and I turn—

It is the pregnant woman. One of her hands under her belly, supporting it. 'Do you need somewhere to rest?'

'No,' I say. 'We're leaving, don't worry, we will not be back.'

'Do not mind Ari,' she says, 'he is an idiot. Aggressive, n'est-ce pas?'

'Yes,' I reply.

'Do you need anything? Help, or a rest?'

'We're fine.'

'Fine, none of us is fine.' She smiles. I notice something on her neck, and I think, for a moment, of my father's necklace, of the knot; but it's a crucifix, tarnished and paled, decades old at a glance. The features on the figure worn soft from the repeated rubbing of a thumb. 'You take care, okay?'

'And you,' I reply.

'Good luck with the baby,' Rhonda says.

'The baby dies,' she says, with a nonchalance that staggers me for a moment; because I forget, maybe, or I haven't considered. Not to this degree. And the pregnant woman goes on: 'There is nothing that can be done. Perhaps if doctors were here, perhaps. I die, the baby dies. It has happened many, many times. Sometimes in the birth, sometimes before. Sometimes we lose the blood.' She does not smile. Her face is still, her lips perfectly closed. 'It is what is meant to happen, I think. Eight months, and then . . .'

She looks as though she wants us to believe that she is used to it. That she is comfortable with what happens. That the death of it, it's been normalised.

Nothing about this is normal. Nothing about it comfortable, or acceptable, nothing about it needs to be accepted. This is not reality; it's only temporary.

Rhonda glances me, then steps up to the woman and holds her. Her arms finding their way around her, dragging them close. And as Rhonda does, I take a cue from her. This woman needs to be held, and I have needed to be held, we all need to be held, in some way. Physical, emotional, whatever. The need is there, waiting. I join the embrace, the three of us standing there, in the middle of this most famous of streets, and we hold each other.

When we are done, she tells us the direction. She orientates us, and we say goodbye; and she watches us leave, her hand never moving from her bump, as she waves with the other.

23

The walk to the tunnel takes forever. Days, as we trudge along roads; as we hold out our thumbs for the few cars that pass us, but nobody stops. One truck slows, stares – at Rhonda, I notice, as I stare back; and I shake my head at the driver, who carries on as if nothing happened – but otherwise, the road is quiet. We find ourselves in Amiens, and we find food, a small hotel, a shower; and the next morning, a continental breakfast, which amazes Rhonda and reminds me of nothing other than terrible hotel breakfasts when I was a child. Stale croissants and tough cheese. But Rhonda loves it, she takes her plate and loads it from the different sections. And Melba toast: hardened to a crisp, and she relishes it, putting cold butter onto the cold bread, biting chunks of it, salty and rich. And the woman who owns the hotel, or who runs it – who acts as if she owns it – barely speaks any English, which makes me apologize over and over, because she tries, and I only really have parlez-vous Anglais and my manners, little more. Pardonnez moi, over and over. Before we leave, I stand in the bathroom of my room, and I stare at the mirror, and I try to coax my sickness to show itself. I try to will the badness out, or not out, but will it to act; so that maybe it won't surprise me on the journey, or maybe it won't come at all, or maybe I will die here and save everybody the trouble of worrying about me any more. Except nothing comes: I lean forward on the sink, eyes into the mirror, locking eyes with myself. Stare at the faint red of the veins, pull down the skin, looking for a trough of blood, pooling in the bottom lid. Picking at the side of my fingernails to make a small hole there, a tear between the soft tissue and the nail; to see if it bleeds, and if it won't stop. I take my hand, curled into one tight fist, and I beat it at my side, briefly; a single thwack, designed to hurt me, to see if it will be the instigator. Because all I want – and I say this, out loud, to myself, quietly, like breathing the words – all I want is to know when it's coming. When it is coming, what it will be. If I cannot stop it. Birdie said, before she left, I don't understand why you're afraid. You'll come back. And I said, But I won't remember. There will be darkness for this version of myself, darkness and nothingness. So write yourself a story, she said, And I can tell you, I can fill in the gaps. I did not have an answer. I did not.

We walk along the roads, all these main roads. Occasional cars zooming past us, as they will; and after a while we stop even with the thumbs, because we're close to the tunnel, and that's strictly foot traffic only. The ground changes as we get closer: scorched, but from fires, not the sun; barbed wire along every trench, and the trenches dug deeper, insurmountable at their sides; and then, in the distances, both distances, large buildings in this army-green finish that seems as though it's designed to blend into a landscape, had that landscape

not been burned to a crisp and were the buildings not quite
so monumental. They are oversized sheds, and I catch Rhonda
staring at one, the similarities to her previous home presumably ringing in her skull as loudly as they are in mine. The
sound in the air of some sort of turbine, in those distances:
of machinery working, perhaps, or a windmill. Something
turning and turning in efficiency.

Then the fences give way to more fences, and more and
more, all that latticework of cheap metal, so dense and layered
– row upon row of it, thin walk-spaces between the fences
– so layered that it's almost impossible to see through it. A
cluster of grey scarring.

'What is this?'

'It's a camp,' I say. She doesn't ask anything else for a little
while. Then:

'For what?'

'People like me,' I say. 'People who are sick.'

'Oh.' She stops walking and steps up to the fence. 'They
put them in here?'

'Yeah. There was . . . Before they knew about how it
worked. So many people died, and they wanted to control
it. They said that they had to put them somewhere. This was
the solution.'

'They let them die here?'

'Stand back,' I say, 'don't get too close.'

'I just, it's so evil, isn't it?' She peers forward, her hands
against the wire, and she presses her face to the mesh, to get
a better view.

'Stand back, Rhonda.' I see him before she does. A movement of red in the distance, a blur of the colour. I grab her
backpack and pull her away from the fence, just in time: he
lumbers towards us, through the lanes of wire fence. It would

be funny, almost, if it weren't so tragic; his hands clinging to the spaces between the wire as he almost pulls himself. And that low growl of his chest as he breathes, the wetness of each inhale, each exhale. I am reminded of my grandfather, with a pipe, blowing bubbles at me. Making me laugh until I felt sick, chasing those bubbles around.

Rhonda stares as this man staggers towards us, like some zombie from a low-budget movie. He groans, this quiet murmur, and I realize that the sound in the air, the sound of the turbine, it's not inanimate at all: it is this same groan, just amplified and multiplied.

'How big is it?'

'Endless,' I tell her. 'I mean, not actually, but it's big. It goes on and on and on.'

The man reaches the final stage of the mesh, and he tries to shout something, but he can't manage the words. His entire outfit is red, stained blood-dark, and it drips from him. He is featureless behind the blood caked onto his face; like that Christ on the pregnant woman's necklace, rubbed clear of details.

'Please,' he says, but there's nothing we can do, nothing that any of us can do.

That doesn't stop Rhonda asking. 'How can we help?' she asks, quiet enough that I doubt he can hear; and he doesn't answer, but he slams himself against the fence, a cheap scare from a zombie horror movie. The metal rattles, and Rhonda steps back again, her backpack pressing into my hand.

'You can't help him.'

'This is terrible.'

'He just has to stay there.' We watch for a moment, as he uses all of the strength that he's got. It amounts to less than minutes, more than moments. His fingers loosening, and then it's bloody palms against the mesh. Then it's the lines on his hand, all split open, cracks turned into fissures.

We watch as he collapses. As he slumps, and doesn't even really try; his arms propping himself up, but more by luck than judgement, the bones not giving. And then he goes forward, his face driving into the ground with a squelch rather than a thud.

Rhonda stares. Has she seen anybody die? Since we've been out here? She reaches for my hand, a fumble at my sleeve, then her fingers interlocking mine.

'Is that—'

'It's fine,' I say. 'I'm fine.'

We stare at his body, and she asks, after a while, when he'll reset. I tell her that it'll be when we stop looking at him, when he's clear and free to move. As if we're giving him agency for that choice. 'And he'll go over there?'

'Somewhere deeper, yes. They got most of the sick – the living sick – they got them here before the Anomaly arrived. Here's where they are, here's where they die, here's where they come back to life.'

'That's not a life,' she says.

'No.' I start to turn away, but she pulls me back.

'We can't stop looking at him.'

'We have to.'

'We can't. It's not fair.'

'It isn't, but—'

'You don't want to come back.'

'I don't want to die.'

'But when you do, you don't want to come back.'

'Not as a stranger. Not without who I am.'

'So why should he?' She nods at me, willing me to agree with her. But her eyes are tilted towards him, and she doesn't blink, doesn't stop him being a fixed part of her gaze. 'Come on,' she says, so I turn back to him – his body, not him, the vessel – and I stare as well.

Minutes pass. She is crying, and I wrap my arm around her shoulders, and I tell her, in as truthful a voice as I can manage, that everything is going to be all right.

'We have to go,' I say, as the sky starts to darken. There's rain coming, and night, and we want to get into the tunnel before it does. 'This isn't somewhere to spend the night, I don't think.' She nods, and we start to walk, but she keeps looking at the man on the ground as we leave, keeping sight of him until we're so far off that he's obscured; and I am no longer looking, but I know that he's gone from there, back to where he was when the Anomaly swallowed our planet whole. The groaning on the air, the sound of pain and fear – of people who are going to die and know it, who can't do anything about it, who have been left, abandoned and alone – the sound picks up again, I think, and louder, his voice part of the cacophony, impossible to distinguish and equally impossible to miss.

The entrance to the tunnel isn't as glorious as you would think. It's a tube, really, a hole in a mound. Darkness on darkness; but lights inside, hanging up, and the telltale hum of a generator, linked to sol2r panels on the hillocks outside.

Rhonda walks in first. She doesn't even hesitate.

24

My days were survival. I have thought, sometimes, of what I did, and why I was doing it. What reason there could possibly be for staying alive as I was, for trudging onwards, waking each day, wondering if that would be the last one. As if, maybe, all I wanted was to see how far I could get. There's an old theory, about exploring, about the human race's capacity for pushing, for forging. This idea that we explore, we discover, because we can. There's no instinct greater in us than to do something, or to try and do something, simply to see if it can be done. And I've wondered: was that my reason? To wake up, to check myself, to read the books and to panic over every tremor, every tremble. Every time my knee felt weak, or my back ached, or my gums bled when I brushed my teeth with a little too much vigour. Was that the start of it? Was I about to crumble? But then I didn't, and the day continued. The sun roared, and I stayed inside, or I went out into the shade of the small courtyard garden, and sometimes I would lower myself into the rectangular length of water that passed for a pool in that part of the sprawl; and then the night would come, and I would have eaten at least two meals, sometimes three, and I would have read a book, or the best part of one, and maybe watched an old film or two, or a television series that I missed the first time around – some of them with Birdie's endorsement pealing out as I dug the boxes from the trunk, her voice reminding me that physical media won't die, that it's worth investing in, even when it's as old as all of this. The internet will go, it'll go, she said, in the later days. We went to yard sales and bought boxes of old digidiscs and flashcards, even ones without cases, even ones that were just files and files downloaded from the internet. And we bought this ridiculous player that could take all sorts of media, all the codecs and file types. She said, It'll pay off, honestly it will, if we have to hunker down. And we did, and it did. Even after she left, it paid off, it was there every day for me. Never broke, this lump of cheap black plastic, and I could watch all of the things I wanted.

So every evening was dinner, then something to watch, as I lay on the sofa, this small patch of it under my heels where I had rubbed the fabric slightly bare, where it had worn back to that exposed undermesh. And then I would go to sleep, on my side of the bed, leaving Birdie's side empty. I do not know what people do when they lose somebody, and that is the only way I could think of it; the bed was a joy to sprawl in when I knew she was coming back, but absolutely too cold and vacant when I believed that she wasn't. And I would shut my eyes, after reading some more by the moonlight; and I would think about sleep, and what would happen if I didn't wake up. What exactly it would feel like, to shut my eyes for that one final time, and to not know any different.

I would pray to whoever was listening: not that I had anything formal there, but I also thought that there could be something. There's no smoke without fire, and people have always believed in something. Maybe not the exact finished article, maybe not the perfect idealized, but the idea of there being something, a creator, a peace waiting at the other end, that feeling is so heartening. So I lay there, and I spoke to God, or god, or whatever it was – even the Knot, at my darkest, when I couldn't stop my brain from wandering there – and I thought to them, If I die, please be gentle on me; because I am not prepared for it. If I go, I will not know; if I wake up again, I will be so lost. There is no Birdie here, she has not come back, and I will be entirely alone.

And that thought would wake me up, more often than not, and I would write myself a note: here's what's happened to you, here's what's happened to the world, here's what you have been through, Birdie is gone, she's not coming back. And then I would sleep, because I was so exhausted I couldn't not. I would lie back, and I would shut my eyes, and I would feel their wetness in the corners, as I tried to not let myself get overwhelmed; and I would run my tongue over my teeth, my gums, one final time, to see if I could taste the telltale blood, before I went.

Come morning, I was still there. I would read the note I left for myself, and I would scrunch it up, and I would throw it away; and I would start my day again, as if it were my last.

25

'How much further?' Rhonda asks. The only light the emergency exit lights, this green glow. Like something haunted, or alien.

'I don't know,' I say, again, again. Every time, because there aren't markers that I can see, and I don't know how far we've gone, and there are no signs of life or light. Only the time we've spent walking, time that I can't even turn into a calculation: walking actually means stepping carefully, treading over and under detritus.

I think of Rebecca, learning to walk: as I held her hands, and she took those tentative steps. Not wanting to let go, in case she couldn't do it.

It was when she couldn't balance that we first spoke to the doctor.

We didn't know it would be anything other than normal. Told, that's normal, go home. They all grow in different ways.

We stop and rest when we find a train car, set aside for repairs in a gulley some way down the tunnel; other people have set it up as a temporary abode, a mattress and sheets and food growing in this curious little farm-come-arboretum, a carriage that's been lain down with soil, carrots and potatoes abundant under lamps hooked up to an old repurposed peloton. *Do your share*, a sign says, *Take what's fair*. There are notes like that all over the place, all in different hands: *Leave me as you'd like me to be found* in the kitchenette, or *You soil them, you boil them!* written about the clean sheets folded on a shelf.

'This is cool,' Rhonda says, and we both sit in absolute silence on the seats, and I shut my eyes; and when I open them next, time has passed, and Rhonda's pedalling for dear life, grinning as the pedals fly around. 'I thought I should do our part,' she says. 'There's a little thing here, you can see how much people have done on their sessions. I figured I'll set a new record, something for everybody who comes after us to aim for.'

'Noble,' I say. I ache, and so much. I stretch, but there's not much room, so I step out of the car and into the dark. From here, it looks like a painting. Some old Hopper or something. The light from inside casting out, and Rhonda there in the forefront of one of the windows, cycling. Everything yellows and greens, before the light gives way to the black, everything around the borders being swallowed up by it. I get my pencil, my notebook. A marker for here, as much as anywhere. As good a way of remembering it as any.

The book falls open on the page with the most creased spine: a drawing that I did of my mother, from memory. I don't know that it even looks like her. Probably the details are wrong, probably the scale of her features, the tone of the skin, the way her hair fell. I remember her with it down. She said, 'I have to wear it up at work, they insist, so I have to mark the difference. I have to feel like there's a change between the two versions of myself: the one that is your mom, and the one that is at work.' She said that, or something like it. Words to that effect. And the picture is her, but split almost; the pencil lines shading a version of her that was as torn as she was. The line of the book down the middle of her: and she is slightly different on either side, slightly changed.

My father said that her choice was easy.

It wasn't easy, I know that much.

I cook something. Carrots and potatoes, fried up. Some small onions we find in the soil, and then replant from a sachet of seeds; and some chillies, they are abundant, chopped up small. All fried together with noodles from a packet, literally decades past a Best Before but also that taste exactly as I remember them tasting.

'Maybe they come back,' I say to Rhonda. 'Maybe the Anomaly's a big noodle fan.' Rhonda doesn't reply, but that's only because she's eating so quickly, wolfing down the food. Or maybe that's not the only reason, but it's the one I cling to.

I shower, and I shave. I sit as much as possible, and rub at my calves, which are sore from the walking. My feet are raw, blisters on my toes. I need walking shoes, or perhaps I needed them. It's late in the day for that now.

Then Rhonda's cleaned, and she's in temporary clothes – a dress – and she says, 'Don't say a fucking word,' then she washes her old clothes, her uniform. I stare at her t-shirt, stretched out across the old carriage railings. A vintage band, but one that I can't say I've heard.

'*The Black Parade*. Like a funeral.'

'I guess.'

'Cheery.'

'Oh, because you don't like anything dark?'

'I didn't say that.'

'They've got good songs.'

'Well, then.' But that's not the end. She goes to her bag, gets her old music player out. There's a stereo here, linked to the bicycle's power supply, and she plays me a song: the words deafeningly sad, even as the singer's projecting happiness, or something like it. The band crashing together at the perfect moment, in perfect synchronicity.

'You see?' she asks, and I tell her that I do, I see.

When she's asleep, I write a letter to my dead daughter. I ask her what she would listen to; what she would say to me, if we would argue, if we would be close. I ask her if she would have come on this journey with me, or if having her there would have been enough to keep me exactly where I was, in that house, in that city, waiting to die instead of chasing somebody who isn't yet a ghost.

PART THREE

'*I said to my soul, be still, and let the dark come upon you.*'

T. S. Eliot, *Four Quartets*

26

Daylight hurts our eyes, but it's incredible: the brightness of it, bouncing off the white chalk of the landscape, making it appear for a moment as if it's snow. 'Woah,' Rhonda says.

'Woah,' I repeat. A sign, looming at the verge of the tracks, where a road runs adjacent: *You Are Now Entering the Kingdom of United England.*

'Kingdom?'

'They have a king,' I say.

'That's old school.'

'It is,' I say. We walk along the tracks, then climb up the grassy bank – she helps me at the end, because it's steep, and her boots make this easier for her than my terrible shoes, my feet stinging in all the wrong places from the incessant rubbing – up the grassy bank, to the road itself, and then we walk along that. We are quiet, because there's only so much anybody can talk when they have had shared experiences, only so much dissecting of the recent past that can be done. Then we come to trucks and cars, pushed to one side of the road, to keep it clear: their bodies stripped, the only things left the husks that aren't of use to anybody. Some of them don't appear as wrecked as the others, but they're decades old now, rusted, gutted, I'm sure.

'Can we use one of these?'

'They're useless,' I tell her.

'They look okay.'

'Looks can be deceiving.'

'We can try. You said I get good with cars?'

'Yes.'

'Well, then, we should try. One of them might, I don't know. Maybe it'll start.' She stops walking. It's what she wants to do. I shrug assent.

'Find one with sol2r panels, then. Best chance of that rather than looking for biogas or whatever.'

'What was it like when people died?' she asks, as she's walking between the vehicles, staring at their roofs. 'I mean, you don't have to talk about it.'

'No, no. It's fine.' I don't know if it is fine. Birdie and I were alone together, huddled and terrified. We watched the news until the news stopped being a thing you watched and started being a thing you listened to; and we shut the lights off and locked the doors when the news said to do that, and we ate every single thing we had in the cupboards or the freezer, in no real order beyond the fresh stuff first, and freezing what was fresh that we couldn't eat, and then working our way through increasingly outlandish dishes – imported British baked beans with sardines; frozen chicken nuggets in pasta, their oil as the sauce; tinned peaches with everything, sweet or savoury, grilled and chilled and roasted, a de facto accompaniment to gussy up any meal – before eventually running out of food, rice for days and days, until we argued, weak as we were, that finally we needed to leave the house.

She wanted to go, told me that it was important to her; and I waited outside, in our little courtyard, for her. Listening for any sound that could have been her in trouble. But she returned, arms full of oranges and tomatoes and bags of dried pasta, orzo, grains and pulses, more rice. 'This will do', she said.

'It was awful,' I say. Rhonda listens. She doesn't say anything, she wants me to go on. 'It was like nothing I've known. There are stories you get taught, or you'll read about, about what happened during wars, or famines, or when the breach broke, or when the climate reached the peak. Or pandemics, they're a good proxy, a good example of what it was like. But it was worse, of course. Because when you engineer these things, they're more efficient than nature. Nature has this thing where a virus exists, but biologically needs to stay alive. It can't cause an extinction event, because then it can't spread itself. We're all built from the same material, the same cloth. We all, really, want to survive, to get to the next stage of whatever it is we're trying to get to. A virus needs to spread, so it can only be so damaging; that is, if it's natural. If it's not, there are no limits. You design a weapon, you only need it to achieve one thing: to damage the people so that they cannot fight back. The people who designed the virus, they wanted it to do three things: infect, spread, kill. People got infected, it didn't have any symptoms for three days, then they dropped down dead. A transmission rate of nearly seven, that's what they thought, or the last statistic I read about it. So every person infected, they infected seven more. And surviving it, that's a one-in-a-thousand chance, maybe more. Genetics played some part. Some people took longer to die, or longer to show symptoms. Some people weren't susceptible. Some people died straight away, some people infected hundreds of others. It took six days to discover that the virus existed. And by then, it was everywhere. The virus was meant to have a gestation period of months, that was the problem. Nobody was meant to die before the Anomaly arrived. We were all meant to be infected, then the Anomaly would be here, and then we would die inside it. In service to it. Bleeding, in tribute. There were these wacky conspiracy theories, leaked papers written by that crank Hyvönen, from up on the space station – and, I thought, when he could have been trying harder to save my mother's life – his rants about time loops and life resetting itself. Birdie had a theory – she was a mathematician by trade, she had a theory, she always had a theory – that it was some old thing. I forget. Some thing, some Einstein thing. Old science. She was terrified, I was terrified. We didn't know what would happen. Everybody died.' I taste the dryness of my own mouth; the sticking sensation of my tongue against the roof of my mouth, the back of my teeth. 'Everybody died, that's all I can say. Nearly everybody.' I feel exhausted. I slump against a car.

'Hey,' she says, 'you okay?'

'Just tired,' I say. 'Talking about it, thinking about it. I'm tired anyway, and then that on top of it. What did you hear about it?' I ask her. 'Did you get the news?'

She shakes her head. 'They told us the news, so we never really heard about how bad it got.' I nod. 'All I knew was what they said.'

'And what did they say?'

'They said that the people who wanted to die from the virus succeeded.' Her voice still and small. 'I think that's what they thought.'

'Probably,' I say, or maybe I don't say, maybe I only think

it, because I am in my own way overwhelmed: at the thought that Rhonda was there for all those conversations, running in the background as she grew, or reading or talking, and her parents, her family friends, aunts and uncles, they were part of discussions about the murder of the human race. She was there. Maybe her parents were not the scientists, they were not the organizers or the propagators, they were not the agitators or the talking heads or the journalists; and they were not the politicians or the leaders or the cabals that were whispered about; and they were not the people on the street who either wilfully refused to listen or who, like my father, fully embraced the ideas, the ideals, giving themselves over to something that they decided was better than their old realities, their old beliefs or religions or feelings. Better than the way that they felt before, trusting in this thing that felt tangible. Forget everything else, forget the old ways; here's something that could punish us, let us pay penitence. No more worrying about believing just in case. This was real; the Anomaly was coming.

Couldn't hurt to worship it. Don't say anything, don't ask too many questions. Let them kill people, be complicit by omission.

I think about my father. Leaving the house as he did every day, those early days. Still reeling from the loss of my mother, or claiming that he was – brushing back his hair with his fingernails, and saying, It's all so senseless, Theo, I just can't quite fathom why the universe would do this; and wouldn't it be better if something righted the course? – claiming he was suffering, when I was suffering, I was truly feeling that she was gone, I was the one who cared. Years without a word, believing that she was dead—

My father strapping his backpack on. Not dissimilar to

Rhonda's, really. The same non-brand genericism, the same too-many zips, the same faded straps, frayed ends. And he'd been wearing it for weeks at a time, every morning, leaving the house with it on. A totem. Increasing weight, or decreasing, depending on the day. Sometimes catching him packing it in the kitchen, transparent bags going into opaque bags. Things that he kept in the garden, or that arrived in the mail, stored in the refrigerator in coloured Tupperware. Never in the house for more than a day, and he would shout at me if I so much as went near them.

It was a shock. Hindsight is everything, of course. But when you're still really only a child, when you're desperate to believe the best of the person keeping you safe. When you don't want to know a truth, because there's no truth more important than: he will look after me. And then, one day, he took me to the airport, and he put me on a plane. Sent me to my stepmother's house, before I even knew that she existed. He left no note. He didn't tell her, not until I was there, and he knew that she would look after me. She was a good person.

I never saw him again. And then, years later, sitting with Birdie and watching the reports of the explosions, before they knew what the first virus was, they showed a clip of a subway car in Chicago. The newsreader, this one woman, said that whoever released the virus there wouldn't have survived. They would be just another one of countless dead.

And in the distance, the bag that the canisters were released from. A rucksack, no branding, no signs of anything other than the fact that it was tattered, and old. No way of tracing where it came from.

But I knew.

'They weren't killers,' Rhonda says. 'They weren't, they

236

weren't . . . I think they didn't know, really. Like, they thought they were part of something distant, maybe?'

'They killed themselves. And they would have killed you.'

'They thought it was the right thing to do.' She's red-eyed. 'It wasn't their fault.'

Was it my father's fault? He was sick, I have come to realize. To understand. He was sick, and nobody noticed; because they were worried about my mother, first, and the world, the universe. The godforsaken Anomaly.

We're silent, both of us. There's too much we don't know, and that we never will. Rhonda will find her own answers, and I have long lost the chance to find mine. I have one answer left to find: why Birdie left.

That's what this is, for me. Not that the answer is that important, or that the question is, but that it's all I have left. One thing, one solitary thing left.

'Oh, hey,' Rhonda says, spotting something. She moves bushes to one side, shuts a rusting car door. There's a panel, a really old one, but a panel nonetheless. 'You think that'll get enough power?

'Try it,' I say.

She gets in. The key's in the slot still, and she presses the button, and the car chokes, coughs, sputters. She tries again, and then it doesn't make an alarming sound, just the soft purr that the engine's getting power.

'Huh,' she says.

We don't dwell on it, don't allow the moment to be anything at all. Here is what we were looking for, so we will simply give ourselves over to it.

The roads are clear; the sun is shining.

27

The suburbs of London have the most distinctive feeling: of being somehow completely pushed to the side of what's important, safe spaces at a tube-line's length. Whole communities kept away from the tourism; from the city, capital C; from the shopping experiences and celebrity restaurants. Martine, my sister, my half-sister, described the city to me as a theme park when I first got here. Fresh off a plane, and in the back of the car, Martine's mother driving us along this green-edged motorway, and I waited for the city to reveal itself; and Martine said, 'We don't even go there, you know. The things you've seen on the movies, or in the news, they're not even for real people. They're for rich foreigners,' and she said it in a way that suggested both a dislike of said foreigners, and that I was one as well. She interrogated my backpack – the same as my father's, a different colour – sifted through the backpack's pockets, looking to see what I thought was important enough to bring with me on the flight. My clothes were being shipped after me, along with some of my father's possessions. But there was nothing of interest – 'A Mickey

Mouse? How old are you, eight?' – so she took to looking out of the window as the motorway gave way to houses and streets, the car being driven slowly, thumping over sleeping policemen in the tarmac. She told me a story about the hill we drove up: 'This is where they buried an elephant, that's why the hill is so big!' And I asked where London was. The London on the aeroplane magazine. She said, 'You don't even see it. I told you: this is the real London.'

The house was old, the bricks and the cement; and I was told not to touch anything, because I didn't know what was worth something yet and what wasn't. Martine's mother – my stepmother, she told me, but it wasn't official, not in any sense – was nice. Her name was Jackie, and she was nice, and then she died when we were eighteen, and there's no story there beyond that. Martine took me to the room that was going to be mine: decorated for visitors, of which I was one, and with nothing that felt like it was mine.

'You'll be okay,' she said, as she left me there, to unpack my bag. 'You will,' she repeated, and I think she meant it.

The house hasn't changed. The bricks, the cement, still old. Maybe more sun-baked, and the vines up the side genuinely tumultuous now. You could climb them, to one of the windows. Probably not safe. Probably wouldn't have been safe, but I don't know how many people live here now. If the ratio's the same, then a few hundred thousand, probably. I look down the street: there is nobody else here. No signs of life.

Maybe it's just her.

The front door has the same stained-glass panels, dirtied in the grit. The doorbell the same ring, that feels like a rattle in a throat trying to clear itself for a cough.

Rhonda stands back, on the path. The tiles a bit chipped and worn. Nobody's bothered to fix them, which feels like Martine's way. She said she was detail-blind, that was always her thing. Didn't notice the little things; sweated about the massive ones. I glance back—

'Are you all right?' I ask, and she nods.

'Are you?'

The door opens before I have time to answer. And there's Martine, looking the same but older. Every bit of the years on her, but in a way that suggests they fell sort of where she wanted them to fall. The same sort of clothes, the same posture. Her hand pressed to the door, holding it open, as if it would absolutely swing, slam!, if she were to let go of it.

'Oh, bloody hell,' she says.

Martine pours tea into mugs that I remember, that I drank out of years ago, decades ago. Mugs that are chipped or stained or faded: one with a little cartoon on it, and that was mine from before, even. One of the things sent with my possessions. That was my cup, and now I drink from it, and it's so strange: the exact heft of it exactly as I remember.

She sits opposite me, but looks at Rhonda. 'So you've just followed him, have you?'

'Martine,' I say, my voice doing that thing that suggests she stop talking.

'No, no. I just want to know what led to you both being here. Ragtag pair of misfits.' She smiles, but it's not Martine's smile. Everything about her is so familiar, and then this: the smile of a woman who's absolutely been destroyed by something that's happened that she will never talk about, or possibly even reference. We don't speak, really. We don't, we haven't.

'Rhonda was a friend of mine.' Barely, doesn't matter. Details don't matter. 'She died, and she reset.'

'And Theo saved my life.'

'Theo?' She laughs. 'Saved your life? Jesus, I never knew Theo to do anything that wasn't entirely for the benefit of Theo.'

'Don't be a dickhead,' I say. And she laughs, this burst of laughter, like a shotgun blast.

'Go on then: how did he save your life?'

'My parents were terrorists,' she says.

'Aren't they all.' Martine's face, tone, lips dry as anything. The smell of some sort of distilled alcohol to the house. Perhaps from her own drink, now, or maybe just lingering. There's a basement that I know she will lock, and will never let me look inside. I don't know that I want to, her life is her life. 'What's that poem? "They fuck you up, your mum and dad."'

'Your mother didn't fuck you up.'

'What, because having an affair – having *you* come and live with us – was evidently a good idea?' She stares at me, this smile on her face: Poke me, poke the bear. 'I didn't think you would actually come, you know.'

'I need to find Birdie,' I say.

'She obviously doesn't want to be found, I genuinely can't believe you actually came.'

'You saw her, where did you see her?'

'I told you, High Street Ken. In the Waitrose.'

'And she didn't say anything to you?'

'I doubt she even remembered me. We haven't seen each other since the wedding.'

'You saw her at Bob's funeral.'

'Oh, Bob's funeral. Same window of time, wasn't it. You wore the same suit, as I recall. That's probably what's thrown

241

me, in my memories. That one cheap little suit.' The smile doesn't break. 'Look, this is a folly. It's an absolute folly, you should just go back to Los Angeles. Or maybe not LA; I have worried. Reading what the papers say.'

'What do they say?'

'That it's a wasteland. Like something from a terrible movie.'

'And London's thriving under Pettersen,' I say, which is passive-aggressive, and she knows it. That is our relationship: we bat words between us, we swipe at them, we swat them down.

'Look, I can't say I like the man, but at least the city's alive. And the tourists still come. There are soldiers, yes, whatever, his police guard or whatever they're called, but still. I think there's something about wanting to see the oldest things, you understand? Time has lost all meaning, except for the linear time that was there before. Tourists, idiots to a man, want old buildings. Some evidence of permanence, the man on the radio said.' She sips from her cup, and I watch as her hand trembles, as her teeth bare at the liquid. A leveller. 'I've seen Birdie a few times. I stay back, of course. Don't want to scare the hen before she's laid the egg, as it were.' She turns her attention back to Rhonda. 'Must be galling, I would think? To make it so far and then be set back to where you began.'

'I don't know,' Rhonda says, 'I don't remember.'

'No. I suppose not.' Martine drains her mug. The gasp of a finish. 'You're welcome, of course, to use the house as a hotel. Come and go as you please, there are keys.'

'I still have mine, if you haven't changed the locks,' I say.

'Oh, but I have,' she replies. 'I did that a long, long time ago.'

* * *

My old bedroom is back to being the vagueness of a room that it was when I first arrived: all character I managed to imprint on it having been stripped out. The walls have these marks on them where the sun has baked the colour around the edges of what were once posters and photographs. Square windows that are slightly less pale than the surroundings. The bed feels the same; nobody's stayed here for any length of time. The mattress still conforming to my body, even as I'm a totally different build now. Semi-starved by my life into a body that looks like fitness, at a glance. I lie back, and Rhonda sits on the old chair that I always said I would reupholster and never did, and she stares at the drabness. I pre-empt:

'Martine's removed every trace of me,' I say.

'I didn't want to judge,' she replies. 'This is awful.'

'It's a spare room.'

'Could at least feel like a home.' A hint of her own pain there; thinking about, I am sure, where she grew up, in the factory. 'Show me the rest.'

The house is the same, otherwise. Martine's room, locked; my stepmother's room an archive of memories and old materials. Her bedspread the same, the curtains the same. Damp on the walls, darkness spreading across the pale rose-coloured wallpaper. But the room feels the same. All of her old photographs on the dresser: rows and rows of her family, going back. As long as she remembered them, as long as they were named in her history, they had a place there. It's something I suppose I inherited, if you can inherit without blood: a desire to surround myself with the safety of knowing what came before.

Rhonda noses around the pictures. 'This your stepmother?'

'Yes,' I say. 'And that's my father next to her.'

'So they took photos together?'

'It was a whole other family. They were in the same place until we went to America, for my mother – my real mother – for her work. That's when the affair became harder, and my father . . .' In my memory, he touches his necklace, the knot, and he leans down, his face close to mine, and he says, Do you want one? Then we can be like each other. His hand runs through my hair, the subtle grab of his fingers on the back of my skull; showing me his power, letting me know that I had no choice. Not that I wanted one, my mother was gone, I wanted to be like him, all I wanted was to be like him.

'So he's where you get your hair from,' she says.

'It used to be darker.'

'He Italian?'

'Greek, going way back.' I pick up a photograph of the extended family. Point to my father's mother. 'This is my Yiayia Elena. My grandmother. I didn't really know her, we were much closer with my mum's side.' The old woman in the photograph is dressed in black, but smart with it, classy. Like this chic take on the classic elderly Greek widow. Her face tight, wrinkled. Peaceful, though.

'She's old,' Rhonda says.

'Over a hundred. Hung on in there. Clung on.' I look for another photo, but there's not one. Everything here focused, trimmed. 'Her husband, my grandfather, I never met him. He was one of the astronauts who first discovered the Anomaly. I say astronauts, he was a journalist, a writer. She used to say that he was who I got my creative spark from. And she lived in London, back then. He abandoned her, left and never came home.'

'What a prick,' Rhonda says, then, 'Sorry, maybe he wasn't.'

'No, I think he was. She tried to get him to stay, they fought a lot. She wasn't very happy, I don't think, and he was just really selfish. He saw an opportunity and took it. I don't think he wanted to discover anything, nothing like that: he wasn't a success in his career, and he wanted the glory. She found out later he was also having an affair or something.'

'So lord-king of the pricks, then.'

'Her brother, my great-uncle, if that's a thing, he told Cormac – that was my grandfather's name – he told him that something really bad had happened. Maybe it had, I don't know, that bit's sort of been kept quiet. Nobody to tell me the truth now.'

'Bad like how?'

'Like she hurt herself. He said he wanted to see if Cormac would leave the mission – he hadn't gone to space, when they spoke he was still able to say no – but he didn't. Like, he had that one last chance to prove that he was a good person or whatever, and he blew it. He was selfish, I suppose, totally selfish. Probably that's a genetic thing, he was selfish, and then my dad was so fucking selfish as well.' I feel myself getting het up; I breathe. 'Anyway, it was Cormac's ship that first went into the Anomaly. They went into it and they never came out. At the same time, Yiayia Elena discovered that she was pregnant, she gave birth, married somebody else. My dad never even knew his father. I don't suppose that matters now, in the long term.'

'Oh,' Rhonda says.

'Sometimes I think: well if he did, would that have stopped him becoming who he did? Like, would it have stopped him being radicalized?'

'He probably would've ended up at the Knot churches right with your dad,' Rhonda says. That makes me smile: I've thought the exact same.

'People in my family keeping fucking off into space and not coming back,' I say. 'My grandfather went into space, my mother went into space as well. Then Birdie left me.'

'Yeah, except she's not in space.'

'No,' I say, 'she's not. Or, at least, let's hope not, I'm not following her up there.' I try smiling, and Rhonda tries returning it. But the house feels wrong. A dead woman's room, a house that won't move on. The bones so old and the innards warped to fit them.

'I'm hungry.'

'Me too,' I say. 'Go and ask Martine if she's got sandwiches?'

'I don't want to,' she says, 'you do it.'

'I need a shower. I stink,' I say. I try the smile again. But I can feel something in my mouth: more wetness than I would like, the taste of iron, of chewed metal.

'Yeah, you kinda do,' Rhonda says, and she leaves the room, down the hall, thumping into the walls as if she's a pinball and they're the bumpers, pranging from side to side.

I rush to my stepmother's en suite bathroom, this smaller room that's coated in thick dust, the bathtub as dry as any I have ever seen. I yank the handle on the shower, my hand imprinting the chrome with the red, and the dust starts to congeal immediately, a gunk of it; the water sputtering at first, then gushing out, just in time, just as I find myself in the tub, peeling my clothes off as fast as I can, letting the water hit me, trying to keep myself as clean as I can. Every pore opening, every pore of my self. I swear that I can feel them, like miniature eyelids, craning to the light: then flooding, spitting blood, crying, and thicker now. It was brighter, and now it's darker, darker, thicker. Squeezing out of me, and I scream, but my mouth pulses with it, and I cannot see anything, and I can't hear, or smell, or taste anything but the flood.

I am on the floor of the bath, I am drowning. Choking, and the water runs over me, and it's freezing cold. And all I can think is of when I was young, the sound of the boiler kicking in: a dense vibration you could feel through every part of the house, the pipes humming, but now they're silent, they're so silent.

28

'You look like shit.' Martine's voice is a balm, in its way. A sign that I'm alive still; that I haven't gone back to the house, alone, confused. 'How much are you bleeding?'

'A lot,' I say.

'I'll have to boil the mug you drank from.'

'Surely the booze will kill the virus,' I say.

'Touché,' she says. 'How long?'

'I have no idea. Not long. It's getting worse, it's progressing. Not long.'

'Okay.' She is sitting on the edge of the bed, the bed I slept in as a teenager. I remember my stepmother sitting in that spot. Telling me that it would get better. That you can only miss a person for so long before your brain takes over. Before it rights itself, restores control. Don't worry, lamb. 'You should have told me it was getting worse.'

'I didn't want you to worry.'

'We were on different sides of the world.'

'What would you have done?'

'Well, I'd have known what had happened if we spoke and you were, I don't know. Juvenile, suddenly.'

'I was never juvenile.'

'Spoken like a true teenager.' She puts her hand on my head. Her palm cold against my skin. I remember this; the same touch as my stepmother's. When we were sick, or tired, or simply needed it. Her hand. 'I cleaned you off. There are clothes here, if you want them. Rest up here for a few days.'

'I need to find Birdie,' I say, but Martine shakes her head.

'You really don't,' she says.

'I have to talk to her.'

'Because she left you.'

I don't reply. Martine doesn't say anything more either. She leaves the room, and I stand, slowly, unsteadily. A pile of clothes on the side, and I muss them up, ready for wearing. Bob, my stepmother's partner, was a big man, I think, bigger than I am by possibly half again, there is no way that they will fit; but they do, they are like a glove. And then I realize that they are – were – my father's, of course. They're not Bob's. They're my father's jeans, his faded t-shirt. A tiny hole under the collar where – and I can see it now – where the knot necklace sat, softly rubbing at the cotton.

I walk to the master bedroom, the shrine. The old wooden dresser that's never been nice, that's never been touched up or painted or treated, just old wood that's always looked old but never felt old. The pictures on top, disturbed from where we looked earlier; lines in the dust. I open my father's drawers, the ones that my stepmother kept for him, in the days he came here regularly, in the days where he held his secret second family closer than he held the Anomaly. Clothes, old wallets, boxes of cufflinks that I never saw him wear. And then, finally: his necklaces. A gold chain I remember pulling on as a child, scratching his skin; a silver thing with a saint on a pendant – Christopher? clutching a stick – engraved *May your travels be safe, and bring you home*; and then, finally, the first knot he owned. He died in the last, which was so much more elaborate. The first was a second chain, wound into a ball around the first. The sort of tangle you accidentally make and find yourself incapable of unpicking. I find myself holding it, tight between my hands, pulling on the chain itself. Pulling harder, the metal digging into my skin, not tight enough to cut, not yet, but tight enough that the blood leaves and the skin pales, and the necklace is tighter and tighter; and the knot, somehow, miraculously, starts to unpick itself, starts to pull itself apart. There is give in the chain, and I pull harder; and I mouth, or whisper, 'You fucking idiot,' but I don't know which one of us that it's aimed at. Grit my teeth, and I feel them grind, the chain hardier than I suspected, given how cheap it is – how tarnished, how the metal colour of the gold has started to peel and chip, revealing the shitty chrome underneath – and I pull, again, and the necklace doesn't just break, doesn't just pull apart, it absolutely shatters. Every single link, it seems like, opens itself, the point where they meet splitting, sending every subsequent link down the chain tumbling, all of them at the same time. Hundreds – less, probably, but in the moment – hundreds of pieces of tony fake gold, chain and knot alike, spilling all over the old floorboards, tumbling under the dresser, the bed, my feet. The crunch as I step back in surprise, feeling them. And I want to do more. I want to take everything in the drawers – the drawers themselves – I want to take it all, and destroy it, rip it apart. Leave it wrecked, and broken, pieces that simply cannot ever be put back together. Permanently done, no way to repair it.

The necklace will be enough. I kick the pieces, I pick up some and flush them down the loo, I scatter others.

And I notice, there, in the middle of the floor, the knot. Freed from the necklace, now sitting there. It looks so small. I pluck it up. Examine it; the same chain, the same cheap workmanship. A lack of care.

An icon in place of actual belief.

I plop it onto my tongue, and I dry swallow it. Feel it in my throat, my gullet. Imagine it hitting my stomach, where the acid will eat it, or I will shit it out, or it will stay there, dying right there along with me.

My mother saying, Your stomach is all knotted. When I was so young, and I would get this worried belly, this ache, this gnawing. Your stomach is all knotted; you need to let whatever it is you're holding inside you go. Let it out—

I gag, but nothing comes.

Stay down, stay down.

29

'The fuck is this place?' Rhonda asks. She means Waitrose, which is back to how it was in my mind, sort of, in this roundabout way. A facsimile of a place that once existed, a chain of shops, supermarkets, aimed at the fairly well-to-do, people who liked to buy nice things, who liked to believe that their food came from better places. To tell themselves that they were being environmentally kind, to the air and the seas and the animals. A pat on the back when they packed their food into their own bags, rather than single-use disposables. Now, people are here, milling about. Not many of them, and it's not the same shop: it's been beaten about, turned into something that feels distinctly last-century, fruit and veg and the butcher's counter like some sort of market. Less super. Everybody here wearing khaki or beige, the telltale sign of Pettersen's curious uniform. Nothing gaudy, nothing too big or showy. Slow fashion, made by hand here. People who have used their time to create something of subtle understatement.

They glance at Rhonda and myself, because we're not in the uniform. We're more like tourists here, which is probably right.

'This is where we used to get food,' I say. 'When I was a child. Didn't you go to somewhere like this?'

'We had Walmart, and we grew the rest,' she says.

'In the desert?'

'Hydroponics.'

'Oh, of course.'

'I mean, we got a lot from Walmart. Lots of mouths to feed, my mom used to say.' She looks at the aisles. Stares down them: half-stacked, the lights too bright. Gigantic freezers chugging in the corners. 'Wasn't like this, I gotta tell you.'

'Okay,' I say, because I don't know what else to say. I am nervous; my fingernail picking at that bit of skin on my thumb. It's sore. I can feel a nascent infection just below the skin, the bubbling of it before the body decides whether to just deal with it or not. Red soreness, the pressure of it swelling a little.

I hand Rhonda one of the photographs. There were only two in the house, both from when we first were together. My stepmother had them, in frames, but they were in a cupboard, I had to root around to find them. I know whose choice that was. 'Explain that she doesn't look like this any more.'

'Unless she's reset.'

'She didn't. She can't have. We were at home when it happened. We were in bed, we missed it.'

'I can't believe you slept through it.'

'Well, yeah. I woke up, and Birdie was standing at the foot of the bed, and I just knew something was wrong. Something had changed.' I can remember her face; how sad she looked. 'We should look for her.'

'Where do we begin?'

'Let's split up. I'll do the exits, you ask the people working at the counters.' She looks over, but she's quiet, silent even.

Her face absolutely still. 'Are you okay?' I ask her, and I follow her gaze, as she says something, probably that she's fine, or that I should look, but I am pre-emptive; and I see her, then.

'I don't think we need to split up,' Rhonda says. Birdie, at one of the checkouts, packing food into a small wicker bag. Birdie, but it takes me a moment to parse her, because this is surely not what she looks like now?

I have spent years, decades, imagining her face: the lines that would appear, that would come, that would change her, dressing her in a different skin, the skin of a woman who couldn't defy time, who couldn't change the path of it. A beacon of linearity in a world robbed of it. Something of an artist's eye: imagining what those changes might look like; how those small lines, creases, crow's feet, would develop. How her smile would ensure their delicate spread; how her laugh might make those lines around her mouth even more ingrained.

But she is young. She is young. It is like looking in a portal: closer in age to the woman who left me that day than the age she should be now. I have pictures, photographs; and paintings that I made myself, my hand – my eyes – recognizing her, seeing her, recreating her.

She does not look how I expected her to look. She's younger. Not much, but she's not as old as I am. Forty, maybe.

She doesn't see me. She waits as an older man scans her food. He's in PPE – risk-averse, don't come too close, see how far I have made it already, don't risk it – in PPE that covers his hands and face, plastic like cling film. Handling the food, bagging it for her, not really engaging. Birdie's staring at the food as he bags it, and then she reaches into her pocket, pulls out notes – old plastic British notes – and she pays for the food, chicken and vegetables and pulses in small tubs, and she moves away from the counter.

'Is that her?'

'Yes,' I say, as she sees me. She doesn't stop walking, she smiles as if she might recognize me, as if we are people who pass each other on the street, that's the entirety of our relationship, people who know each other, who smile and nod, How are you, I am well, we do not need more than that. It isn't until she's a few feet away that she realizes, and understands. An honest mistake, because why should I be here? Here, now?

She doesn't run. This isn't some movie. She stops walking, and she stares at me, and then down at Rhonda, and then back at me. I see her hand: clutching the hand of a young girl, ten or eleven years old, maybe.

But this is about Birdie.

'Jesus Christ, Theo,' she says. Her voice the softest bullet. A memory that sounds exactly as it should. A tone that burrows deep inside me, that carves a path right through me. Into my guts, my soul. 'What are you doing here?'

'I came to find you,' I say.

'No,' she says, 'don't say that.'

'I did. I don't— You're young.'

'Don't, Theo, not here.'

'You're young. How are you young?' Rhonda's hand is on my arm then. Her hand saying, Come on, come on back, wherever you're going.

'You shouldn't be here,' Birdie says, and she starts to walk, and I follow her. 'Go home, Theo,' she barks.

'I came to find you,' I say, I hear myself saying, 'I was worried about you.'

'There is literally nothing to worry about.'

'I—'

'How dare you. How dare you.'

People are staring. I don't mind. Rhonda's let go of my arm, she's standing a little way back herself. She doesn't like the attention, neither do I, neither will Birdie. People, these people. The people she smiles at, that she nods at, have a nice day. 'I had to come,' I say, 'I needed to know. I needed to know, Birdie.'

My mother left me. I didn't know why, I tell myself that I did nothing wrong, that she understood she needed to try and save the world. But still she left, still she never came back. My father left, because he was so weak, so swayed, and his priorities put me below his fantasies. Then Birdie left: one day, disappeared, and I was alone.

Alone with just that fucking Knot.

'I left you, Theo. I left you, I came here.'

'I need to know why,' I say.

'I told you,' she says. 'I told you, I said, so many times. We were so unhappy,' she says, but she – this Birdie, this version of her – she cannot possibly remember that. She cannot know that, she is too young.

'We argued, Theo—'

No.

'We had an argument, I told you I was leaving.'

No, no, no.

'We didn't,' I say. This isn't me forgetting; this isn't time erasing a narrative from my mind. This is her. 'What did I do?' I ask her. Now, I ask this Birdie. I don't need her to tell me what's happened: she's come back, not once or twice, but multiple times; and she's seen the message, and she's believed her own lie. That's how close she was to being able to do it; even if she couldn't quite pull the plug. 'Why did you leave?'

'Because you couldn't move on,' she says. 'You didn't listen, it was like you couldn't hear me. When we spoke, Theo, you were so selfish. That's the word. You couldn't move past where we were, or what happened. The Knot arrived, and you couldn't see what was in front of your face. Directly there, Theo!'

'I couldn't move past our daughter dying. That's why you left me.' It kicks at me. 'How did it happen?'

'I came here. Time passed, I got older. I wanted children, I wanted a future, and staying with you, well that wasn't one. I'd been robbed of a future, Theo. You were stuck, trapped or by choice, I don't know, but I couldn't stand it. So I left, I came here. And then I was too old, when it was my time— So I did what I had to do.'

'You killed yourself? You came back?'

She beams, a smile I remember. 'Of course. I sent myself notes, letters. I started a correspondence, with a woman who didn't yet exist. I wrote them, put them in a box. Arranged it, on the side: *Open this when you wake up.* I was awake when the Anomaly happened. You were asleep. I was awake, staring out at the darkness, and I could see that wall, outside our house. That wall, just this slab of concrete. It meant nothing, it was just a wall; but in that moment, it meant everything. I painted the graffiti on the wall, so that I would see it when I got out of bed. Because I wanted to leave, Theo, but I needed to find the strength.'

I picture the graffiti on the wall opposite my back gate.
Time means nothing.
You are free.
Don't look back.

'I put the box where it needed to be, right by my bedside, and I did it. In the bathroom, I did it, I assume, that's what the letters to myself said I was going to do; and then I opened my eyes for the first time in this loop. I saw the words on the wall, and the box was at my feet, and I read the letters to myself. I left that night; before you could wake up and persuade me to stay. You were always persuasive, always so gentle, and that is such a lure.'

You are free.

Not a message to the city, or to me. A message from Birdie, to herself.

Don't look back.

'I was gone before you even woke up, before you realized what had happened. I knew, down inside. You have to move, and you have to keep moving. Don't you see? The Knot, it provides a gift, Theo. It's stasis, but stasis can be used. Should be used. We are stuck in place, so you have to keep moving in place. That's what we are proving to it: that we're worthy of moving. It has given us time. It has given us chances. It has given us everything we needed. Rebecca died, and she could not come back, and you couldn't move forward.'

'She died.'

'And you couldn't move forward,' she says again.

'Why did you come back here?' I ask.

'I knew it. It felt safe to me, that was one of the reasons. And then I met Josie's father, and, well, here we are.' She shuts her eyes, this languid gesture of false deep thought. 'I have seen so much, Theo. We all understand.'

I feel as if I am dying. A different sort of dying. Heat death of my universe. 'And now you follow the Knot.'

'Don't call them that. Ashley doesn't call them that.'

'Ashley?' Pettersen. Ashley Pettersen. First name terms.

'He's such a good man, such a wise man.' She looks around her, around us. 'This is his city, Theo. He rebuilt it, and he's in control of it. The people here, we understand what he offers, and what he – and the Anomaly – provides. It's time, Theo. Nobody ever has enough time, and now? Now it's all we have.'

'You didn't believe in the Knot,' I say.

'No, you didn't. I was always open. And now, I know the reality of it.' Her smile, placating. Patronizing. 'Because of the Knot, I met Ashley. Because of the Knot, I was reborn; and because of the Knot, we made Josie.' She looks to the girl standing near. Her daughter. 'I see now that my cycle is a gift. It's my way of being able to prove I am worthy of progression. I birthed her, and here we both are.'

I glance at Rhonda. She's blinking more than she ought. Holding back. 'You're with Pettersen,' I say. I stare at the girl, trying to see Rebecca; but she's not Rebecca. Familiarity, in what she got from Birdie; but after that it's different.

'We're all with Ashley,' she says. 'All of us, he's the father of our new mankind,' as if that's the most normal thing in the world: to pursue a cult leader across the world, to have his baby. Her and however many hundreds of women. Thousands. Could that be possible? 'We're a part of the many blessed. He loves her, and he loves me. We have everything here, Theo. We have time, Theo. We have endless time. The best parts, we relive them. We revel in them. We change ourselves. I was older, but I wanted a child, so I sent myself back again.'

I interrupt her. 'Again? When again?'

'Ten years ago. I timed it perfectly: the same box of things to tell me of my future here, but better. Even more persuasive. I didn't even need the words on the wall, the graffiti, to establish myself. I came to Los Angeles, I wrote myself a letter, and I left it; and then I died, right there, moments before I reappeared. It is the most beautiful experience. Transcendent.'

'This is insanity,' I said.

'It's natural. It's all natural! When Josie wants to, we will send her back. When I decide that it is time, I will send myself back again. We document everything, you should see it, Theo. All of the hours, all of the hundreds of thousands of hours. All of us.'

Rhonda's voice trembles. 'You – you all kill yourselves.'

'If we need to, if we want to. It's a personal choice, this is all about personal choice. Who are we hurting? Nobody, not if we choose it, not if we are not being hurt. Think about what you miss, the things that happen to us, that we want to relive; and then, well, we have the chance to have those moments again. I've been thinking: we will both die, soon, and we'll relive it all. Josie's first time walking!' She touches her daughter's head. 'Imagine being able to hold Rebecca again for the first time,' she says. I feel dismal, as if I am being beaten from the inside. My body wanting to fold in on itself. I feel absolutely fucking bereft. 'It'll bring us closer, and closer; and we'll all have so much time.'

'You're sick,' Rhonda says, 'this is all so sick.'

Birdie stares at her. Her eyes sliding to that half-closed style they did – they do – when she's wanting to prove a point. As if she is so tired that this can't possibly be anything but the final clause in the argument. 'This isn't a sickness. It's rolling with the gifts that we have been given.' She steps close to Rhonda then, and she uses her hand to push Josie forward as well. An advance front. 'You tell her she doesn't have the right to her childhood again. Look? She's happy.'

'She doesn't look very happy,' Rhonda says. And she's right: the girl doesn't seem to be much of anything to me, barely reacting, staring as we speak but as if the conversation has nothing to offer her.

I think about my father when I was a child. The border-line abuse of forcing me to wear that necklace, to listen to those sermons. To listen to Pettersen.

And I see Rhonda, shaking: her own childhood gone thanks to people who wanted something for her that she had no choice in. A lack of freedom.

Rhonda said to me that she was evidence we can change.

It's harder than that, I think. Sometimes, the world doesn't want us to.

Birdie stares at Rhonda for too long. Doesn't take her eyes off her. She speaks, though, to me: 'Theo. Go home. I don't care what you wanted from this trip, but you won't find it. Go home, go home.' She starts to walk away. 'Get out of here, this place isn't for you. I don't know where is.'

She walks past us, out of the shop. Away from us, fast as she can, little girl behind her, clutching onto her hand as it holds the wicker shopping bag. I feel my breath, I hear my breath. Through my nose, the only way I can control myself. My body doing it for me. I stare, I stand there and stare, but Rhonda doesn't. She follows, and fast, rushing after Birdie, and I hear her, shouting almost: 'He came to find you! He's dying, you get that? You understand that?'

They're outside, then, on the street. And through the window, the glass that runs the length of the building, I see them outside, as I struggle for my breath, even as I can hear it, as I can feel it. I watch Birdie turn, pushing Josie back against the window of the shop, keep her out of harm's way, and I watch Rhonda approach, and Birdie grabs her arm, and she says something I don't hear, that I will never know, and she shakes Rhonda's arm, Get off me. Rhonda says something else, and Birdie walks, and Rhonda reaches for her.

Birdie shoves her. Hard, her arm this lash of tensed muscle. Rhonda falls backwards, to the road, into the road.

The car that hits her isn't going fast. It's not racing, it's not doing anything it shouldn't. It's just there, suddenly, and so is she: two bodies filling the same space, the same physical space. Rhonda thumps, tumbles across the ground. A tumble-weed weighed down by bones, by flesh. I think I scream. I race, and Birdie's standing at the side of the road staring at Rhonda's body – her body, not moving; and when does a person become a body? When is the person gone? Is it before you even know? – and Rhonda's body is perfectly still, and there's no blood, no terribly bent limbs. No horror but the sight of her there.

I'm outside, I'm past Birdie, I'm at Rhonda's side. Her eyes shut, as if somebody's already closed them: two fingers, softly brushing them down, as if that somehow might mean she has found peace.

Birdie shuts her eyes. She raises her hands to the sky, and she shakes her head, a smile on her face. Her daughter does the same, and other people here: the staff from the shop coming out to the street, to intentionally stop staring at Rhonda. To say, Take her, take her. 'Let her begin anew,' Birdie says, her voice quiet, but everybody else is quieter.

I do not blink. I feel for a pulse, and there is one; and I scream for an ambulance, I shout for somebody to get me one. Nobody moves, they stand there, palms skyward, and I scream it again.

'She isn't dead,' I say, and Birdie speaks to me, eyes open for one moment, that fucking slitted stare:

'Let her go,' she says, but I can't, I don't, won't.

There's no ambulance. Nobody wants to help her, because she should just come back. That's easier than helping somebody, easier than saving them: to assume that they will simply have another go at it.

So I stare at her, in case she dies, because I don't want her to leave yet; and everybody around me lifts their hands to the heavens and waits, waits, waits for me to give up.

30

The biggest problem with the Anomaly – outside of the death, the murder, the violence, the terror and pain, the cycling, the lack of anything resembling a true death, a lack of actual peace – the biggest problem was the misinformation. The lies. The same problem as with the bleeding sickness, as with everything in the years before those happened to us. The scientists were first against the wall, it seemed. Their importance a target on their backs, their fronts, their heads and necks. Strung up, purposely infected. Factories across the world, in Brussels and Detroit and Beijing and Hanoi and Vancouver, all barricaded, the virus being released inside their walls. The scientists left there to die; but then never leaving, of course, because the Anomaly arrived, and they began their cycles, trapped in the massive grey boxes, days at best, over and over, inside those walls. The factual vacuum was enormous, in those early days; and as others fell, as governments collapsed, as people lost their ability to rationalize, misinformation ruled. Chaos fell: people scrambled, as if they could run away from this thing, this achingly slow bowling ball that was advancing towards us, as we advanced towards it. It moved slow enough that we should have died; and one theory in the years afterwards – that I heard over and over, that might have been true, that there is no way to disprove – is that it was so slow that we were in it, and our orbit meant we were crushed against the inner wall of the Anomaly as we carried on with our orbit. That it's a semi-permeable membrane, and we can enter but not exit. A whole planet of people crushed, unable to remember that crushing because of the nature of the reset; but that presumably happened, over and over and over. That's the theory. If you start to think too hard about the theories, your head hurts. Because there's something unexplainable, and it will only ever be unexplainable, and nobody will ever know the truth.

My mother's co-workers, from up on the New International Space Station, they arrived in the days before the Anomaly swallowed the planet. Only a few of them: a medic, a security officer, an assistant to the prick who ran the operation. The prick who took them up there, who knew more than he was letting on—

It doesn't matter, it doesn't matter. They came down, and I don't know what they expected: a parade, or crowds, but there was nothing. A camera crew, but it wasn't even reported there and then, because there were other things to worry about. To concern ourselves with. The world wasn't the same as when they went up there.

And they knew, this is the worst part. The trust was kept from us. There were rumours, but they only ever felt like rumours, not like things that could actually be true, because we didn't have the tools to understand them. We didn't have the evidence. So: time is different in the Anomaly? The rules of death are different in the Anomaly? The Anomaly is alive, somehow? Rumours, the sort of conspiracy that fuelled division and hatred. That fuelled the Knot, of course, that helped it to grow. Those rumours, those tenets of their faith: that it would arrive, and restore us anew. Die, that it might bring you back. Remember the stories of Jesus; surely, the Anomaly is the true God.

Killing Christians in their churches. Killing Muslims, Jews, atheists, everybody alike. Bombs, the virus in water bottles and aerosols and small glass capsules, cracked like stink bombs. Doors barricaded, people locked inside. Left to become infected.

'There is no chance for repentance', Pettersen was quoted as saying. The signs were there, this is not about conversion. It is about understanding through demonstration. They will die, they will be reborn; and that will be incontrovertible proof.

His face on televisions, before the networks went cold. His voice on casts, his eyes on billboards. His hands, wrapped around the world, squeezing the life to nearly dark until the day that the Anomaly came.

31

Rhonda coughs, and I leap from my chair. Her tube was removed a few hours ago, her breathing has been stable. Her skin is a pale that you never see in the healthy; a pale I know from my own, from wiping down myself in bathroom mirrors. In the six weeks I've been here in the hospital with her, I have done it four times. The last time was yesterday. The time before, a week ago. It is coming, it is coming for me, I know. An acceleration.

But this moment is not about me. It is about Rhonda, and she needs water, so I fetch her a glass, and I hold it for her like I might have seen people do, two hands as she sips, there, steady, have you got it. Sit up a little, move the pillow for her. There are no nurses to do this for her, no doctors if I press a button. When I got her here, carrying her from that awful street, people frozen, their eyes looking away from her, muttering that she will come back, I stumbled upon the few medical professionals left here, people who still want to help the hurt, the dying. People who saw your life as sacred; who took an oath.

They did what they were going to do, they got her here. Now, as one of the nurses told me, it's up to her.

And me, I suppose. 'There,' I say, 'not too fast,' because she's guzzling the water, dribbling it, and I start to say something but I hold myself back.

'What?' she starts to ask, but there's no other sentence there. There's a lying back, her eyes shutting, her lips in this motion that's nearly speaking, until these wisps of breath sneak out instead. And she's asleep, and I am back to waiting.

She wakes me, then, much later, asking me where she is. I calm her, and I explain – because in this moment, she's absolutely conscious, and absolutely alert, as if she's not been in here at all, as if she wasn't critically injured – I explain that we're in the old hospital, that there's nobody else here. That I'm looking after her, that she's okay. It was touch and go for a while, I say, but I don't tell her the scale: about the need for transfusions, how hard it was to get blood, the need for emergency surgery, for the coma that they induced and couldn't promise me they could drag her out of on the other the side.

I don't tell her any of that, because it doesn't matter. It doesn't help her to know.

But she's awake now, and for a while. Hours. We sit, and I tell her: that I've been here, looking after her, making sure she's okay – I don't say, making sure that she doesn't die alone, but I'm sure it's implied – that she's okay, doesn't need anything, doesn't hurt. Painkillers, when she seemed like she was struggling: the face scrunching up, even as she wasn't conscious. Her pulse racing.

She tries to stand, and I help her, and the act of getting

to her feet is enough, wipes her out, back to laying, back to sleep. And then I sleep on that chair, a chair that's imprinted on me as much as I'm imprinted on it.

We walk around the outside of the hospital: a riverside bank that's been kept tidy and clean and orderly by a group called, per the little bronze sign fastened to the building's wall, *The Friends of the Riverbank*. Little flowers, and herbs, this smell of summer from when I was a child, in my grandmother's garden: oregano, thyme, herbs that grow in dry environments. The river itself perfectly still. A turbine fails to churn on the south bank, by the old power station. Rhonda walks back and forth, the slowest pacing.

'I didn't know if I did the right thing,' I say, eventually. We haven't spoken about her death yet, or her lack of it.

'Of course you did,' she says. 'I don't want to go back there.'

'That's what I thought, but I didn't know.'

'There should be a thing. Like a ticket you can carry, a card. Like *Do Not Resuscitate*.'

'*Save my life please*.'

'*Do not let me loop*.' She grins at me. 'You did the right thing.' Then, looking at the river – at the perfectly still turbine, no wind, no movement in the water at all – looking out, she carries on. 'What do you want?'

'When I die?'

'Yeah. I figure I'll be with you. I mean, look, do you want me to try and save you? Keep you alive?'

'I don't know if you'll be able to. When it happens, I mean.'

'Okay.'

'You can try, but I think when it's my time, it's my time.'

'So you'll just give up?'

'No,' I say, 'Jesus! You're so antagonistic. Even when you've just nearly died.' I smile, trying to get one from her, but I can't. 'I just mean: I think it's out of my hands. I've stayed alive this long, and I don't know why. When I die, it'll be time. I won't know why, and it won't matter. It'll be time.'

'You ever wonder if the Anomaly's kept you alive?' she asks.

'No,' I say, but that's a lie, and I immediately correct it. 'I have, maybe. I want to buy into those crackpot theories that it's here to save us. I don't know.'

'What do they say?'

'It's all because of the sun. Before it got here, you know how hot it was? It was unbearable. It must have been, where you lived.'

'It was. It was like, you didn't go out. People died if they were outside for too long.'

'And whole parts of the world were utterly uninhabitable. And then the Anomaly came, and because of it, because of whatever it is, the sun's been dampened a little. Just a little.' I glance up at it: there, always there. I remember watching an eclipse with my mother when I was a kid, through this little device we made out of cardboard, to keep our eyes safe.

Now, you can just look at it.

'So, you know, maybe. Maybe. But then everybody's died.'

'We're still here,' Rhonda says. 'But you will die.'

'Yes,' I say. 'I think I will.'

She breathes in deeply, and she holds it. One, two, three; then out through her mouth. 'I want to go back inside now,' she says, so I take her arm, help her up the stairs, to the ward, empty as it is; to the room, where I turn down the bed for her, as if this is a hotel, and she settles in to sleep, and I sit, as much a part of the room as any of the furnishings.

*　　*　　*

Days and days we don't see anybody, living off tinned foods I prepare in the kitchen: a sprawling canteen of chrome that is somehow both absolutely sight-clean and also immeasurably dusty. Surfaces all wiped down, but the edges caked. I warm tinned spaghetti, I defrost and then try to not burn meals on trays in the ovens. A trove of pudding cups, all with use-by dates that have happened but that also, in their own curious way, haven't come to pass yet; and I remember Birdie saying, when we were eking out our own supplies, that those dates were something that the agencies had to use, rather than anything representative. That they weren't even real, that there simply needed to be something to prevent the public thinking that the preservatives made the foods somehow immortal. Because immortality was something to be afraid of; we are meant to decay, as are all things. But you opened those tins or those pudding cups, and inside the contents were just as they would have been decades ago. Somehow.

'Can we have something else?' Rhonda asks one day. She's healing: she winces less, her bruises are faded. The scratches are new skin now.

'Like what?' I ask. She shrugs.

'Like anything. A burger, oh man, a burger. I would murder for a cheeseburger.'

'Okay,' I say, and I start to head out. I'm nervous: I am waiting for a bleed, on edge that it's about to happen. I have been for a few days now.

'You'll be okay,' she says.

'Okay,' I repeat. And I walk through the corridors, following the green line to reception, then the convergent rainbow of lines to the exit, heavy automated doors that aren't automated any more, that require a crowbar in them to prise them open. A chair wedged between them when you're outside. I should drain the hydraulic fluid, really. A hole in the tank, let it seep out.

The streets are quiet. The river's quiet. Nobody around here, really. I walk towards where there used to be a large train station, but it's quiet now. No trains in and out of London. But there were shops there, and a market, just across from it. I walk there, and I find the shop, the burger place I remember. It's different now, I'm sure, like in New York, like everywhere. Branded but independent. A franchise without money behind it. A boy behind the counter, sixteen or seventeen. Reading something, and he doesn't look up, but I'm the only one in here, so I clear my throat. Order three burgers, a large fries. Out of fries, so an extra burger, please. He nods, and walks around the counter, starts to cook them.

'Where's everybody else?' I ask him.

'What do you mean?'

'There are people,' I say. 'There should be people.'

'All fucked off, didn't they,' he says. 'To Ecuador or whatever.'

'Ecuador.' All I do is repeat, I think. Repeat what somebody else has said, desperate for clarity, when I don't quite understand.

'Where the guy is. Was. The dead guy, the climber.' He watches as my face doesn't shift. As it's clear to him that I don't know what he's talking about. 'You been in a hole? The climber man, Ames or something, whatever his name was. He died up there, didn't come back. They think it's leaving, so everybody's gone there, like, I don't know. Pay homage or shit. He climbed, he fell, he died. He didn't come back. They all looked away, his body just stayed there.' The

272

sizzle of the patty on the grill. I watch him slice a bun. 'You want ketchup?'

I race back, small brown bag in hand, to the hospital: past the bit where the walls are stained yellow and won't get better, past the collapsed entrance to the old train station, the coffee shop, the bicycle shop – that appears to be in business, if not closed today – past all the shops, to the entrance. The chair slightly warped under the strain, but it won't buckle. I know that it won't. Through reception, the rainbow exploding into the lines that race off in every direction. The purple line: past elevators and stairwells, past waiting rooms and cancer wards, past a second security desk. Down, past the kitchens, a staircase that only goes down at the very back of the hospital, no way up from here; to a door that I have chained shut, that I have locked with multiple bike locks, heavy-duty, unbreakable really. The combination in every one, the same as all of my combinations, a reminder; and then the door, heaved open, the tape I lined it with to block out sound really sticking today. Must be the heat, the adhesive. Through to another room, big metal doors. The morgue, kept cold for the bodies, except the fridges don't have power any more, all still sealed, no sense in opening. I don't want to know what's inside. And another door, an office, and a door that needs a code to enter, but 1-2-3-4 worked, of course it worked, and so I changed it, as if it was a combination to a hotel safe. I beep in my code, and the door clicks open, and he looks up at me: this desperate pleading in his eyes, a dog so happy to see his master. I have taken everything from this room, every single thing, every shelf and book and bit of fabric, and all of his clothes. He doesn't have the strength to bludgeon himself.

I read a story once, when I was young, about how pigs

will commit suicide. In a slaughterhouse, or in the bit before the slaughterhouse, when they're basically shoved into this small space, left there suffering, being fed to fatten them up, eating to stay alive. And they all, one day, seemed to make this choice: to stop eating. Let themselves starve. Whether they communicated that to each other, or it just sort of happened, they all stopped. So the owners of the factory forced them to eat, first holding their mouths open, then injecting them with replacements and substitutes. Giving them injections to fuel their hunger. And so the pigs took another option: they started killing themselves, and each other. Tearing at each other, ripping at necks, trying to trample each other to death. Hooves smashing into thick skin. But that was also unacceptable, so the factory owners split them off, building them all tiny pens instead of the one massive encampment. All alone, being fed, the pigs had one choice: they all beat their heads against the walls of their pens, one, two, three, smashing their faces, their skulls, against the walls or the fences, finding anything that they could to end their existence. To leave their bodies there, dead, useless.

Except, of course, when the factory owners found them, they weren't useless at all. They were still, in that terrible moment, meat.

I have taken all of his things. He doesn't have it in him: to bow his head, to stand back, to charge at the walls and to allow his skull to connect, to crack, to bleed. He is too weak to say no to food, too desperate to live to allow himself to fade. I wouldn't force feed him, I couldn't. He does it for me, because he can't not. He got hungry enough, and the need takes over.

He looks up at me as I open the door. Does that little scurry thing, where he pushes backwards, close to the wall.

I have never hurt him. I have never laid a hand on him, but he acts as if this is just some great act of abuse. And I explain to him, again, as I have seemingly had to do every day, over and over again.

'Don't be scared,' I say to Pettersen. 'I only want you to live.'

32

I did not know if Rhonda would survive, that's the first thing to understand. I wanted her to, and she wanted to, I know – she fought, that's what the doctors said – we both wanted her to, but I knew it was unlikely. I needed something to do, to occupy my days. The hospital had an imminent room, where families were taken to be given the bad news that they were inevitably going to be given, and there was a small shelving unit in there, stuffed with books. All of a type: either novels to take your mind off the situation at hand, novels that you'd heard of but not read; or they were there for the supposed betterment of your thoughts, of your mind. It was the latter that I read. I worked my way through them all: a book about the positivity of grief, written by somebody who clearly had not endured their fair share; a book about mental health betterment, by a writer with no qualifications or medical training, offering plaintive purple prose in lieu of actual medical advice; a book called *Buck*, about a man with cancer who overcame it through simple acts of positivity and the medicine he seemed unwilling to credit with his cure. And then, when they were all done, Pettersen's final books: one, pre-pandemic, called *Let It Be*, and one published during the pandemic, called *Let It Go*. I read them with rising self-disgust – as if the other books hadn't been enough, but then these two – self-disgust and self-hatred, that I was putting myself through this. But more than that: hatred of this man, this wreck of a human. Whose message seemed to be that we should give up, from the start. That what will be will be, like some old song, that there is no point in trying to change our lives, our lot. His hatred, his bile, for those who had worked, who had moved heaven and earth to adapt their lives to be what they needed them to be. Across lines of genre, of sex, across prejudices, jobs and environments, countries and borders and political beliefs, families and loved ones and enemies. I read these thinly veiled diatribes from this man who believed that we are who our pasts say we are; that there's no room for change at all. This man who bought into the rumours of the Anomaly before it arrived, who placed all his chips on it being some sort of gateway to a state of ascendance, and then won big when it was; who then decided that his life, his deaths, his rebirths, they were the gift he had been granted. Wives and children and a lack of repercussions. And in his writing, this sense that he was chosen, somehow. That he knew it was coming, that he was the one blessed with foresight.

And what is a messiah if not a leader, blessed with the knowledge to bring their people from the darkness, into the light.

I hated it. Every page, every word. I would read it, as distraction from my concerns about Rhonda. In her room, sitting there, waiting, terrified. Changing the bag the doctors fitted to her; giving her the drugs they told me I had to give her, to stave off infection. Back to the pages, the terrible pages. Drawing the view from the window. Drawing Rhonda's medical equipment; the point where the cannula entered her hand, the little tape over it, the small blackened glue-marks from the previous piece of tape. Drawing her eyes, fluttering, half open. Drawing myself: in the mirror, in that tiny adjacent bathroom, thinking that I should leave myself something, some evidence of how I looked, in case I reset. Something for me to find; for Rhonda to give me when I returned.

In the back of *Let It Go*, he mentioned Birdie. He wrote a list in lieu of his acknowledgements. I always skipped them, every book, I never wanted to know anything beyond where the text ended; but I read them here. A long list: *The people that I could not have survived without.* And Birdie's name was right there, seventy-something names into the list. That's how important she was to him, that was it. And then, at the bottom: *For now.*

For now.

I was incensed. Furious.

And I knew, in that moment, that I needed to see him. To talk to him. In person.

There was, as far as I was concerned, only one way to find him. His biography – . . . *lives in London* – told me nothing I didn't know already, which left me with detective work. Detectives start by tailing, and I knew where Birdie and her daughter shopped. I told Rhonda I would be back, I left her a note in case she woke up, and I left. I expected, honestly, that she wouldn't be there when I returned: that she would have gone, stolen back by the Anomaly, back to a situation she desperately wanted to escape. I took a bag with me, water and food in case I had a long time to wait, and chloroform from the hospital store.

I think I always knew what was going to happen.

Birdie wasn't watching for me, or even on her guard. I think she assumed I would have left, that Rhonda died and I quit whatever mission it was that I had been on. I saw her and Josie, and I stood on the far side of the street and watched as they shopped, as they filled their bags; and then I followed them, out of the shop, down the street, turning up towards the houses, away from the high street. The crunch of the produce in their bags as they walked, listening for it so that I could stay far enough away from them. Listening to them as they walked, Josie not much of a talker, Birdie more than making up for it. Talking about where they had just been, the things that they purchased. Talking about what Ashley would like, about the food he'll eat, the things he will say to them. Some predicted pats on their heads. I followed them, staying nearly a full block back from them. Wearing a coat I found in the hospital lost property, a hat, even in the heat; holding back, using doorways if I needed them, or waiting at the corners while Josie dawdled, and her mother said, in a tone I absolutely recognized, 'I wish you'd hurry up.' Repeatedly said it, as if that was her default when Josie became distracted.

And then they turned off, up the stairs to this incredible mansion block by the Albert Hall, this stretching row of houses and flats, all joined together, curving around the roads, Mars-red brick and white window frames. The windows all flung open, sounds of children and laughter and talking from inside, the sonorous spread of men's voices cutting through. I looked through the windows, to see walls taken down inside: long stretches of corridor, going on and on and on.

So I picked a door, and I tried it, and it opened. Children running in the distance, and those voices, those men's voices coming from upstairs. I walked through, white walls, marked up with pictures drawn by what must have been hundreds of children: a modern nuclear family, Pettersen-style, all of these faces, hundreds of them. So many mummies, and then there the man himself was: arms wide open, dressed in white – like me, like my uniform of hospital-rescued clothes – dressed in white short sleeves, khaki trousers, his face smiling, unerringly, in every single drawing. I walked through, past these. The murmurs coming through the floorboards. The sonorous sound of them. I took the stairs, an empty staircase. The thumping of feet across the entire place; and then a window, through which I could see the gardens, all divisions removed, every child running, playing, trampolining. Sandpits and bicycles and hide and seek. Up the stairs some more, and I saw the mothers of these children: all those women, dressed the same, in nice skirts and nice blouses and nice cardigans, as if there was a uniform, a rack of clothes for them to choose from in the mornings. Those that weren't playing were exercising, preparing to run, or many of them doing yoga, stretched out on the lawn. Smiling, and happy, and I thought, in that moment, of how Pettersen had turned this into a playground, and this was all his. Some return to a way that had long since gone.

I thought of Rhonda, her car. Saving me, and not wanting thanks for it.

It's just what you do, isn't it.

I went to the next corridor, and the voices were louder here. I could hear them arguing about something. Not the heated argument of near-violence, but a disagreement of opinion. Outside the door, then – a massive door, double

280

doors, varnished – outside the door I waited, and I listened, as they debated, that was the tone, about art, and philosophy, and life. Debated. These men, Pettersen and his friends, debating some bullshit about whatever the fuck they were talking about. 'Does the creation of something really entitle the bearer to ownership of the idea?' one of them wittered. And then Pettersen's voice:

'Now, now, I think there's really two different arguments happening here. First, you're arguing that creation stands extant from the seed, which is simply not the case. And then you, Dee, you're arguing that creation of something means the absolute entitlement, even if somebody else has commissioned said creation? What about if it's you, if you, on another go-round, make something, and it outlasts you? I mean, you call your children your children, do you not?' Laughter among them all. 'My children are my children, there's no sense of loss, I don't feel? No sense of othering in my parental rights. And I created them, didn't I?'

I waited there and listened to them, the argument spiralling, on and on. And then, eventually, they agreed to disagree, but in such a way that it was clear Pettersen had won, and the doors clicked to open. I rushed into a side room, a small bathroom, shutting the door behind me. Suddenly gutless, no plan; and I listened as the men walked off, still talking. Down the stairs, the clip of smart shoes on the wood. I left, thinking to rush out, past the room, past the double doors.

Pettersen was standing there, back to the doors. Leaning over a book he was noting something in, a fountain pen in his hand. Expensive, the sort you don't see any more. I took the chloroform out from my pocket, this tiny bottle, and I tipped some onto a cloth, like I had seen them do on TV shows.

He heard me, and he turned, and he saw me. Didn't clock what I was doing. Just stared at my face.

I expected recognition. As if we had had any sort of history. But he didn't know that he had been there in my life since my father first brought his pamphlet home. His necklaces, his iconography, his words, his books. And then all over the television, the news, his idiot prophecies. He didn't know that he had stolen my father, that he'd stolen my wife, that he'd stolen every part of my life, somehow. All my dreams of what could have been, thieved away by him, this charlatan, this liar, this terrible human being.

'Can I help you?' he asked.

'Yes,' I said. 'I think so.' I marched over to him, grabbed him. My hands around his neck; my fingernails, weeks past needing a trim, on the skin, on the flesh under that beard of his. He gasped, and he tried to speak.

'Who,' he started, but I clamped my hand over his mouth.

And I thought, I could kill you. There were windows there, big Crittall windows, black metal frames, thin single panes of glass. He would fall so easily: thumping to the ground outside, watched by his many children. I could escape, in the chaos, to the street, and be back with Rhonda, if she was still there.

But he would come back. His files: everything that had happened to him, I realized. He was writing a transcription, his memories of the events, of the conversation I had listened to. I could see the words, and I squeezed harder, my nails breaking his skin. For a moment, the blood made me think I had exploded, somehow. I had reached my own end.

I let go of him, and I stepped back, and he said, 'You maniac,' and he tried to move past me, but he was gasping, in pain, out of breath. I had taken skin from his neck, actual skin picked off, peeled off. Chunks of it. I pushed him, shoved him, but away from the window, towards the wall, and he thumped against the books, and they fell, and fell open, and I realized that these were all volumes – an entire library! – all volumes of his writing about his life, in seemingly infinite detail.

'I won't let you die,' I said to him, and I grabbed him, and I slammed his head against the wall, hard but not too hard; and then I pressed the chloroform rag to his face, and he slumped, so hard; and I picked him up, from the floor, and I dragged him to the stairs, my hands in his armpits, then thump thump thump, down the stairs, expecting to find all of his family – every single one of them, every wife, every child, all of them – I expected to find them all there, waiting for him, to pull him away from me, to raise him up in a sea of hands as they dragged me down, tore me apart, turned me inside out. But they were not there, I was alone with Pettersen, hauling his body, my own body burning, my lungs howling at me, my every muscle tensing, stinging; and then dragging him across varnished wood, to the door, opening it with one hand, and then hoisting him up, onto my shoulder. A flash of a memory, then, of my daughter in that same pose; clutching onto my shoulder, my neck. Carrying him; waiting until it was dark, and then carrying him, hours and hours it took, and when he stirred I knocked him out again, slowly making our way across London. Slowly, so, so slowly.

When he woke up, tied to a chair in the room that would eventually become his prison, he tried to scream, but there was nobody to hear him, the walls thick, and only I was there, and I said, 'Don't scream, it's such a waste.' He told me he would kill himself, that he would get there, that he would come and find me, and he would make me pay.

'You won't,' I said, 'but you won't.'

33

The story is flaky, hard to get actual details on, but: a climber called Ames Pink went up to the peak of Mount Chimborazo, free climbing, as that is all they do now, no ropes or harnesses, just taking chances and understanding that you can come back and try again, that your worst case is a reset, as if this is all a video game. He was with friends, a team of them, all climbing without any sort of protection, and then he reached the peak, and he decided, in that moment, that he would take – and the quote is flaky here, a few different opinions and voices changing the words – but the crux of what he said was, 'I'll take the fast route down'. He hurled himself off, wing suit opened far too late, and he smacked into the rocks on the side of the mountain, the stone as immovable as anything that's ever existed. His body spread.

The friends assembled around him, as they did: a ritual when one of their number died, they kneeled in a circle around them, and they shut their eyes at the same time, to allow them to pass. Except, it didn't work. They wondered if Ames might still be alive, somehow, but there was no chance. One of the friends reported him as being destroyed; another said that there was no part of him left intact. They shut their eyes, over and over, some physical incantation, but he didn't go anywhere. His body there, his blood staining the snow, his torn clothes – the wings from the wing suit – fluttering like flags on jagged spikes of rock.

He didn't leave, and they wondered what that could mean. They waited and waited, and eventually they splintered off, leaving him there; and the next morning, in a helicopter, they went to look for him, and they assumed he would be gone, or covered by snow, impossible to find; but his body was still there, like evidence waiting to be cleaned up.

He died. He died, he didn't come back.

The first person for whom that was the case for decades.

Since before the Anomaly.

The first person to find a way out.

34

Pettersen is violent, even though he would tell you that his violence is just. He spits invective, even though he would say that it's totally reasonable, that opinions are only opinions. He tells me that he hopes I suffer, that he wishes me pain, that he wants me to be in agony – an agony that lasts a lifetime – and that when this is over, he will torture me. He tells me all these things, and all I have done is strip him and leave him, and tell him that I won't let him die. I'm like a nurse, tending to small wounds. I give him antibiotics, because there are still some here, a massive fungal farm out the back for all the doctors who want them to use, stored in enormous fridges. I protect him, which feels strange: as he runs for me, biting and snarling, trying to get me to attack him, to fight back. And I don't, I won't. I haven't.

I stand at the doorway, and I tell him what I've learned. 'They think it might be leaving. Finally, it's going.' He stares at me, as if I've said something stupid. 'The Anomaly, people are— They're dying. On mountains, at the highest points.'

'Oh,' he says.

'You didn't think it would leave,' I say. 'In your book, you said, *This is the new normal now, this is life moving forward; a cyclical event, a way to reset, to have no repercussions.* You said that.'

'Words to that effect,' he says.

'Those exact words,' I tell him. 'I memorized them. For this moment, you understand.' I love it: watching this man's face, and seeing the realization that he's built something on a lie. The realization that it's over.

'So, what,' he asks, this bolshy defensiveness to him. 'So, you're going to, what? Kill me?'

'No,' I say, 'I couldn't. I don't have that. In me.'

'So why are you so fucking happy?'

'Because I know you're going to die,' I say. 'Because I know, finally, absolutely, that this won't last forever.'

Rhonda is up and dressed when I get to her room, moving slowly until I walk in, and then she acts as if she's better than she is. She says, 'I want a walk,' so I suggest the gardens, but she says, 'I want to do a proper walk. I feel up to it, let's go somewhere. Do something.'

'Like what?' I ask her. I can hear, I think, the sound of Pettersen listlessly throwing himself against one of the plain, slightly office-soft walls. Of course, I can't actually hear that, but also, it's there: like that telltale heart from the story, pulsing down below. Pettersen, wall to wall. Atrium to atrium, to ventricle. Thump. 'Where should we go?' I ask.

'Like, I don't know. The river? The market, the aquarium thing? That old boat they've got down there? I don't care, just let's do something.'

'Okay,' I say, so we go: I help her downstairs, out of the building, along the way that I know is best to walk.

'Quiet here,' she says.

'Less than two per cent of London means—' I start, but I stop myself, and I tell her. She is not sitting down, perhaps she should be. 'This is ending,' I say. 'I think it's always quiet, but also, this is ending. It happened, I just found out.'

'What happened?' She seems afraid, almost. The news, whatever it is.

'This, all of it, it's ending.'

'What is?, Jesus, Theo—'

'The Anomaly. Maybe. There's some people it seems, in Nepal and Italy and New Zealand, they think that maybe people are dying again.' Saying it feels so false; like a lie we tell ourselves, to give reassurance.

'Oh,' she says. Relieved? Maybe? 'Like, here?'

'No. High up, altitude. The points, something about the height of them. Above sea level, that's the theory. That seems to be the theory.'

'Shit.'

'It's incredible, really. I think that's why it's quieter. I think some people have gone there, to try and, I don't know.'

'To die. For good.'

'Maybe, yes.'

'Do that many people really want to die?' she asks.

'I don't know.'

'I mean, if they're sick, maybe.' She looks at me, but doesn't realize I catch her. Her eyes, so quickly passing over me it's barely registrable. 'But everybody else, they want to live, right? So why are they going?'

'Maybe they're not. Maybe they're dying one last time.'

'One last time.'

'If you knew you could, one last time, and have most of your life left. If somebody made it to fifty, and they could lose decades by resetting where they were, who they were; and then the Anomaly would be gone, it would be like it had never even been here in the first place. Like a blip.'

'Maybe.'

'Would you?' I ask her.

'I'm in this one now. I got saved, I've got to make this one last. Would I die again? End up back with my mom and dad? No.' She doesn't speak for a moment then, and I know why: she is processing what I have already thought. That everybody who is in a death loop, that loop would end. Her parents' factory would end with tens of hanging souls, with gunshots and poison and actual finality, and they will likely never even know. She would come back, they would all die, that would be it. She would be left there, with the blood around her, the bodies, and she would never recover from it.

If we didn't have the loop, how would we ever recover?

'So this means that when you die,' she starts to say, and I cut her off.

'If I'm inside the Anomaly, I come back. If I'm not. Well.'

'But you come back sick.'

'Yes.'

'But you'll live another thirty years.'

'Something like that. Maybe. Assuming the virus behaves the same.' I have wondered, but this is not the time for it, if the virus cells die and are reborn, if there's something about the Anomaly that's tweaked it. Not in every case, but in mine, maybe. I feel like I'm prodigious, when others died so fast, and here I am, clinging on to life. Clinging on, fingers peeling slowly away from the carapace.

'And that doesn't appeal to you?'

I would come back, in my home in Los Angeles. Birdie would be gone; and maybe I would come to understand that she was never really there in the first place. Maybe I would still go looking for her, find her. Work it out. Rebecca would be gone, still; and the pain of that would still feel so fresh. I would look for Birdie, but not far, because I would want to know what caused her to leave, where she had gone. I would be young, and in love with her, or with the idea of her, or the idea of what we were; and our shared grief propelling us – no, dragging us, against everything inside us that said to curl up and sob and wait, but we were dragged into the Anomaly, into the future. Without that, without Birdie, without Rebecca – without the time I have spent in my grief, and out of it, if you ever truly come out of it. And I wouldn't have left, finally, eventually. I wouldn't have adventured, and met Rhonda, and met Rhonda again, and seen this version of the world on this path to this place.

I would still be sick. There's no cure, not for any of it. Maybe it would be faster, more brutal. Maybe I would infect more people: my sickness spreading as my end came. Maybe I would be the thing that killed the rest of the world. Free of the Anomaly, suddenly, and then here it comes: the virus, the weapon, back to finish us off.

And then also: if I were to come back, loop again, I would not have had this, any of this; my last gasp.

I would not have Pettersen.

'No,' I say, finally. 'I don't think that's what I want. No.'
'So what do you want?' she asks.

We are on the South Bank. Where the steps go down to the old market, where the landscape is blotted by towers of ego, where tramlines swoop off, running alongside the river and under the river, both of them, like twin snakes, wrapped around each other. Constraining. We are there when the blood comes, and like a flood. I wonder, as I collapse, how much the body can lose. Is that how people finally die, is that it, actually; that they have lost enough, that there is no way back from this, because all of what we are is spilled out and all over this, over ourselves, semi-permeable; can my pores not simply open enough and drink it back in, like a hungry mouth held under a tap, lapping at it, trying not to spill a drop?

35

It's still not over. It's never over. I am in the bed that Rhonda was in, and she's been looking after me; but she's not here now, as I wake up, as I drag myself out from the pink-tinged covers, to the bathroom, and I wash myself, caked-on blood under the shower, my body gasping for the water, and I drink it, my mouth open, my head tilted back, drinking from the faucet. I get out, into the comparative cool of the room, the chill of an air-conditioning system that somehow still works, presumably hundreds of thousands of hours since it was last serviced. I dress in clothes that have been left for me on the chair, I know that they must have been left for me, because they're laid out, and it's the sort of thing Rhonda would do. I dress in them, the khakis and pales, a white shirt and sports coat, pale socks, loafers. Like that broken example of humanity in the basement, I think, looking at myself, smoothing over the hair softened by the water here, by the antibacterial hospital pump-soap that smells distinctly of rubbing alcohol. I leave the room, calling Rhonda's name, but she doesn't answer, and my voice echoes in these corridors. So then, the elevator down, to the lobby, and I get out into that space, and I call her again. There's a clock on the wall, hardwired, one of those with a little thing of the date that ticks over, and I don't know if it's right – I can't imagine it accounts for leap years, which means it's probably off, probably; not that dates really mean anything any more, not really. Or at least not yet – but it's been a day, that's all. And I am not dead. I head to the exit when I hear her voice, through the PA system. Clearing her throat before she speaks, some relic of another time entirely.

'Are you dangerous?' she asks.

'No,' I say, a reaction. I am not. I freeze. I look around. There's a speaker, a camera. She's in the basement, watching on the old security monitors. 'I've found where you've been keeping Pettersen,' she says. There's no anger or disappointment in her voice, it's curiously flat. I look at one of the cameras. Try and hold my gaze on it.

'Okay,' I say.

'Were you going to kill him?'

I shake my head. 'No, absolutely not.'

'Do you even have a plan?'

'No.'

'They'll be looking for him. His family, his wives. He's got soldiers, right? Guards, whatever.'

'An army,' I say.

'An army.' She's quiet for a while. As if she's waiting for me to pull back on this, to cancel the plan. Set him free, let him run out into the wild, we'll all be fine. There'll be no repercussions.

'I want to see this through,' I say. 'I don't know what that means, but I want to see it through. I'm dying, I want to die. He's dying, just much slower, and I want him to know that he's going to die. I don't want to kill him, I just want him to know. I want him to understand that he's done, and gone, and that what he's done, created, whatever, the world that he's made: it means nothing. Like in a horror film where the last person alive wants the bad guy to know that they lost, wants to see them watch somebody survive them. I want him to know that he was wrong: that the world has survived him.' I slump against the wall, because it's a relief, to be able to say this stuff. 'I don't want to kill him. There's so much terror in the world, and so much terrible stuff, and I just want to know that there's some penance for it. I don't want him to be in pain, I don't want to hurt him. He changed his tactic, he pivoted, and he succeeded. He conned the world, and he won. I want him to lose, Rhonda. More than that, no, no: I want him to know that he lost, and that there is only one way for him, in the end. The same as all of us.' I shut my eyes. I wonder if she can tell that I'm being honest, if that's coming across. 'Are you there?' I ask her.

'Yes,' she says.

'I toyed, you know, with giving him this. What I've got, cutting our palms and doing blood brothers, or spitting in his mouth, or making him, I don't know. Drink my blood, like some fucking parasite, and then he would die of it. That's how far gone I am, Rhonda. I thought about that, but that's murder, and I don't have that in me. There are people, and when bad people die, they said – I remember this, from before the Anomaly came, after some of the suicides – well, good, glad that they're dead. As if their death meant less to those who loved them. They were mentally ill, or they were radicalized, or they were just desperate for something that they didn't have, but their deaths didn't mean less. They were people, and they died, and it was tragic. They couldn't be helped. My father was sick. He had to have been sick. But that didn't mean I wanted him to die. I don't want to kill Pettersen. I don't want Birdie to suffer, I don't want his children to suffer. I don't want anybody sad, or lost, or torn away from themselves or their loved ones. I don't want pain, I want the pain to end. But I want him to know what it *feels* like. I want him to know that he was wrong. That this isn't infinite, it isn't our destiny, we don't have control, or mastery, that we're not the ultimate. That *he* isn't.'

The door at the end of the hallway, the one that leads downstairs, opens, and Rhonda's standing there, listening to me in person. I look at her. 'I want to die, and I want to know, when I die, that he understands: that he will die, one day, and that this is all over, and will be all over. And he was wrong. That we will go back to how we were before.'

She listens, and she nods. She's a kid, really, but she looks as if she absolutely understands. How rare it is to understand; to listen, to understand.

'They're looking for him,' she says. I don't know how to reply. 'There are a lot of men with guns out there. His *army*. I went for a walk, it didn't feel very safe.'

'No,' I say, agreeing with her.

'It's in the newspaper, which, I don't know, does he print that? It's all about him, anyway. They know he's somewhere, because apparently there's a chamber where he reappears when he's dead. The room he was in when the Anomaly came, he's turned it into this sort of panic room thing, that's what it seems like.'

'Oh.'

'And he's not there, so they know he's still alive.' She seems afraid, genuinely afraid. Like I don't know that I've seen her before. 'There are a lot of them, Theo. They're looking everywhere, they're really turning the city over. They'll find him.'

'London's big.'

'They're here. There's this.' She pulls a folded piece of paper from her back pocket. A picture, hand-drawn, beautiful, really, artistic. The work of a portrait artist, albeit not a very talented one: a crude early sketch, but clearly me, clearly my face. 'So I don't know, Theo. They'll find you, I think, and him, and me.' Terror. That's what makes her look so young. It's not a look people often have. I remember seeing it on Birdie's face, when Rebecca— 'I don't want to die, Theo. They'll find him, and they'll kill us.'

'I don't know what to do,' I say.

'Send him back. They'll stop looking, and we'll have the time to run. Look,' she says, 'come on,' and she holds the door as I go to it, and we go down, to the basement; and there, Pettersen's room, and she says, 'He's fine in there, I've fed him,' like he's a pet rat, and then we go through another door, and another, down a corridor that runs the length of this entire building. A door with a keypad that she's smashed apart, she tells me, sheepishly – as if I'm going to disapprove – and then to larger doors, and a button she mashes with her hand as she walks past. A grille lifts, and there's the ambulance bay. One of the vehicles opened, the back doors wide, and the inside rifled through. She holds out the keys. 'I found these,' she says, 'so we should use it.'

'Use it.'

'Take it. Go to wherever we can. We send him back, we go wherever. If the Anomaly's leaving, I don't know, we go there. Eventually, probably, won't we be outside it or whatever?'

'Send him back. We can't just let him go, he'll get them, the soldiers. He'll tell them.'

'If he makes his way back, to the house, he won't remember.'

I realize what she's saying. 'No,' I say, 'we can't.'

'It's not that bad! He'll come back!'

'It's murder,' I say, but even that feels weak. He won't die. He won't feel it, won't remember it. The repercussions are few.

'But we can't stay here,' she says.

'I need to think,' I say, and I walk away from the ambulance bay, past his door – he throws himself at the window, and he stares at me, and I think I see, in his eyes, the frantic madness of somebody who understands what we're discussing, who knows what we're thinking about doing to him.

In the lobby, I stare through the doors at people, walking past for the first time; and I lock the doors, hide at the back as they peer through the glass, unable to see me, clearly wondering what's going on in here, back there, downstairs, upstairs, a hospital waiting to be explored.

36

I talk to Pettersen. I ask him what he wants. He is on the floor, tired, eating soup by drinking it straight from the bowl. Remarkable how quickly we go feral. He answers, red tomato dripping from his chin. 'I want to go home,' he says. 'I want to be allowed to get the fuck out of here,' and the soup spits as he speaks, blowing out from his lips. His voice having lost some of the refined accent he's cultivated: here, he sounds normal, like anybody else. Just a man.

'But what do you want? In the bigger picture, I mean. In the scale of things, when this is all said and done. What's your endgame?'

'You know, you're a nasty piece of fucking work,' he says. He contemplates, and then delivers, his next lines as if they will shake me to my core. 'I see you, you know. I see deep inside you. Your weakness, your self-worth. I was just like you, a man just like you. I was sad, and I was depressed, and I did things. I could have died.' His story is a mesh of lies, twisted and warped. That changed when he became famous, when he started printing it for posterity. Print makes things tangible; an audience makes them permanent. And so his story solidified, and he uses it now: the way he talks to the lonely, the lost, the searching. Finding common ground; trying to turn me; to radicalize me. 'I was no stranger to pain, and I see that pain, in you. Do you feel it? Because there's freedom, you know. In accepting that the Anomaly is here to save us. God, to be free of the shackles of permanence! Have you accepted it yet? You strike me as a man who simply hasn't. Not can't, but won't.' He wipes his mouth with the back of his hand, and pushes himself to standing. 'Let me— Take me, back to my house. And I can help you, you get me? I can help you turn this all around.' He holds out his hand for me to shake, a vestige of the old world.

'The Anomaly is leaving,' I say. 'You're an infection, that's all. And one day, you'll be cured. Gone for good.'

He fixes me in the eyes, and he stares, and then he jabs his finger at me, as if to punctuate his words. 'Nasty man,' he says. 'You nasty, nasty man, you can't possibly know that,' and he rants, and I understand entirely: I don't want him to die, to reset; I want to watch him know the truth. I want to witness him as he understands: that he's the same as everybody else, not better, not worse especially. Not special, and his knowledge, his house of lies, they're not a gift, they're not marking him out as a prophet. I want him to see that.

But I am dying. I am dying. I do not know how many more fits – is that even what they are? Eruptions, more like – I have left.

I go to leave him, and there's a banging from upstairs, almost perfectly timed with my shutting the door on Pettersen. Hammering, more like; and then I hear Rhonda, running down the stairs, her boots thumping—

'We have to go,' she says, 'they're here.'

'The soldiers?'

'We have to go,' she says again, and then she's at the bottom of the stairs, and she grabs my arm, and she starts to pull me away from Pettersen's prison. Upstairs, the rattling of the doors; and then the smashing of glass, I picture a brick, hurled.

'I can't,' I say. I only have this, I think, before I die; I have this one thing left. 'I don't want to leave him.'

She stares at me. The scuffing of soft-soled shoes on the treated floors above us. 'We take him, then.'

'What?'

'In the ambulance. We take him. I can drive, he goes in the back with you.'

'You can't drive an ambulance,' I say, 'I'll do it,' but she shakes her head.

'If you have a thing, what do you call it, an *episode*, then we crash, and we die. I can drive.' She opens the door to Pettersen's room. 'Come on,' she says, 'help me.'

We grab him. We move him, and he starts to shout, to yell, that he's a prisoner, trapped here; so Rhonda grabs some gauze and shoves it into his mouth, and we strong-arm him to the ambulance she's prepared. We strap him to the bed in there, tight straps, and I sit in the back with him, and she shuts the doors, and I think, for a moment, that they'll catch us; but then she starts the engine, and I hear the big metal doors retracting, and the car moves, that silent rumble, that pinging charge of the sol2r panels as the light hits us, and she says, muffled, 'Hope you're all right back there,' and I reply, we are, panic in Pettersen's eyes, his mouth unable to scream, but I know he would if he could. And we drive, and we drive, and I see nothing, really, out of the rear doors of

301

the ambulance. Just the streets that I knew once, vaguely; as we leave the city, and then the land turns from grey to green.

Rhonda laughs, and the sirens blare, briefly. Nobody follows us, nobody chases us, this is not that story. That is not how stories end any more, not with a chase, not with the world bearing down as everything explodes.

We are on the road, and I am going to die very soon, and I would like it to be as quiet as possible; and as final as possible.

37

The service station coffee tastes like water that's been dashed with gravel, with mud and scraping, and looks it, but the woman behind the stand doesn't seem as if she'd have any sway over the *No Refunds* sign hanging on the front of her van. Coffee is hard to get, that's a universal truth now. Places that make things, they hold stock of them. If we were in South America, Ecuador or Colombia, I'm sure that the coffee would be exceptional. Here, in England, little middle England, there are root vegetables, home-grown produce. Meat labs in Kent likely still running, and the country always had pharmaceuticals, always had wheat and corn. Nothing like America used to be, but the heat only helped us where it killed theirs. America: with plains of grains, all through the heart of it; with plants that are not indigenous but have been forced to take the soil. With cows; with factories designed to take advantage of the looping life cycles of cattle, red meat for everybody. But no coffee: the soil is wrong, the plants are wrong, the rain, the heat, every bit of it slightly wrong. Coffee in the places that were taken for granted, and now this: freeze-dried, like it apparently used to be.

But I drink it, of course. I still drink it.

Pettersen is in the back of the ambulance, his feet thumping these little trills against the thin metal of the gurney he's strapped to. The gurney is fastened into place, he is not going anywhere. Rhonda sits on the back step, the door pulled to, and she says, 'Do you want to drive?' which isn't really a question, because she knows the answer. The roads up here are steep and winding, and there's barely any room for error: the sides, the verges, are littered with chunks of vehicles, with tyres and wing mirrors and door handles and tiny cubes of shattered safety glass.

'We can't risk crashing now,' I say.

'I know.'

'We're so close.'

'Okay, I get it. I'm just tired, that's all.' That's all, tiredness. I don't know if the tiredness outweighs the chances of my degradation. We were near Bristol when I had an episode: frothing in the seat, and she braked, and stopped. The motorway not nearly as busy as it once might have been, but still: we were in the middle, idling, and she was grabbing old gauze from troughs and trying to stem blood that was simply coming from everywhere; and then she was wiping my eyes, because I couldn't see, there was that much blood; and I could hear myself breathing, because there was a rattle of liquid coming from deep inside me. Like an echo of a breath. A memory of one, repeated, got wrong.

I wonder: what is a death rattle? They call it that. Is that the lungs?

She wiped me, cleaned me. I retched on the side of the road, and darkness came up: so much that I think you're not meant to lose. Not just blood, but material. Windscreen wipers and collapsed exhausts abandoned at the side of the road; pieces of me lying with them.

I wonder: how much can you lose? Is that how it ends?

I have never been sure, not what the actual final blow will be. Not how that works. Is the body overwhelmed?

Flooded?

Emptied?

My grandmother died peacefully in her sleep. What does that actually mean? Did she not wake up? Or did she wake up, a moment alone in bed, and *know* what was happening to her? That it was her time, that her death was to be right then?

With Rebecca, she didn't know. We did. You make a decision, to switch something off. To switch off a piece of machinery that's doing a job that the body no longer can. There are, after that moment, hundreds of ways – thousands of ways – that the body can do whatever it is going to do. I remember Birdie asking the doctor if it was possible that she would breathe, by herself. Without the machine. And the doctor said, Anything is possible, but it's unlikely. Improbable. Birdie, with tears in her eyes, tears that seemed like they had formed a permanent barrage wall against her bottom eyelids in those days, saying, That means there's a chance. And of course, there was a chance. Infinitesimal, but the body could do things. Could, optimal word. Wouldn't. I knew it wouldn't, the doctor knew it wouldn't.

You turn something off, there's an inevitability. Fucking heartbreaking, absolutely completely fucking devastating. Because that's a choice you have made.

It's not the same as killing somebody, except, in the darkness, at my worst, I heard myself saying that it absolutely was. It was murder. Another six hours, maybe she would have breathed by herself. Maybe the howl that Birdie made – a howl that detuned itself, that turned into a hum, a low-level constant murmur in our lives, until the Anomaly breezed in and removed it with other concerns – maybe if we had let her live longer, maybe that howl would have dissipated.

They say that grief happens sometimes even when the person is alive.

They say.

Rhonda drives, and I sit very still. The seat is wiped down, but still: the red in the grooves of the fabric, staining the little threads on the trim of the seats, pooled in the footwell, crusted on the strange felt material there by the sun. Sun that somehow has reached it, even as shaded as it is.

In the back, he screams, but muffled. There was a mask in a drawer in the back that must have been to stop people who were frothing at the paramedics. Like something from a horror movie, an institution movie, a muzzled dog. I can make out words, but they're really not important: all things telling me what I will regret, because he doesn't understand: if this works, I will have no regrets. And he will have nothing but: life after life lived with no permanence, just this idle frippery, wishing it away, washing it away.

38

At a pub in a town called Cowbridge – a long stretch of old shops on a hill, bucolic and idyllic and perfect – we see television footage of a mountain. Not the first, not the highest, but a mountain where, it's alleged, you can die. We see the crowd at the pub with the television as we're looking for somewhere to buy food; park the ambulance up, walk across to see what the commotion is all about. We ask a man and he tells us: people are dying, this is the footage of it. Bodies, lying still on rocks. Hurling themselves off, all in the name of actual finality.

We buy a sandwich from a shop where the person selling them can't believe it, can't believe that this is happening, we'd all heard rumours . . . And we sit on the back step of the ambulance, and we watch the people watching the footage.

'It's mad,' Rhonda says.

'But it's real,' I say.

We tell Pettersen he can have a sandwich if he promises to be quiet, and Rhonda pulls the muzzle from him, and he tries to bite her, so we put it back on, leaving the sandwich next to him. Cruel, tempting. I feel like I might be the bad guy of this story, but also: fuck him.

'What do you think'll happen?' Rhonda asks.

'Exodus,' I say. 'There will be an exodus. There's a history of it: we like to move in groups, I think. All of us, in large pilgrimages. Or convoys, there's a song, a really old song that my dad used to sing. "Convoy!" Like that.' She stares at me as if I've revealed too much. Embarrassed for me. I remember that feeling.

'I mean: what do we do?'

'About? I don't understand, I feel like I'm missing something.'

'You want to go?' She looks at the crowd. There's happiness there, and terror. Faces that are both somehow obvious and yet devastatingly hard to read. 'There's a mountain and the thing's leaving, and you could die.'

'Oh.'

'I mean, you said you wanted to.'

'I did, no, that is totally what I said. I did.'

'How far is the mountain? I mean, any of them? How close is the nearest one?'

I think about how it felt, convulsing on the passenger seat. Hours between fits, now. Between episodes. Another will be along in a moment, and another, and then I will have bled all I can bleed, I'm sure. How the body can keep going, I don't know. I must be so weak; adrenaline doing its job. Pushing me onwards, ever onwards. 'It's too far,' I say.

'Okay, then, something else. Like, a building? There must be skyscrapers here,' she says. She looks around. 'In a city.'

'Not really,' I say. 'And the land needs to be high, it's not—'

I was barely a teenager, or barely not a child any more. I

hadn't lived in London that long, and my stepmother took Martine and I on a trip. In a caravan, like this little Volkswagen van, bright orange, bought secondhand. For a week, she said, won't it be nice? The three of us, forced to get along. Driving along the motorway, and then up into the hills. Parked up, higher and higher, eating bacon rolls from a van at the side of the road, looking out over the valley. Nothing, really, out there: just the green, rolling to the edge of itself, if the edge is the horizon, where the world tips over itself. Then higher still: the green giving way to scrub and scrag, and we climbed, wrapped in scarves and wearing inappropriate shoes, but it was something: to push up, and my stepmother telling us that there was no difference between mist and cloud, they were fundamentally the same thing. Higher and higher. I have no idea if we reached the top, or if it was something worth reaching. A mountain, not a hill, that's what my stepmother said. Never forget, you climbed a mountain, not a hill. Doesn't matter what anybody else says, you define the rules. I remember her voice cracking, as she spoke to me quietly. Your father, she said, but that was all the sentence I got. Your father; and then she broke off, and then she made a joke with Martine, and we went down a slope, and then we found a pub and she got Martine a shandy, and I had a sip of it, and we ate pub lasagna, cheese and pasta and meat and chips and salad. How empty the pub was.

The crowd outside the pub starts dissipating, people going to the few cars parked along the street here, or to their home. Not a rush, but clearly headed somewhere, clearly something to do. The whole crowd, and then they're gone, and there's just the pub, empty, the front opened up to a world that suddenly doesn't want anything to do with it.

'Where are they all going?' Rhonda asks, and I know, I already know.

We drive for hours, and there are other vehicles on the road: an old commandeered double-decker at one point; cars and motorbikes, sol2r panels strapped to the sides of them; and then people on foot, sandals or boots and walking sticks or thick branches. Older people, mostly: a wash of bald heads, of veins, of liver spots. Not quite me, but not quite not. Rhonda drives, stable as always, and Pettersen beats his feet in this simple rhythm – let! me! go! let! me! go! – that's absolutely ineffective, that only seems to fit into the moment of this. Like a war drum, these people ascending.

We drive slower as we pass one group, mostly middle-aged, some elderly, as they walk, as they wheeze. They smile at us, nod, laugh. An ambulance, up here. The lilted shout of one of the men: 'I've seen enough of you to last a bloody lifetime, no more, cheers!'

We pass them, and the others. Not quite in front, but in front enough to hit mist; and I say to Rhonda, 'It's the same as cold, really,' and then the wash comes over me, the second time in this ambulance, the right place for it; my hand smacking on the window, and I see the bloody handprint, like some old horror story, trails from my fingertips down the glass, before I pass out.

39

Up the mountain, the road just sort of comes to an end, concrete fading to patchwork concrete with grass and then dirt track and then the grass and the rest of the green overwhelms whatever was there at all; and Rhonda says, 'This is where we walk, I guess?'

There have been so many people here. The ground trampled as they walked before us, as they climbed. Cars abandoned at the sides of the road, and the sun is nearly completely hidden by cloud here, mostly, leaving this grey that starts twenty feet in front of your face and seamlessly reaches up and around you, everywhere you look. The ripple of the sky only partly visible through it all: the swirls of ink as if they have been watered down. Storm weather. She helps me out, and I stand with her on the side, on the verge. 'What do we do with him?' she asks.

'Scout it first?' I say. He's asleep, I can see, looking through the little glass windows. That glass that's designed to shatter, a lattice of metal wire running through it. The door is locked, as well, the locks hardcore enough that people can't break

311

in and take anything to sell. So we walk, up the hill, seeing markers of people – their litter, their footprints, dog turds and scuffed grass, pathways made where there were none – and hearing their voices on the wind, higher and higher.

The sky is darkening, the storm coming. I picture the rain as we walk up, coming down in buckets, flooding these pathways, rushing down them as if they're galleys built for it, gutters, a river that scoops us all up, hurls us down the mountain, deposits us in a brand new lake at the bottom.

'So,' says Rhonda. She is absolutely efficient, her breathing, her conditioning. Living in the desert will do that, I suppose. I am not: I wheeze, and I creak. I am barely old, but at the same time: I feel every moment of my years.

And the blood, I sense it pooling. At the bottom of my lungs, simmering. A volcano, far from dormant, waiting for the moment.

'So?' I ask.

'What if this doesn't work? What if it's not real?'

'Then it's not real,' I say.

'And so you, just, what? You die.'

'I die, I come back.'

'And that's okay.'

'There is literally no other choice. It's not okay, but—' A fatal illness was something to scream against. In the past, it was a thing that made you howl, made you want to live. I understand how selfish this may seem; how cruel I might seem to those who don't know. To be given a chance again, and yet to know exactly how it ends.

I hear Birdie's voice, perennially: What if they find a cure?

'I don't want to live through this again. I don't want to live knowing that I will be sick, that I will die. There are inevitables, but some things are too inevitable. I don't want the pain of not having dealt with Rebecca. I have processed my grief, I think I have processed it? Thirty years, Rhonda. I don't want to know I am dying again, and go through that pain again. Maybe the Anomaly kept me alive longer, maybe, no doctor's ever looked at me, so it could be – I'm a freak of nature, that's a possibility. But it's not just me, it's the world. The world has been in pain, and we need to move forward. We need to keep moving, if we're trapped, that's all we feel. We keep running, or walking, or whatever, moving the best we can, but there's no way through, no way out, no exit. We need to know we're not working in vain, we're not growing in vain. It needs to have a point, all of this. It can't be that it doesn't, because we need to feel something else. We need to feel something else; that who we are is worth it. I need to feel that I have worked, and changed, and grown, and that I am *me*, Rhonda. Not the man I was thirty, forty, fifty years ago. That I am me *now*.' She stares at me. She takes my hand, her small hand, soft in mine.

Rebecca's hand, limp in mine. Holding it, as we made the choice that we had to make.

I will never stop hurting from that. And that's okay.

'You're a good person, Theo,' Rhonda says.

'You grew up surrounded by maniacs and cultists,' I remind her, 'your levels are off.'

We both laugh. What else is there to do?

The road plateaus off in front of us: the storm has taken hold, like a microclimate at the top of the mountain. I am reminded of the end of superhero movies from the past, that I loved when I was a child, when they all ended in some cataclysm, in swirling maelstroms of cloud and lightning. Thunder, and the sky rippling with light, except that this light is thick blue, like trails of ink, like painted hands plunged into clean water. Like contrails, except there are no planes. We stare, because there is not much else to do. The people up here, a party. We went to Burning Man once, when we hadn't been in LA long. That's what you do, when you're young, and not yet pregnant, or don't have kids, and there are friends – who would die or disappear when push came to shove – friends who told you that it was incredible, that you'll forget life, that it's just you and the plains. And the caravans and the RVs and the motorhomes and the metal constructions, temporary homes and stores and tattoo parlours and art sanctuaries and safe spaces, where whatever you want to do, whatever you are into, that's where you can do it. Birdie and I were not into much, some drugs, recreational. I took some ancient something or other, which was definitely not ancient, but was in fact brewed in a lab in one of those old RVs. In the desert there I saw colours and shapes and chaos and sand and the sky, this skybox, stretching off forever and ever, clouds bursting into stars as the night settled in. Birdie said, afterwards, that she saw nothing. Nothing, just like she hadn't taken anything at all. And I wondered: did I? Or did I simply want to?

Now, the storm settles in. People in disposable or folddown anoraks, because we don't have cold-weather coats now, not really, so they're all shivering, and this is like Niagara Falls, in a boat, close enough to the crash to get soaked, to pose for photographs that can only be taken by an official photographer, collect your token and pay when you exit. We walk towards it, and there's a line where it seems to start, as we climb a little outcrop and step over. Drenched to the skin, and Rhonda holds her hand over her eyes, and she says, 'This is insane,' or screams it, really, because the wind is beating up here with a force like I haven't seen outside of hurricane videos. Those poor people, uprooted, displaced. And yet here we are, up a mountain, of our own volition. The sky, those contrails, those entrails, inky blue against the crashing grey. White and black smashed into each other.

This is where it ends, a sign reads. People holding them, the paint running. I try a headcount, hundreds of us, all on this little verge, this little outcrop. Not the top of the mountain, but the top of something. Hundreds of them, and more down the road, more down the valley, because some people are walking.

There's a little camper van, this old Renault, converted and converted, power supply to power supply, and I'm amazed that it still works, but it must; and there's a man at the back, making coffee from a little flask with his wife. They are dressed for walking, like this is a life that they understand: up the hill, down the hill. In the back of the van, two boys tumble and fight and play, grinning, sleepless. The man stares at me, and he's got this smile across his face like he's almost drunk.

'It's working,' he says, 'fucking hell, this is working.'

'What?'

'The, the, the Anomaly. It's— Here.' He thrusts a little radio towards me. I listen, through crackly static, to a voice speaking German. Excitable barking, the man on the report clearly thrilled.

'What's he saying?'

'He's saying— Hang on, this bit, Don't be afraid, you don't need to be afraid any more, something like that. And then, Reports from Zugspitze, that's a mountain, in Germany, reports from there that people are out of the Anomaly, somehow. On the other side of it. It's fucking gone! It's

315

fucking gone, it's amazing.' He runs his hand through his hair. 'It'll be here soon enough. Germany now, so what, a few hours? What's the time difference?'

'Two,' I say. 'Is that how it works?'

'Who the fuck knows,' he says. That big grin again. 'We're here until it does, I reckon.' He looks at his little family. So complete here in this moment. 'No sense in going anywhere. There's walks, there's coffee. Might as well kick back, make a trip of it. You want a coffee?' He leans back, pours me a cup from the flask. 'It's real coffee,' he says, 'this is real Ugandan coffee, there's a microclimate pod there, they made it, and it costs an arm and a leg, so watch it, don't let the rain water it down, yeah?'

'Thank you,' I say.

'No problem.' He grins, then turns back to his family. There's a story here, I know. We all have stories. They are here, the kids are young.

I drink the coffee.

This might be the last cup I drink.

My insides are churning. Like they know. That subtle undercurrent: hunger, almost. Burbling away, and knowing, utterly knowing, that it is coming.

'What do we do?' Rhonda asks.

I say, shout, yell, 'We go back down and get Pettersen.'

So we turn away from the revellers – that's the feeling, this intense sense of excitement – and walk back down the hill, the water rushing back with us, lapping at our heels, faster than we can walk.

The back of the ambulance is broken open; the gurney toppled.

Pettersen is nowhere to be seen.

40

Rhonda shouldn't be here. This isn't fair on her. I say to her, as we sit, as I try and work out what happens next, that she should leave.

'Where would I go?' she asks. 'You said I was—' And she describes herself, as I described the older version of her. Like this rebel who never grew up. This person who was absolutely, utterly in control of themselves, of who they were, are, who they always would be. A person who begins at a fixed point, and that point never shifts, and neither does the person. So the person is unflappably themselves, their path is written. There is a track and they are fastened to it. Rhonda is the person, the track, the path. I can see her older self in the younger, and vice versa. 'So where would I go?'

'You would go anywhere,' I say, 'do anything. I don't think being here—'

'What do you want?'

'I want to die,' I say.

'And Pettersen?'

'Fuck him,' I reply. 'He's gone.'

'Okay then.' She smiles, and she takes my hand. 'Let's go, old man. Let's get you dead.'

41

The top of the hill, the mountain, whatever this thing is, it's swarming even more by the time we reascend; by the time we've eaten sandwiches and tinned mandarin segments, and climbed up, slower, slower. As we reach the top I can feel my lungs thrumming. My clothes, the fifth – sixth? seventh? – change since we began this journey, and they are clinging to me now, sweat that tricks me into thinking it's blood for a moment. Damp to my back, and the rain, the drizzle until we ascend, and then it's pulsing, lashing, water that comes in thick sheets. But there's a celebratory sense, a sense of something ending and beginning simultaneously. These people here, and us, trying to witness something that's brought us to an end, and restarted us. And my end— My end will be sometime, I pray now, I don't want to live this over again— The people drinking, and laughing. A sign, written in thick bold mud on cardboard: *Fuck off, and don't come back.*

Because what was this? How will we ever unpack it? How will people, moving forward, onward, picking up and rebuilding, how will they ever reconcile what's happened to them with what life is actually like? I think, in this moment, that it feels like a hoax. Like the days when it arrived: when the chaos set in, and we hid, and the reports felt like they were going to be revealed as something other. A story, a strange piece of narrative. An experiment that draped the world in terror, *The War of the Worlds* on the wireless radios of the past, pushed to a degree that nobody would be comfortable with.

My grandmother, my Yiayia Elena, telling me stories of my grandfather, of Cormac the Explorer, as he went off to the stars and never came back; and how when he was a child, he had been obsessed with old science fiction, with stories of places and creatures and beings and presences other than this.

He left her. He abandoned her, just like people do. She needed him, she was suffering, and she needed him; and he still left. He thought she was dying, or dead, and still: he sat there on his spaceship, and he did something he felt was more important. His priorities so fucked up, and the world thinks of him as this hero, one of the first who tried; but the reality is, he wasn't. He was a weak little man who the world will never understand.

But this is not his story. It isn't a story where there's an antagonist waiting to be offed; the antagonist is here, yes, but he won't be killed, he will simply be allowed to ultimately die, which would have happened anyway but I will get to look into his eyes as he understands the truth, that his world is built on lies, and always was, and those lies have crumbled. It isn't one where there's a love story, because the woman I loved left me, and then I found her, but she was gone, there was no coming back, there was no second chance. It isn't one where I find a cure, because there is no cure; there is a sickness that pervades, that sits and waits, that nearly died out but still lives inside me, and there are no scientists or specialists or last-minute cures for it, or ways to keep it at bay, this is not that sort of story. It isn't a story about my daughter, where I find some way to bend the mechanics of reality, to bring her back somehow, or to make the pain of what happened to her any less. It isn't one where Rhonda asks me to adopt her, or where she gives me some answer to something that I have been wanting, some great quest for a truth that only she can provide, some quest that ends with her opening the treasure chest, F#, E, A#7, B7, the music that plays when you open the treasure chest to find the jewel, the power, the ability that allows you to continue. It isn't a story about me finding some truth about myself, where I begin afraid and end less afraid, as I am still afraid, and I will always be afraid, until I die, until that moment; because maybe I will be back, maybe I won't, but either way there's something so deeply unknowable, so unfathomably mysterious, that fear is the only option I have left, really. This is not a story about Pettersen, or people like him, men like him, who try to bend the world to their will, to their way of thinking.

It is not a story about people at all, not really; about their beginnings and their endings, their circles and cycles. This is not a story about chaos, about order, about trying to fathom the universe out; there is nothing to be fathomed, as best I can tell. This isn't a story about faith, as some have it, and some do not; and some preach it, and some do not; and some believe it, and some do not. It's not a story about the discovery of something in space, about spaceships and science and science fiction; about a creature, a life form, a being, something the size of an entire solar system, maybe, pulsing and pulsating through the stars, swallowing planets whole – I remember

Galactus, from old comic books, this god that ate entire planets, and the herald that preceded them, the Silver Surfer, riding through the cosmos – this is not that story, I do not know what the Anomaly is, and I don't think that I ever will.

I don't think it matters. Maybe this is a first-contact story; but even if it is, it's about us, primarily. If we met something, if we met an alien presence, we should learn who we are. We should take something from it that helps us to grow. Anything that feels like our world is getting larger, or smaller, expanding or exploding or compressing or condensing, anything like that: we should take from it. Move forward. Keep moving forward.

This is a story about time, because there is not enough of it, and yet also somehow too much of it; and I am rushing, pushing, to try and move through it before it is gone, or before it is taken, or I am. Time, enough to do some things, enough to do nothing, not nearly enough for everything. Cross your fingers, and hope. And now, some of these people celebrate: drinking, drugs, waiting, singing, singing these songs I haven't heard in years, songs that exist as part of something more global as a memory than local, that transcend the individual. Imagine what it takes to reach that point? To become something more than the individual? Here they are, the songs, sung by these voices, out of tune with each other, losing the melody, finding it again. Butchering it and somehow, in that butchering, rendering it perfect.

I say to Rhonda that I want to sit, to paint this, and I do. She helps me to a little outcrop, uncomfortable but who cares, really. She hands me my notebook, and I start to draw it all out: the lines, the frame first, of the peaks, and the clouds, and then the people, as shapes, formless, like a mass.

One shape, really, all of them. The clouds, closer, heavier. Actually weighed down, struggling under the weight of what they're unleashing. The torrent soaking the pages, so Rhonda leans over and provides some cover for it. I say that the pages are waterproof, that the booklet, it's one that Birdie got me way back, designed for – ha! – permanence, nothing lost, nothing erased. She doesn't listen, or doesn't hear, or doesn't pay attention, anyway, she stays there, her arms sheltering the paper. She tells me it's good as I draw, and I think that she might be right: because the people aren't people here, not yet, they are a surface, they are a coating. They are a part of the land, and the land goes on and off, and the sky, about to rain, is punctured by the peaks in the distance. The signs above the heads of the people collapsing into, I don't know, degrading. Falling apart in their hands. Part of the land, the cardboard degrading, turning to mulch, mulch into mud, mud into this grass, barren and patchy and sun-burned, the soil turned to grit, unable to drink the water, so it runs. There will be a flood, I'm sure, somewhere; the landscape giving way, avalanche and landslip. This place has had tragedies, there will be more, there will always be more. But I draw, hand making the lines. Keep your fingers as a tripod, and follow the fingers, and your heart, and your eyes. A perfect tripod. The people, the land, the sky; and the Anomaly.

Imagine it, that this sky is all of it. Draw the sharp darkness of it, the dark lines, slashes, jagged slashes, deep fucking scores across the sky. Blue ink of its tendrils, its contrails, its tendrils. What would it be like to be in the heart of this storm, to see it? Is it different, how is it? The picture, charcoal-grey, but every colour— And the red, now, on my finger. Drawing it in, the blood running down to my nail. Along the wood, along the lead, to the page. Like: a tattoo, an inscription, a feathered quill, a fountain pen, a deep red thread being drawn through fabric that's designed to last forever. The red runs across the page, flows down, and I think of the artists who spent their careers working in inks, red and black and grey, those three colours alone, there is nothing that cannot be drawn – achieved – with those three colours. White paper, red ink. The grooves from the pencil perfect gutters for the flow, and it's as if I have intended this: blood from the lines between fingernail and flesh, blood from the cracked skin of my knuckles. Blood from my eyes, running down my face, and my hands, my eyes, all red. I think of stigmata; of statues of the Virgin Mary, bleeding as people worship at their feet.

Rhonda urges me to keep going, but the pencil is slipping from my hand, and she shouts something to some of the other people – help us, please – and they come over, with their signs, and their disposable waterproof sheaths, and they start crowding, asking what we need. She tells me to keep drawing, and I do, my hand slippery, wipe the blood on my clothes; and feel, through the clothes, the blood soaking back the other way. Nowhere to wipe it, nowhere that's clean. The people asking if I'm sick, and she tells them, but we are nearly fucking over, so they stay because what's the risk, really. The drawing, the hills, the mountains, the valleys. The far off, and the further off, imagined, really. The sky there, and the ink, and the— I stare at it, looking up. Past the rain. Past the darkness. My eyes are bloody, my eyes are weeping, they are— But up there, up there is nothing and everything. I imagine: seeing the angels coming from the heavens, in the days of the old testaments, stories without words, seeing myself dragged to a light, seeing the darkness and nothingness that's swallowed everybody who went into it, that's broken everybody who tried to come out. It is leaving.

Everybody else here is staring at me, at Rhonda, to allow me to finish this one piece of drawing, this art, my final. My hand working automatically, I don't know what it's doing. It won't reach the edges— Rhonda screams at me that Pettersen is here, bumbling about, totally fucking lost, and I look at him, and he's a bit away from the rest of the people, over at an edge; and he's howling, about to throw himself off, but I can tell he simply doesn't have it, the guts, the strength, the fortitude, whatever it takes to understand the actual power of your own life and death, he is missing that entirely. I watch him, and he turns back, and I'm sure he sees us, all of us, standing here, and that makes me laugh, spitting blood— The light, the line of the sky, the clouds, they're parted. Sunlight there, and I realize – from here, eyes darkened – that the quality of the light is totally, utterly different. We got used to it, that's what I said, what we all said. We got used to it, like watching a film. Everything toned slightly off, askew, and yet here, suddenly, the light past, the near-far off, is different. Clear, like— Breathable, clean air, breathable air. The light moves, a wave, washing over the land, and the land – the scrub – it's green again, in the wake. Like: it's reborn, made anew. Green plants, shrubs, grass. The rock glinting with a freshness, and the landscape seeming to shift. Rain bends light, light refracts, everything can look different in the rain, but it feels so tangible! Pettersen stands there, and he sways, and he's about to leap, maybe, or telling himself that he can, as the wave hits him, crashes over him.

I wondered what it would look like: it is something pulled through water, that slight tugging of the edges of a substance designed to be permeated. It sucks around Pettersen, then plops back into place, and he is outside it, finally: gasping, heaving in air, an air that his lungs are not built to take. The light had been different, the air had been different. He is standing there on grass, as flowers spiral and curl around his ankles, growing in this bucolic future. And the others here turn and look, and eyes widen, lighten. This is really happening, the man with the van says, he holds his wife and kids tight, and he stares at it; and he's crying, and Rhonda's crying, and I feel my insides. They lurch, and blood comes. I feel myself draining, this is horrifying. The worst moment, the worst image, and yet: it is happening. I put down the drawing, the blood covering the page, soaking through every page, every grooved pencil mark, every etch lined with it, stained with it. Dyed. My guts, my legs. The pores, can you imagine feeling your pores? Actually feeling them as they seep? That is how it feels, as the light scrapes along the landscape, like a shaver, a thin sharp blade. How long since I shaved last? Those pores, fit to burst. Hairs pushed out for blood. The Anomaly scraping the landscape, dragging itself away. Everything popping out of it, and the green, the light, the blue of the sky, as blue as it was just painted, as blue as if it was just created. The people turn and look, all of them, they're not on me any more, even Rhonda looking away, which I understand – and I say to her, 'Don't look at me, look away from me, there's no —' But the words are done, there's not a single new word from my mouth, it doesn't exist.

The notebook falls from my hands, I feel my muscles done, gone, blood gone from them, blood gone from my bones and my skin, pooling on the floor, the palest red, like washing a small cut under a tap, running the water and the water runs pink until the water runs clear. I am sinking, my body a mulch, a puddle. There is so much blood, blood like I have never seen, blood like has never existed. It is extravagant, to feel like this, to be this utterly broken and gone, the last person on Earth with this sickness, maybe, certainly the last who hasn't yet died from it, and I made it, I fucking made it, careening towards death as the thing sweeps towards us. Then it passes, the grass so verdant, the land so clean, and I feel my lungs, collapsed, full of mess, as they can't breathe anyway, let alone this clean, clear air, this clear, clear land.

I fall to the ground, it passes over me, it feels like fingers plucking at my skin, pulling, tugging, the tiniest sense of being ushered through and into something else. A splinter being pulled, that relief; a spot popped, a boil lanced. Sitting on a counter as my mother picked grit from my knee with a needle: a sense of something being taken, being left complete, empty, clean. That absolute relief, that's what it is, relief. I am on the ground, I am on the ground, the grass is so clean.

My hand: feeling Rebecca's hand in mine. A twitch of it, like when she was younger still, from before. The warmth of it, in mine.

It's Rhonda's hand, I see. She smiles at me. I thank her, I say the words aloud, I think I do. Maybe I can't speak; this rush of sound, this deluge of noise, of wind.

I shut my eyes for a moment, and then open at them again. All around us, the land looks perfect, somehow.

Everything as if it has changed. The darkness, even if it wasn't darkness, even if it was a veil, is gone, and it is like: it was here, and time changed, and it changed *this*. As if it paused it, held it, close and tight. A period where we could not destroy the land, where we could not destroy ourselves, where what makes us *us* could not be destroyed.

Where the land healed, where we healed. Where we learned that life was precious, that we should not waste it. Where we were in a bubble, wrapped, embraced, and on the other side, the world was kept for us; until we were ready.

My fingers, red as they are with my blood, wet as they are with my blood, feel the grass. I should be empty, there is so much of it; but I cannot see my blood anywhere. I look at my hand: the red gone, and now there is only water, the softness of rain. My tears on my face, and Rhonda's hand, still in mine, and I can feel it.

Time means nothing.

With my other hand, I touch the soft grass beneath me: to be able to feel it, to really be able to feel it. The land, cold, but the warmth of sun on me, on it. Warming it up. The warmth of the sun, not the heat, not the blazing heat. I look up at that sun, our sun, and it hurts my eyes: with how bright it is.

You are free.

How new it seems.

Don't look back.

I breathe, and as I take that breath in, and I hold it, I feel it being held, I wonder: how is it that I am still breathing?

Acknowledgements

Thanks to everybody at HarperCollins UK, past and present, who has believed in this series, who has fought for it. I'll always appreciate getting to tell the story I wanted to tell. Thanks especially to Eleanor Goymer for her thoughtful edits, and to Jack Renninson for shepherding the novel to publication.

Thanks, as always, to Sam Copeland and all at RCW; to Katie Haines and Jonathan Kinnersley and all at The Agency; to Matt Hill and Cath Steptoe for their thoughts and answers to my constant queries; and to Amy McCulloch for being there from the very start, and seeing it through until the very end.

Eternal gratitude to the fans of the books. The emails and messages I get from you have meant the world to me, I can only hope that this ending satisfies.

And lastly: thanks to Ben North. Ben was Creative Director of HarperCollins UK. He was a sci-fi fan; we spoke at parties, chatted over drinks. It was at one of those parties, years ago now, that he asked me how I felt about my writing, my career up until that point. I told him I was seriously thinking about giving up on the Anomaly books, ending the series after two entries. He told me that I shouldn't. He told me to write exactly what I wanted to write. To tell the stories I wanted to tell. He had belief in me, at a time when I had little in myself.

As it happened, I wrote this book in two extended stretches: the first, the section that runs up until Rhonda's journal, was written before the pandemic, at the end of 2019. I returned to the book nearly a year later, not long after getting the news that Ben had died. I wasn't sure I could write it – it was about a pandemic, after all, even if said pandemic was very different to our own; and my own anxieties had taken a toll on my mental health – but I thought of him, telling me to write the story I wanted to write. Spurring me on. So I did. This novel – about death, and life, and grief, and memory, and *time* – is a novel that very likely only exists because of him, and his belief in me. I'll never forget it.